# ONE NIGHT
# @
# THE CALL CENTER

### Chetan Bhagat

_Rupa & Co_

Published 2005 by

*Rupa & Co*

7/16, Ansari Road, Daryaganj,
New Delhi 110 002

*Sales Centres:*

Allahabad Bangalore Chandigarh Chennai
Hyderabad Jaipur Kathmandu
Kolkata Mumbai Pune

The Bhagvad Gita quote on Page 289 is taken from www.krishna.com,
copyright © The Bhaktivedanta Book Trust International, Inc. His
Divine Grace A.C. Bhaktivedanta Swami Prabhupada, International
Society for Krishna Consciousness

'Flower of Life' on Cover by Chetan Bhagat and Samantha Holyoak
(sam@kreativ.com.hk). Combining science with art, this circular flower
pattern is often cited in the field of sacred geometry and is also present
in the 5000-year-old temple of Osiris at Abydos, Egypt.

Typeset in 12 pts. AmericanGaramond by
Nikita Overseas Pvt. Ltd.
1410 Chiranjiv Tower
43 Nehru Place
New Delhi 110 019

Printed in India by
Gopsons Papers Ltd.
A-14 Sector 60
Noida 201 301

*To my baby twin boys
and the wonderful woman
who created them*

*with a little bit of help from me

# Contents

| | |
|---|---|
| *Acknowledgements* | *xi* |
| Prologue | 1 |
| From #29 | 11 |
| #1 | 13 |
| #2 | 19 |
| #3 | 34 |
| #4 | 39 |
| #5: My Past Dates with Priyanka—I | 46 |
| #6 | 52 |
| #7 | 58 |
| #8 | 68 |
| #9 | 75 |
| #10: My Past Dates with Priyanka—II | 84 |
| #11 | 93 |
| #12: My Past Dates with Priyanka—III | 99 |
| #13 | 111 |

#14                                            120
#15                                            125
#16                                            130
#17                                            134
#18: My Past Dates with Priyanka—IV           140
#19                                            146
#20                                            154
#21                                            159
#22                                            167
#23: My Past Dates with Priyanka—V            177
#24                                            181
#25                                            188
#26                                            194
#27                                            203
#28                                            210
#29                                            220
#30                                            225
#31                                            238
#32                                            243
#33                                            252
#34                                            260
#35                                            268
#36                                            271
#37                                            277
#38                                            283
Epilogue                                       285

Before you begin this book, I have a small request. Right here, note down three things. Write down something that

    i) you fear,

    ii) makes you angry and

    iii) you don't like about yourself.

Be honest, and write something that is meaningful to you.

Do not think too much about why I am asking you to do this. Just do it.

*One thing I fear:*

_____

*One thing that makes me angry:*

_____

*One thing I do not like about myself:*

_____

Okay, now forget about this exercise and enjoy the story.

**Have you done it?**

If not, please do. It will enrich your experience of reading this book.

If yes, thanks. Sorry for doubting you. Please forget about the exercise, my doubting you and enjoy the story.

# *Acknowledgements*

hang on a minute here, in case you are thinking this is just
book. It is never one person's book alone, and in my case,
many people supported me. In particular, I would like to
k:

Shinie Antony——for her scrutiny and standards when she
s me feedback. I said it the last time, she is my mentor, guru
friend.

My call center cousins, sisters-in-law and friends——Ritika
n, Shweta Sarin, Akhil Sarin, Nikhil Sarin, Nithin and Jessica.
thout you, this book would be nowhere. Thank you for
ping me snoop around call centers at night, providing
ormation, stealing various training materials and arranging
etings with so many people. Most importantly, thank you for
ring your life with me. I can never claim to know as much
the people who work in call centers night after night. But
think I do understand your feelings——considering how much
iting this book moved me. Still, if you find me lacking in some

aspects, please consider me as another normal, imperfect human being and forgive me.

My one particular ex-boss. My life when I worked for him was living hell, and was probably the worst phase of my life. I used to wonder why this was happening to me. Now I know. Without that experience I could not have done this book. Thank you Mr Ex-boss for making me suffer. On the same note, I want to thank all the women who rejected me (too many to name here). Without them, I would not have known the pain of rejection.

My family—Anusha, Ishaan, Shyam, Ketan, Anand, Pia, Poonam, Rekha, Kalpana and Suri. They are still with me and support me despite my craziness, which alone deserves to be recognized.

My publishers Rupa & Co, an unpretentious, hardworking, high quality and caring company that holds its own despite head-on competition with every other foreign publisher in town. Such companies make India proud. I specifically thank the people there who worked extra hard on my last book. It was beyond commercial reasons sometimes—they just wanted my story told. Stay that way guys (but yes, you can pay me more).

Mr Bill Gates and his Microsoft Corp again, for MSWord. I cannot write without this software. Besides, it has a great selection of fonts which I think we've been able to use to effect here. Of course, this time I have to thank them for another reason—which you will figure out when you read the story.

With that, I hope you are ready to spend—one night @ the call center!

# Prologue

THE NIGHT TRAIN RIDE FROM KANPUR TO DELHI WAS THE most memorable journey of my life. For one, it gave me my second book. And two, it is not every day you sit in an empty compartment and a young, pretty girl walks in.

Yes, you see it in the movies, you hear about it from friends' friends but it never happens to you. When I was younger, I used to look at the reservation chart stuck outside my train bogie to check out all the female passengers near my seat (F-17 to F-25 is what I'd look for most). Yet, it never happened. In most cases I shared my compartment with talkative aunties, snoring men and wailing infants.

But this night was different. First, my compartment was empty. The Railways had just started this new summer train and nobody knew about it. Second, I was unable to sleep.

I had been to IIT Kanpur for a talk. Before leaving, I drank four cups of coffee in the canteen while chatting with students. Bad idea, given that it was going to be boring to spend eight insomniac hours in an empty compartment. I had no magazines or books to read. I could hardly see anything out of the window in the darkness. I prepared myself for a silent and dull night. It was anything but that.

She walked in five minutes after the train had left the station. She opened the curtains of my enclosure and looked puzzled.

'Is coach A4, seat 63 here?' she said.

The yellow light bulb in my compartment was a moody one. It flickered as I looked up at her.

'Huh...' I said when I saw her face. It was difficult to withdraw from the gaze of her eyes.

'Actually it is. My seat is right in front of you,' she answered her own question and heaved her heavy suitcase onto the upper berth. She sat down on the berth opposite me, and gave out a sigh of relief.

'I climbed onto the wrong coach. Luckily the bogies are connected,' she said, adjusting her long hair that ended in countless ringlets. From the corner of my eye I tried to look at her. She was young, perhaps early to mid-twenties. Her waist-length hair had a life of its own: a strand fell on her forehead repeatedly. I could not see her face clearly, but I could tell one thing—she was pretty. And her eyes—once you looked into them, you could not turn away. I kept my gaze down.

She re-arranged stuff in her handbag. I tried to look out of the window. It was completely dark.

'So, pretty empty train,' she said after ten minutes.

'Yes,' I said. 'It's the new holiday special. They just started it, without telling people about it.'

'No wonder. Otherwise, trains are always full at this time.'

'It will get full. Don't worry. Just give it a few days,' I said and leaned forward, 'Hi. I am Chetan by the way, Chetan Bhagat.'

'Hi,' she said and looked at me for a few seconds. 'Chetan...I don't know, your name sounds familiar.'

Now this was cool. It meant she had heard of my first book. I am recognized rarely. And of course, it had never happened with a girl on a night train.

'You might have heard of my book, Five Point Someone. I'm the author,' I said.

'Oh yes,' she said and paused. 'Oh yes, of course. I've read your book. The three underperformers and the prof's daughter one, right?' she said.

'Yes. So how did you like it?'

'It was all right.'

I was taken aback. Man, I could have done with a little more of a compliment here.

'Just all right?' I said, fishing a bit too obviously.

'Well...' she said, and paused.

'Well what?' I said after ten seconds.

'Well. Yeah, just all right...okay okay types,' she said.

I kept quiet. She noticed the expression of mild disappointment on my face.

'Anyway, nice to meet you Chetan. Where are you coming from? IIT Kanpur?'

'Yes,' I said, my voice less friendly than a few moments ago. 'I had to give a talk there.'

'Oh really? About what?'

'About my book—you know the just okay-okay type one. Some people do want to hear about it,' I said, keeping a sweet tone to sugarcoat my sarcasm-filled words.

'Interesting,' she said and turned quiet again.

3

I was quiet too. I didn't want to speak to her anymore. I wanted my empty compartment back.

The flickering yellow light above was irritating me. I wondered if I should just shut it off, but it was not that late yet.

'What's the next station? Is it a non-stop train?' she asked after five minutes, obviously to make conversation.

'I don't know,' I said and turned to look out of the windows again even though I couldn't see anything in the darkness.

'Is everything okay?' she asked softly.

'Yes, why?' I said, the tone of my 'why' giving away that everything was, in fact, not okay.

'Nothing. You're upset about what I said about your book right?'

'Not really,' I said.

She laughed. I looked at her. Just like her gaze, her smile was arresting too. I knew she was laughing at me, but I wanted her to keep smiling. I dragged my eyes away again.

'Listen. I know your book did well. You are like this youth writer and everything. But at one level...just forget it.'

'What?' I said.

'At one level, you are hardly a youth writer.'

I turned silent and looked at her for a few seconds. Her magnetic eyes had a soft but insistent gaze.

'I thought I wrote a book about college kids. That isn't youth?' I said.

'Yeah right. So you wrote a book on IIT. A place where so few people get to go. You think that represents the entire youth?' she asked and took out a box of mints from her bag. She offered me one, but I declined. I wanted to get this straight.

'So what are you trying to say? I had to start somewhere, so I wrote about my college experiences. And you know the story is not so IIT-specific. It could have happened anywhere. I mean, just for that you are trashing my book.'

'I am not trashing it. I am just saying it hardly represents the Indian youth,' she said and shut the box of mints.

'Oh really...' I began, but was interrupted by the noise as the train passed over a long bridge.

We didn't speak for the next three minutes, until the train had returned to smoother tracks.

'What represents the youth?' I said.

'I don't know. You're the writer. You figure it out,' she said, and brushed aside a few curls that had fallen on her forehead.

'That's not fair,' I said, 'that is so not fair.' I sounded like a five-year-old throwing a tantrum. She smiled as she saw me grumbling to myself. A few seconds later, she spoke again.

'Are you going to write more books?' she said.

'I'll try to,' I said. I wasn't sure if I ever wanted to talk to her again.

'So what is it going to be? IIMs this time?' she said.

'No.'

'Why not?'

'Because it does not represent the country's youth.'

She started laughing.

'See, I am taking feedback. And now you laugh at me,' I said.

'No, no,' she said. 'I am not laughing at you. Can you stop being so over-sensitive?'

'I am not over-sensitive. I just want to take feedback,' I said and turned my face away.

'Well, well now. Let me explain. See, I just felt the whole IITian thing is cool and all, but what does it all mean in the broader sense?

Yes, the book sells and you get to go to IIT Kanpur. But is that what it is all about?' she said.

'Well, then what is it about?'

'If you want to write about the youth, shouldn't you talk about young people who really face challenges? I mean yes, IITians face challenges, but what about the hundreds and thousands of others?'

'Like whom?'

'Just look around you. What is the biggest segment of youth facing challenges in modern India?'

'I don't know. Students?'

'Not those, Mr Writer. Get out of the student-campus of your first book now. Anything else you see that you find strange and interesting? I mean, what is the subject of your second novel?'

I turned to look at her carefully for the first time. Maybe it was the time of night, but I kid you not, she was one of the most beautiful women I had ever seen. Everything about her was perfect. Her face was like that of a child. She wore a little bindi, which was hard to focus on as her eyes came in the way.

I tried to focus on her question.

'Second novel? No, haven't thought of a subject yet,' I said.

'Really? Don't you have any ideas?'

'I do. But nothing I am sure about.'

'Inte....resting,' she drawled. 'Well, just bask in your first book's success then.'

We kept quiet for the next half an hour. I took out the contents of my overnight bag and rearranged them for no particular reason. I wondered if it even made sense to change into a nightsuit. I was not going to fall asleep anyway. Another train noisily trundled past us in the opposite direction, leaving silence behind.

'I might have a story idea for you,' she said, startling me.

'Huh?' I was wary of what she was going to say. For no matter what her idea was, I had to appear interested.

'What is it?'

'It is a story about a call center.'

'Really?' I said. 'Call centers as in business process outsourcing centers or BPOs?'

'Yes, do you know anything about them?'

I thought about it. I did know about call centers, mostly from my cousins who worked there.

'Yes, I know a little bit,' I said. 'Some 300,000 people work in the industry. They help US companies in the sales, service and maintenance of their operations. Usually younger people work there in night shifts. Quite interesting, actually.'

'Just interesting? Have you ever thought of what all they have to face?' she asked, her voice turning firm again.

'Uh, not really...' I said.

'Why? They aren't the youth? You don't want to write about them?' she said, almost scolding me.

'Listen, let's not start arguing again...'

'I'm not arguing. I told you that I have a call center story for you.'

I looked at my watch. It was 12.30 a.m. A story would not be such a bad idea to kill time, I thought.

'Let's hear it then,' I said.

'I'll tell you. But I have a condition,' she said.

Condition? I was intrigued. 'What? That I don't tell it to anyone else?' I asked.

'No. Just the opposite in fact. You have to promise me to write it as your second book.'

'What?' I said, almost falling from my seat.

Wow! Now that was something. Okay, so I meet a girl who appears interesting and has a nice pair of eyes and looks like she can tell me a story to kill time. However, it does not mean I will spend two years of my life turning it into a book.

'Like a full book? Are you kidding? I can't promise that. It's a lot of work,' I said.

'Up to you,' she said and turned silent.

I waited for ten seconds. She did not speak.

'Can't I decide after you tell me the story?' I said. 'If it is interesting, I may even do it. But how can I decide without listening to it?'

'No. It is not about choice. If I tell you, you have to write it,' she said.

'A whole book…?' I asked again.

'Yes. Like it's your own story. In first person—just like in your first book. I'll give you the contacts of the people in the story. You can meet them, do your research, whatever it takes, but make it your second book.'

'Well then, I think it's better if you don't tell me,' I said.

'Okay,' she said and became quiet. She got up to spread a bed sheet on her berth, and then arranged her pillow and blanket. I guessed she was planning to go to sleep.

I checked my watch again. It was 1:00 a.m., and I was still wide awake. This was a non-stop train, and there were no stations to look forward to until Delhi in the morning. She switched off the flickering yellow light. Now the only light in the compartment was an eerie blue one; I couldn't figure out where the bulb was. It felt strange, like we were the only two people in the universe.

As she was sliding under her blanket, I asked, 'What is the story about? At least tell me a little bit more.'

'Will you do it then?'

I shrugged in the semi-darkness. 'Can't say. Don't tell me the story yet—just tell me what it is about.'

She nodded and sat up. Folding her legs beneath her, she began talking.

'All right,' she said, 'it is a story about six people in a call center on one night.'

'Just one night? Like this one?' I interrupted.

'Yes, one night. One night at the call center.'

'You sure that can be a full book? I mean, what is so special about this night?'

She heaved a sigh and took a sip from her bottle of mineral water.

'You see,' she said, 'it wasn't like any other night. It was the night there was a phone call.'

'What?' I said and burst out laughing. 'So a call center gets a phone call. That is the special part?'

She did not smile back. She waited for me to stop laughing and then continued as if I hadn't said anything. 'You see, it wasn't an ordinary phone call. It was the night...it was the night there was a phone call from God.'

Her words had me spring to attention.

'What?'

'You heard me. That night there was a phone call from God,' she said.

'What exactly are you talking about?'

'I just told you what the story was about. You asked, remember?' she said.

'And then...how...I mean...'

'I'm not telling you anymore. Now you know what it's about, if you want to hear the story, you know my condition.'

'That is a tough condition,' I said.

'I know. Up to you,' she said and lifted her blanket again. She lay down and closed her eyes.

Six people. One night. Call center. Call from God. The phrases kept repeating in my head as another hour passed. At 2:00 a.m. she woke up to have a sip of water.

'Not sleeping?' she asked, with eyes only half open.

Maybe there was a voltage problem, but this time even the blue light in the compartment started flickering.

'No, not sleepy at all,' I said.

'Okay, goodnight anyway,' she said, and began to lie down again.

'Listen,' I said. 'Get up. Sit down again.'

'Huh?' she said, rubbing her eyes. 'Why? What happened?'

'Nothing. You tell me what happened. Tell me the story,' I said.

'So you will write it?'

'Yes,' I said, with a bit of hesitation.

'Good,' she said, and sat up again. The cross-legged position was back.

The rest of the night, she told me the story that begins from the next page. It is a story about six people, three guys and three girls who worked at the Connexions Call Center. I chose to tell the story through Shyam's eyes. This is because, after I met him, I found him the most similar to me as a person. The rest of the people and what happened that night—well, I will let Shyam tell you that.

# From #29

$O$THERWISE?' ESHA SAID.

'Otherwise we die,' Vroom said.

We stayed quiet for a minute.

'Everyone dies one day,' I said, just to break the silence.

'Maybe it is simpler this way. Just end life rather than deal with it,' Vroom said.

I nodded. I was nervous and I was glad Vroom was making small talk.

'My main question is—what if no one finds us even after we die. What happens then?' Vroom said.

The vultures will find us. They always do. I saw it on Discovery Channel,' I said.

'See, that makes me uncomfortable. I don't like the idea of sharp beaks tearing my muscles, cracking my bones and ripping me to shreds. Plus, my body will be smelling like hell. I'd rather be burnt in a dignified manner and go up in that one last ultimate puff of smoke.'

'Can you guys stop this nonsense. At least be silent,' Esha said and folded her arms.

Vroom smiled at her. Then he turned to me. 'I don't think Esha will smell too much. Her Calvin Klein perfume will keep her carcass fresh for days.'

I WAS SPLASHING MY HANDS IN THE WATER POINTLESSLY IN THE sea. I can't even swim in a pond, let alone in the Indian Ocean. I was in the water while my boss Bakshi was in a boat next to me. He was pushing my head down in the water. I saw Priyanka drifting away in a lifeboat. I screamed even as Bakshi used both his hands to keep my head submerged. Salt water filled my mouth and nostrils as I heard loud beeps at a distance.

My nightmare ended as my cell phone alarm rang hard in my left ear and I woke up to its *Last Christmas* ring tone. The ring tone was a gift from Shefali, my new semi-girlfriend. I squinted through a half-shut eye and lifted the cell phone.

'8:32 p.m.' surrounded by little bells flashed on the screen.

'Damn,' I said and jumped out of bed.

I would have loved to analyze my dream and its significance in my insignificant life, but I had to get dressed for work.

'Man, the Qualis will be here in twenty minutes,' I thought, digging matter out of my eye. I was still tired, but scared to sleep more because I was getting late. Besides, there was a serious risk of Bakshi making a comeback in my dreams.

By the way, hi. I am Shyam Mehra, or Sam Marcy as they call me at my workplace, the Connexions call center in Gurgaon. (American tongues have trouble saying my real name and prefer Sam. If you want, you can give me another name too. I really don't care.)

Anyway, I am a call center agent. There are hundreds of thousands, probably millions of agents like me. But this total pain-in-the neck author chose me, of all the agents in the country. He met me and told me to help him with his second book. In fact, he near as well wanted me to write the book for him. I declined, saying I can't even write my resume or even other simple things in life, there is no way I can write a whole damn book. I explained to him how my promotion to the position of team leader had been put off for one year because my manager Bakshi had told me I don't have the 'required skill-set' yet. In my review, Bakshi wrote that I was 'not a go-getter'. (I don't even *know* what 'go-getter' means, so I guess I'm not one for sure.)

But this author said he didn't care—he had promised someone he'd do this story so I'd better cooperate, otherwise he would keep pestering me. I tried my best to wriggle out of it, but he wouldn't let go of me. I finally relented and that's why I'm stuck with this assignment, while you are stuck with me.

I also want to give you one more warning. My English is not that great—actually, nothing about me is great. So, if you are looking for something posh and highbrow, then I'd suggest you read another book which has some big many-syllable words. I know only one big, many-syllable word, and I hate that word—'management'. But we'll get to that later. I told the author about my limited English. However, the pain-in-the-neck author said big emotions do not come from big words. So, I had no choice but to do the job. I hate authors. For now, let us go back to the story. If you remember, I had just woken up at my home.

There were noises in the living room. Some relatives were in town to attend a family wedding. My neighbor was getting married to his cousin...er sorry, I was too groggy to figure this out—no, my cousin was getting married to his neighbor. But I had to work, so I could not go to the wedding. It doesn't matter, all marriages are the same, more or less.

I reached the bathroom still half-asleep. It was already occupied.

The bathroom door was open. I saw five of my aunts scrambling to get a few square-inches of the wash-basin mirror. One aunt was cursing her daughter for leaving the matching bindis at home. Another aunt had lost the little screw of her gold earring and was flipping out.

'It is pure gold, where is it?' she screamed into my face. 'Has the maid stolen it?' Like the maid had nothing better to do than steal one tiny screw. Wouldn't she steal the whole set? I thought.

'Auntie, can I use the bathroom for five minutes. I need to get ready for office,' I said.

'Oh hello, Shyam. Woke up finally?' my mother's sister said. 'Office? You are not coming for the wedding?'

'No, I have to work. Can I have the bath...'

'Look how big Shyam has become,' my maternal aunt said. 'We need to find a girl for him soon.'

Everyone burst into giggles. It was their biggest joke of the day.

'Can I please...' I said.

'Shyam, leave the ladies alone,' one of my older cousins interrupted. 'What are you doing here with the women? We are already so late for the wedding.'

'But I have to go to work. I need to get dressed,' I protested, trying to elbow my way to the bathroom tap.

'You work in a call center, right?" my cousin said.

'Yes.'

'Your work is through the phone. Why do you need to dress up? Who is going to see you?'

I didn't answer.

'Use the kitchen sink,' an aunt suggested and handed me my toothbrush.

I gave them all a dirty look. Nobody noticed. I passed by the living room on my way to the kitchen. The uncles were outside, on their second whiskey and soda. One uncle said something about how it would be better if my father were still alive and around this evening.

I reached the kitchen. The floor was so cold I felt I had stepped on an ice tray. I realized I had forgotten soap. I went back but the bathroom door was bolted. There was no hot water in the kitchen, and my face froze as I washed it with cold water.

Winter in Delhi is a bitch. I brushed my teeth and used the steel plates as a mirror to comb my hair. Shyam had turned into Sam and Sam's day had just begun.

I was hungry, but there was nothing to eat in the house. Because they'd be getting food at the wedding, my mother had felt there was no need to cook at home.

The Qualis horn screamed at 8:55 p.m.

As I was about to leave, I realized I had forgotten my ID. I went to my room, but could not find it. I tried to find my mother instead. She was in her bedroom, lost in more aunties, saris and jewellery sets. She and my aunts were doing some major weight comparisons of which aunt's set was heaviest. Usually the heaviest aunt had the heaviest set.

'Mom, have you seen my ID?' I said. Everyone ignored me. I went back to my room as the Qualis honked for the fourth time.

'Damn, there it is.' I said as I finally located the ID under my bed. I pulled it out by its strap and strung it around my neck.

I waved a goodbye to everyone, but no one acknowledged me. It wasn't surprising, I am only cared for so much. Every cousin of mine is becoming a doctor or engineer. You can say I am the black sheep of my family. Though I do not think that expression is correct. After all, what's wrong with black sheep—don't people wear black sweaters? But you get an idea of my status in my clan. In fact, the only reason people somewhat talk to me is I have a job and get a salary at the end of the month. You see, I used to work in the website department of an ad agency before this call center job. However, the ad agency paid horrible money. Also, all the people there were pseudos, more interested in office politics than websites. I quit, and all hell broke loose at home. That is when the black sheep term was tagged onto me. I saved myself by joining Connexions, as with money in your wallet the world gives you some respect and lets you breathe. Connexions was also the natural choice for me, as Priyanka worked there. Of course, that reason was no longer relevant.

My aunt finally found the gold screw trapped in her fake-hair bun.

The Qualis horn screamed again, this time in an angry tone. 'I'm coming,' I shouted as I ran out of the house.

## 2

'W HAT SAHIB. LATE AGAIN?' THE DRIVER SAID AS I TOOK THE front seat.

'Sorry, sorry. Military Uncle's place first?' I panted to the driver.

'Yes,' he replied, looking at his watch.

'Can we reach the call center by 10:00 p.m.? I have to meet someone before their shift ends,' I said.

'Depends if your colleagues come on time,' the driver replied laconically as he drove towards Military Uncle's house. 'Anyway, let's pick up the old man first.'

Military Uncle hates it if we are late. I prepared myself for some dirty looks. His tough manner comes from the Army background, from which he retired a few years ago. At fifty plus, he is the oldest person in the call center. I do not know him well, and I won't talk about him much. But I do know that he used to stay with his son and daughter-in-law before he moved out (*read—thrown out*) to be on his own. The pension was meager, and he tried to supplement his income by working in the call center. However, he hates to talk and is not a voice agent. He sits on the solitary online chat and email station. Even though he sits in our room, his desk is at a far corner near the fax machine. He rarely speaks more than three words at a time. Most of his interactions with us are limited to giving us condescending *you-young-people* glances.

The Qualis stopped outside Uncle's house. He was waiting at the entrance.

'Late?' Uncle said, looking at the driver.

Without answering, the driver got out to open the Qualis back door. Uncle climbed in, ignored the middle seat and sat at the back. He probably wanted to sit as far away from me as possible.

Uncle gave me an *it-must-be-your-fault* look. Older people think they have a natural right to judge you. I looked away. The driver took a U-turn to go to Radhika's house.

One of the unique features about my team is that we not only work together, we also share the same Qualis. Through a bit of route planning and driver persuasion, we ensured that my Western Appliances Strategic Group all came and left together. There are six of us: Military Uncle, Radhika, Esha, Vroom, Priyanka and me.

The Qualis moved to Radhika Jha, or agent Regina Jones's house. As usual, Radhika was late.

'Radhika madam is too much,' the driver said, continuously pressing the horn. I looked at my watch anxiously. I didn't want Shefali to throw a tantrum.

Six minutes later Radhika came running towards us, clutching the ends of her maroon shawl in her right hand.

'Sorry, sorry sorry...' she said a dozen times before we could say anything.

'What?' I asked her as the Qualis moved again.

'Nothing. Almond milk for mom-in-law. Took longer to crush the almonds,' she said, leaning back exhausted in her seat. She had taken the middle seat.

'Ask mom-in-law to make her own milk,' I suggested.

'C'mon Shyam,' she said, 'she's so old, it is the least I can do, especially when her son is not here.'

'Yeah, right,' I shrugged. 'Just that and cooking three meals a day and household chores and working all night and...'

'Shh...' she said, 'forget all that. Any news on the call center? I'm scared.'

'Nothing new from what Vroom told me. We have no new orders, call volumes are at an all time low—Connexions is doomed. Just a question of when,' I said.

'Really?' her eyes widened.

It was true. You might have heard of those swanky, new-age call centers where everything is hunky-dory, clients are plenty and agents get aromatherapy massages. Well, our Connexions was not one of them. We live off one and only one client—Western Computers and Appliances. And even their call flow had dwindled. Rumors that the call center would collapse floated in every day.

'You think Connexions will close down? Like forever?' Radhika asked.

Uncle raised an eyebrow to look at us, but soon went back to brooding by himself in the back seat. I sometimes wished he would say more, but I guess it's better for people to shut up rather than say something nasty.

'That, or they will do major job cuts. Ask Vroom,' I said.

The Qualis moved painfully slow as it was a heavy wedding date in Delhi. On every street, there was a wedding procession. We edged forward as the driver dodged several fat grooms on their over-burdened horses. I checked the time again. Shefali would do some serious sulking today.

'I need this job. Anuj and I need to save,' Radhika said, more to herself. Anuj was Radhika's husband. She married him three years ago after a whirlwind courtship in college. She now lived in a joint family with Anuj's ultra-traditional parents. It was tough for daddy's only girl, but it's amazing what people do for love.

The driver drove to Esha Singh's (or agent Eliza Singer's) place next. She was already outside her house. The driver kept the Qualis ignition on as he opened the back door.

Esha entered the Qualis and the smell of expensive perfume filled the vehicle. She sat next to Radhika in the middle row and removed her suede jacket.

'Mmm...nice. What is it?' Radhika said.

'You noticed...' Esha was pleased. 'Escape, by Calvin Klein.' She bent her knees and adjusted the tassels at the end of her long, dark brown skirt.

'Oooh. Went shopping?' Radhika said.

'Call it a momentary lapse of reason,' Esha said.

The driver finally reached a stretch of empty road and raced the Qualis fast.

I looked at Esha again. Her dress sense is impeccable. Esha dresses better on an average day than I ever did in my whole life. Her sleeveless coffee-colored top perfectly contrasted with her skirt. She wore chunky brown earrings that looked edible and her lipstick was a thick cocoa, as if she had just kissed a bowl of chocolate sauce. Her eyes had at least one of these things—mascara, eyeliner and/or eye-shadow (I can't tell, but Priyanka told me they are all different things).

'The Lakme fashion week is in four months. My agent is trying to get me an assignment,' Esha said to Radhika.

Esha wanted to become a model. She was hot, at least according to people at the call center. Two months ago, some agents in the Western Computers bay conducted a stupid poll in office. You know, the secret ones that everyone knows about anyway. People vote for various titles, like who is hot, who is handsome and who is pretty. Esha won the title of the 'hottest chick at Connexions'. She acted very dismissive of the poll results, but from that day there's been just this tiny hint of vanity in her. But otherwise, she is fine. She moved to Delhi from Chandigarh a year ago, against her parents' wishes. The call center job helps her earn a regular income, but during the day she approaches agencies and tries to get modeling assignments. She's taken part in some low-key fashion shows in West Delhi. But apart from that and the hottest-chick in-house title, nothing big has come her way so far. Priyanka once told me (making me swear that I'd keep it to myself) that she thinks Esha will never make it as a real model. *'Esha is too short and too small-town for a real model'*—is what she said exactly. But Priyanka doesn't know crap. Esha is five-five, only two inches shorter than me (and one inch taller than me with her heels). I think that is quite tall for a girl. And the whole *'small-town'* thing, that just went over my head. Esha is only twenty-two, give her a chance. And Chandigarh is not a small town, it is a union territory and the administrative capital of two states. But Priyanka's geography is crap as well. I think Priyanka is just jealous. All non-hot girls are jealous of the hot ones. Priyanka wasn't even considered for the hottest chick. Now, I do find Priyanka nice looking, and she did get a nomination for the 'call-center cutie award', which I think is just because of her dimples and cute round face. But Priyanka didn't win. Some girl in HR won that.

We had to pick Vroom next; his real name is Varun Malhotra (or agent Victor Mell). However, everyone calls him Vroom because of his love for anything on wheels.

The Qualis turned into the lane of Vroom's house. He was sitting on his bike, waiting for us.

'What's the bike for?' I said, craning out of the window.

'I'm coming on my own,' Vroom said, adjusting his leather gloves. He wore black jeans and trekking shoes that made his thin legs look extra long. His dark blue sweatshirt had the Ferrari horse logo on it.

'Are you crazy?' I said. 'It's so cold. Get in, we're late already.'

Dragging the bike he came and stood next to me.

'No, I'm stressed today. I need to get it out of me with a fast ride.' He was standing right beside me and only I could hear him.

'What happened?'

'Nothing. Dad called. He argued with mom for two hour Why did they separate? They can't live without screaming th guts out at each other?'

'It's okay man. Not your problem,' I said.

Vroom's dad was a businessman who parted from his wife two years ago. He preferred banging his secretary to being with his family, so Vroom and his mother now lived without him.

'I couldn't sleep at all. Just lay in bed all day and now I feel sick. Need to get some energy back,' Vroom said as he straddled his bike.

'But it's freezing, dude...' I began.

'What is going on Shyam sahib?' the driver asked. I turned around. The driver looked at me with a puzzled expression. I shrugged my shoulders.

'He's coming on his bike,' I told everyone.

'Come with me,' Vroom said to me. 'I'll make you reach in half the time.'

'No thanks,' I said, and folded my hands. I was not leaving the cozy Qualis to go anywhere.

Vroom bent over to greet the driver.

'Hello, driver sahib,' Vroom said.

'Vroom sahib, don't you like my Qualis?' the driver said, v s bly dejected.

'No Driver *ji*, I am in a mood to ride,' Vroom said, and offered a pack of cigarettes to the driver. The driver took one. Vroom signaled him to keep the whole pack.

'Drive the Qualis if you want,' the driver said and lifted his hands off the steering wheel.

'No. Maybe later. Right now I need to fly.'

'Hey Vroom. Any news on Connexions? Anything happening?' Radhika asked, adjusting her hair.

Apart from the dark circles around her eyes, you would say Radhika was pretty. She had high cheekbones and her fair skin went well with her wispy eyebrows and soot-black eyes. Her sleep-deprived face still looked nice. She wore a plain mustard sari, as saris were all she could wear in her in-laws' house. This was different apparel from the jeans and skirts Radhika preferred before her marriage.

'No updates. Will dig for stuff today but I think Bakshi will screw us all. Hey Shyam, the website manual is all done by the way. I emailed it to office,' Vroom said and started his bike.

'Cool, finally. Let's send it in today,' I said, perking up.

We left Vroom and moved to our last pickup at Priyanka's place. It was 9:30 p.m., still an hour away from our shift. However, I was worried as Shefali finished her shift and left by 10:20 p.m.

Fortunately, Priyanka was standing at her pick-up point when we reached her place.

'Hi,' Priyanka said, as she entered the Qualis and sat next to Esha in the middle seat. She carried a large, white plastic bag apart from her usual giant handbag.

'Hi,' everyone replied except me.

'I said hi, Shyam,' Priyanka said.

I pretended not to hear. It is strange, but ever since we broke up, I find it difficult to talk to her. Even though I must think of her thirty times a day.

I looked at her. She adjusted her dupatta around her neck. The forest green salwar kameez she was wearing was new, noticed. The colors suited her light brown skin. I looked at h nose and her nostrils that flared up every time she was ups I swear tiny flames appeared in them when she was mad.

'Shyam, I said hi,' she said again. She gets really pissed if people don't respond to her.

'Hi,' I said. I wondered if Bakshi would finally promote me after he saw my website manual tonight.

'Where's Vroom?' Priyanka said. She has to know everything all the time.

'Vroom is riding...vroom,' Esha said, making a motorbike noise.

'Nice perfume, Esha. Shopping again, eh?' Priyanka said and sniffed, puckering up that tiny nose.

'Escape, Calvin Klein,' Esha announced and struck a pose.

'Wow! Someone is going designer,' Priyanka said and both of them laughed. This is something I will never understand about her. Priyanka has b :ched fifty times about Esha to me, yet when they are with each other, they behave like long-lost sisters.

'Esha, big date coming?' Radhika said.

'No dates. I'm still so single. Suitable guys are an endangered species,' Esha said and all the girls laughed. It wasn't that funny if you ask me. I wished Vroom was in the Qualis too. He is the only person in my team I can claim as a friend. At twenty-two he is four years younger than I am, but I still find it easiest to talk to him. Radhika's household talk is too alien to me. Esha's modeling trip is also beyond me as no one is ever going to pay me for my looks. I am certainly not good looking: my day is made if someone describes my looks as 'slightly above average'.

Priyanka was a friend and a lot more until recently. Four months ago, we broke up (Priyanka's version) or she dumped me (my version).

So now I try to do what she wants us to do—'move on'— which is why I hang out with Shefali.

Beep Beep. Beep Beep.

Two pairs of loud beeps from my shirt's pocket startled everyone.

'Who's is that?' Priyanka said.

'Oh sorry. It's my SMS,' I said and opened the new message.

```
Where r u my eddy teddy?
Come soon—curly wurly
```

It was Shefali. She is into cheesy nicknames these days. I replied to the SMS:

```
Qualis stuck in traffic
Will b there soon
```

'Who's that?' Esha asked me.

'Nobody important,' I said.

'Shefali?' Radhika said.

'No,' I said and everybody looked at me.

'No,' I said again.

'Yes, it is. It is Shefali, isn't it,' Esha and Radhika said together and laughed.

'Why does Shefali always babytalk?' I heard Esha whisper to Radhika. More titters followed.

'Whatever,' I said and looked at my watch. The Qualis was still on the NH8, at the entrance to Gurgaon. We were ten minutes away from Connexions.

Cool, will meet Shefali by 10:10, I thought.

'Can we stop for a quick tea at Inderjeet? We will still make it by 10:30,' Priyanka said. Inderjeet dhabha on NH8 was famous for its all-night tea and snacks among truck drivers.

'We won't get late?' Radhika crinkled her forehead.

'Of course not. Driver *ji* saved us twenty minutes in the last stretch. Come Driver *ji*, my treat,' Priyanka said.

'Good idea. Will keep me awake,' Esha said.

The driver slowed the Qualis near Inderjeet dhabha and parked it near the counter.

'Hey guys, do we have to stop? We will get late,' I protested against the chai chorus.

'We won't get late. Let's treat Driver *ji* for making us reach fast,' Priyanka said and got out of the Qualis. She just has to do things I don't want to do.

'He wants to be with Shefali, dude,' Esha elbowed Radhika. They guffawed again. What is so damn funny, I wanted to ask, but didn't.

'No, I just like to reach my shift a few minutes early,' I said and got out of the Qualis. Military Uncle and the driver followed us.

Inderjeet dhabha had *angithis* next to each table. I smelled hot paranthas, but did not order as it was getting late. The driver arranged plastic chairs for us. Inderjeet's minions collected tea orders as per the various complicated rules laid out by the girls.

'No sugar in mine,' Esha said.

'Extra hot for me,' Radhika said.

'With cardamom for me,' Priyanka said.

When we were in college together, Priyanka used to make cardamom tea for me in her hostel room. Her taste in men might have changed, but obviously not her taste in beverages.

The tea arrived in three minutes.

'So what's the gossip?' Priyanka said as she cupped her hands around the glass for warmth. Apart from cardamom, Priyanka's favourite spice is gossip.

'No gossip. You tell us, things are happening in *your* life,' Radhika said.

'I actually do have something to tell,' Priyanka said with a sly smile.

'What?' Radhika and Esha exclaimed together.

'I'll tell you when we get to the bay. It's big,' Priyanka said.

'Tell now,' Esha said, poking Priyanka's shoulder.

'No time. Someone is in a desperate hurry,' Priyanka said, glancing meaningfully at me.

I turned away.

'Okay, I also have something to share. But don't tell anyone,' Esha said.

'What?' Radhika said.

'See,' Esha said and stood up. She raised her top to expose a flat midriff—on which there was a newborn ring.

'Cool, check it out,' Priyanka said, 'someone's turning trendy.'

Military Uncle stared as if in a state of shock. I suspect he was never young, was just born straight forty years old.

'What's that? A navel ring?' Radhika asked.

Esha nodded and covered herself again.

'Did it hurt?' Radhika said.

'Oh yes,' Esha said. 'Imagine someone stapling your tummy hard.'

Esha's statement churned my stomach.

'Shall we go,' I said, gulping down my tea.

'Let's go girls, or Mr Conscientious will get upset,' Priyanka suppressed a smirk. I hate her.

I went to the counter to pay the bill. I saw Vroom watching TV.

'Vroom?' I said.

'Hi. What are you guys doing here?' he said.

I told him about the girls' tea idea.

'I arrived twenty minutes ago man,' Vroom said. He extinguished his cigarette and showed me the butt. 'This was my first.'

Vroom was trying to cut down to four cigarettes a night. However, with Bakshi in our life, it was impossible.

'Can you rush me to the call center? Shefali will leave soon,' I said.

Vroom's eyes were transfixed on the TV set on Inderjeet dhabha's counter. The NDTV news channel was on, and Vroom is a sucker for it. He worked in a newspaper once and is generally into social and global issues and all that stuff. He thinks that just by watching the news, he can change the world. That, by the way, is his trip.

A TV reporter was speaking in front of Parliament house, announcing elections in four months.

'Hey, I know that guy. He used to work in my previous job,' Vroom said.

'The newspaper?'

'Yes, Boontoo we used to call him—total loser guy. Didn't know he moved to television. Check out his contact lenses,' Vroom said, as both of us paid the bill.

'Let's go, man. Shefali will kill me.'

'Shefali. Oh you mean curly wurly,' Vroom laughed.

'Shut up man. She has to catch the Qualis after her shift This is the only time I get with her.'

'On one hand you had Priyanka, and now you sink to Shefali levels,' Vroom said, and bent his elbow to rest his six-feet-two-inches frame on the dhabha counter.

'What's wrong with Shefali?' I said, shuffling from one foot to the other.

'Nothing. Just that it is nice to have a girlfriend with half a brain. Why are you wasting your time with her?'

'I'm weaning myself off Priyanka. I'm trying to move on in life,' I said and took a sweet from the candy jar at the counter.

'So what's Shefali, a pacifier? What happened to the re-proposal plan with Priyanka?' Vroom said.

'I've told you. Not until I become team leader. Which should be soon—maybe tonight after we submit the website manual. Now can we please go?' I said.

'Yeah, right. Some hopes you live on,' Vroom said, but moved away from the counter.

I held on tight as Vroom zipped through NH8 at 120 km an hour. I closed my eyes and prayed Shefali would not be mad, and that I would reach alive.

Beep Beep. Beep Beep. My mobile went off again.

```
Curly wurly is sad
Eddy teddy is very bad
I leave in 10 min : (
```

I jumped off the bike as Vroom reached the call center. The bike jerked forward and Vroom had to use both his legs to balance.

'Easy man,' Vroom said in an irritated voice. 'Can you just let me park?'

'Sorry. I'm really late,' I said and ran inside.

# #3

'I'M NOT TALKING TO YOU,' SHEFALI SAID AND STARTED PLAYING with one of her silver earrings. The ring-shaped earrings were so large, they could be bangles.

'Sorry Shefali. My bay people made the Qualis late.' I stood next to her, leaning against her desk. She sat on her swivel chair and rotated it ninety degrees away from me to showcase her sulking. The dozens of workstations in her bay were empty as all the other agents had left.

'Whatever. I thought you were their team leader,' she said and pretended to work on her computer.

'I am not the team leader. I am due, but not one yet,' I said.

'Why don't they make you team leader?' she turned to me and fluttered her eyes. I hate this expression of hers.

'I don't know. Bakshi said he's trying, but I have to bring my leadership skills up to speed.'

'What is up to speed?' she said and opened her handbag.

'I don't know. Improve my skills I guess.'

'So you guys don't have any team leader.'

'No. Bakshi says we have to manage without one. I help with supervisory stuff for now. But Bakshi told me I have **strong future potential.**'

'So why doesn't your team listen to you?'

'Who says they don't? Of course they do.'

'So why were you late?' she said, beginning her sentence with a 'so' for the third time.

'Shefali come on, drop that,' I said, looking at my watch. 'How did your shift go?'

'Shift was okay. Team leader said call volumes have dropped for Western Computers. All customers are using the troubleshooting website now.'

'Cool. You do know who made that right?'

'Yes, you and Vroom. But I don't think you should make a big deal out of it. The website has cost Connexions a lot of business.'

'But the website helps the customers a lot, right?' I said.

'Shh. Don't talk about the website here. Some agents are very upset. Someone said they would cut people.'

'Really?'

'I don't know. Listen, why are you so unromantic? Is this how Eddy Teddy should talk to his Curly Wurly?'

I wanted to know more about what was going on at Connexions. Bakshi was super-secretive—all he said was there were some **confidential management priorities.** I thought of asking Vroom to spy some more.

'Eddy Teddy?' Shefali repeated. I looked at her. If she stopped wearing Hello Kitty hairpins, she could be passably cute.

'Huh?'

'Are you listening to me?'

'Of course.'

'Did you like my gift?'

'What gift?'

'The ring tones. I gave you six ring tones. See, you don't even remember,' she said and her face turned sad.

'I do. See I put *Last Christmas* as my tone,' I said and picked up my phone to play it. Vroom would probably kill me if he heard it, but I had to for Shefali.

'So cute,' Shefali said and pinched my cheeks. 'So cute it sounds, my Eddy Teddy.'

'Shefali...'

'What?'

'Can you stop calling me that?'

'Why? You don't like it?'

'Just call me Shyam.'

'You don't like the name I gave you?' she said, her voice transcending from sad to tragic.

I kept quiet. You never tell women you don't like something they have done. However, they pick up on the silence.

'That means you don't like the ring tones either,' she said and her voice started to break.

'I do,' I said, fearing a round of crying. 'I love the ring tones.'

'And what about the name? You can choose another name if you want. I am not like your other girlfriends,' she said and tiny tears appeared in her eyes. I looked at my watch. Three more minutes and time will heal everything, I thought. I took a deep breath. A hundred and eighty seconds and she would have to leave for sure. Sometimes counting seconds is a great way to kill time through a woman's tantrums.

'What kind of girlfriends?' I said.

'Like,' she sniffled, 'bossy girls who impose their way on you. Like you-know-who.'

'Who? What are you implying,' I said, my voice getting firmer. It was true; Priyanka could be bossy, but only if you didn't listen to her.

'Forget it. But will you give me a name if I stop crying?' Her sobs were at a serious risk of transforming into a full-fledged bawl.

'Yes,' I said. I'd rename the rest of her family if she stopped this drama.

'Okay,' she said and became normal. 'Give me a name.'

I thought hard. Nothing came to mind.

'Sheffy? How about Sheffy?' I said finally.

'Nooo. I want something cu eeer,' she said. Shefali loves to drag out words.

'I can't think of anything cute right now. I have to work. Isn't your Qualis leaving soon too?' I said.

She looked at her watch and stood up.

'Yes, I better leave now. Will you think of a name by tomorrow?' she said.

'I will, bye now.'

'Give me a kissie,' she said and tapped a finger on her cheek.

'What?'

'Kissie.'

'You mean a kiss? Yeah sure.' I gave her a peck on the cheek and turned around to return to my bay.

'Bye bye, Eddy Teddy,' her voice followed me.

# #4

THE OTHERS WERE ALREADY AT THE DESK WHEN I RETURNED from Shefali's bay.

Our bay's name is the 'Western Appliances Strategic Group' or WASG. Unlike the other bay that troubleshoots for computer customers, we deal with customers of home appliances such as refrigerators, ovens and vacuum cleaners. Management calls us the strategic bay because we specialize in troublesome and painful customers. These 'strategic' customers call a lot and are too dumb to figure out things (actually the latter applies to a lot of callers).

We feel special, as we are not part of the main computers bay. The main bay has over a thousand agents and handles the huge 'Western Computers' account. While the calls are less weird there, they miss the privacy we enjoy in the WASG.

I came and took my seat at the long rectangular table. We have a fixed seating arrangement: I sit next to Vroom, while

Priyanka is right opposite me; Esha is adjacent to Priyanka and Radhika sits next to Esha. The bay is an open plan, so we can all see each other. Military Uncle's chat station is at the corner of the room. At each of the other three corners, there are, respectively, the restrooms, a conference room and a stationery supplies room.

However, no one apart from Uncle was at their seat when I sat down. Everyone had gathered around Priyanka.

'What's the news? Tell us now.' Esha was saying.

'Okay, okay. But on one condition. It doesn't leave the WASG,' Priyanka said, sitting down. She pulled out a large plastic bag from under her seat.

'Guys,' I said, interrupting their banter.

Everyone turned to look at me.

I pointed at the desk and the unmanned phones. I looked at my watch. It was 10:29 p.m. The call system routine backup was about to finish, and our calls would begin in a minute.

Everyone returned to their chairs and put on their headsets.

'Good evening, everyone. Please pay attention to this announcement,' a loud voice filled our bay. I looked up. The voice came from the fire drill speaker.

'I hate these irritating announcements,' Priyanka said.

'This is the control room,' the speaker continued. 'This is to inform all agents of a fire drill next Friday at midnight. Please follow instructions during the fire drill to leave the call center safely. Thank you. Have a nice shift.'

'Why do they keep doing this? Nobody is going to burn this place down,' Esha said.

'Government rules,' Vroom said.

Conversation stopped mid-way as two beeps on the computer screens signaled the start of our shift.

Calls began at 10:31 p.m. Numbers started flashing on o common switchboard as we picked up calls one after the oth

'Good afternoon, Western Appliances, Victor speakin how may I help you?' Vroom said as he took one of his first calls.

'Yes, according to my records I am speaking to Ms Smith, and you have the WAF-200 dishwasher. Is that right?' Esha said.

Esha's 'memory' impressed the caller. It was not a big deal, given that our automated system had every caller's records. We knew their name, address, credit card details and past purchases from Western Appliances. We also had details on when they last called us. In fact, the reason why her call had come to our desk—the Western Appliances Strategic desk—was because she was a persistent caller. This way the main bay could continue to run smoothly.

Sometimes we had customers that were oddballs even by WASG standards. I will not go into all of them, but Vroom's 10:37 p.m. call went something like this:

'Yes Ms Paulson, of course we remember you. Happy Thanksgiving, I hope you are making a big turkey in our WA100 model oven,' Vroom said, reading from a script that reminded us about the American festival of the day.

I could not hear the customer's side of the conversation, but Ms Paulson was obviously explaining her problem with the oven.

'No Ms Paulson, you shouldn't have unscrewed the cover,' Vroom said, as politely as possible.

'No, really madam. An electrical appliance like the WA100 should only be serviced by trained professionals,' Vroom said, reading verbatim from the WA100 service manual.

Ms Paulson spoke for another minute. Our strategic bay hardly had a reputation for efficiency, but long calls like these could screw up Vroom's response times.

'See madam, you need to explain to me why you opened the top cover. Then perhaps we'll understand why you got an electric shock…so tell me….yes…oh…really?' Vroom continued, taking deep breaths. Patience, key to becoming a star agent, did not come naturally to him.

I looked around; people were busy with calls. Radhika helped someone defrost her fridge; Esha assisted a customer in unpacking a dishwasher. Everyone was speaking with an American accent and sounded different from how they had in the Qualis. I took a break from the calls to compile the call statistics of the previous day. I did not particularly like doing this, but Bakshi had left me with little choice.

'See madam,' Vroom was still with Ms Paulson, 'I understand your turkey did not fit and you did not want to cut it, but you should not have opened up the equipment…. But see that is not the equipment's fault…. I can't really tell you what to do…I understand your son is coming, madam…. Now if you had the WA150, that is a bigger size…' Vroom said, beginning to breathe faster.

Ms Paulson ranted on for a while longer.

'Ms Paulson, I suggest you take the oven to your dealer as soon as possible,' Vroom said firmly. 'And next time, get a smaller turkey…and yes, a readymade turkey will be a good idea for tonight…. No, I don't have a dial-a-turkey number. Thank you for calling Ms Paulson, bye.' Vroom ended the call.

Vroom banged his fist on the table.

'Everything okay?' I said, not looking up from my pap~~~

'Yeah. Just a psycho customer,' he mumbled as anoth~~ number started flashing on his screen.

I worked on my computer for the next ten minutes, compiling the call statistics of the previous day. Bakshi had also assigned me the responsibility of checking the other agents' etiquette. Every now and then, I would listen in on somebody's call. At 10:47 p.m., I connected to Esha's line.

'Yes sir. I sound like your daughter? Oh, thank you. So what is wrong with the vacuum cleaner?' she was saying.

'Your voice is so soothing,' the caller said.

'Thank you sir. So, the vacuum cleaner…?'

Esha's tone was perfect—just the right mix of politeness and firmness. Management monitored us on average call handling times, or AHTs. As WASG got the more painful customers, our AHT benchmarks were higher at two-and-a-half minutes per call. I checked my files for everyone's AHT—all of us were within targets.

'Beep!' The sound of the fax machine made me look up from my papers. I wondered who could be faxing us at this time. I went to the machine and checked the incoming fax. It was from Bakshi.

The fax machine took three minutes to churn out the seven pages he had sent. I tore the message sheet off the machine and held the first sheet up.

From: Subhash Bakshi
Subject: Training Initiatives

Dear Shyam,
Just FYI, I have recommended your name to
assist in accent training as they are short
of teachers. I am sure you can spare some time
for this. As always, I am trying to get you
more relevant and strategic exposure.
Yours,
Subhash Bakshi
Manager, Connexions

I gasped as I read the rest of the fax. Bakshi was sucking
me into several hours outside my shift to teach new recruits.
Apart from the extra work, I hate accent training anyway. The
American accent is so confusing. You might think the Americans
and their language are straightforward. Far from it—with them,
each letter can be pronounced several different ways.

I will give you just one example—T. With this letter
Americans have four different sounds. T can be silent so 'internet'
becomes 'innernet' and 'advantage' becomes 'advannage'. The
second way is when T and N merge—'written' becomes 'writn'
and 'certain' is 'certn'. The third sound is when T is in the middle.
There, it sounds like a D—'daughter' is 'daughder' and 'water' is
'wauder'. The last category, if you still care, is when Americans
say T actually like a T. This happens when T is the beginning of
the word like 'table' or 'stumble'. Man, it drives me nuts. And this
is just one consonant. The vowels are another, more painful story.

'What's up?' Vroom said, coming up to me.

I passed the fax to Vroom. He read it and smirked.

'Yeah right. He sent you an FYI. Do you know what an FYI is?' Vroom said.

'What?'

'Fuck You Instead. It is a standard way to dump responsibility on someone else.'

'I hate accent training man. You can't teach Delhi people to speak like Americans in a week.'

'Just as you can't train Americans to speak with a Punjabi accent,' Vroom said and chuckled. 'Anyway, go train-train, lose your brain.'

'What will I do?' I said, beginning to walk back towards our desk.

'Go train-train, lose your brain,' Vroom said and laughed. He liked the rhyme, and repeated it several times as we walked back to the bay.

I was back at my seat, Vroom's words—'train, train'—echoing in my head. They were making me remember another kind of train altogether. It brought back memories of the Rail Museum—where I had a date with Priyanka a year ago.

# #5:

# My Past Dates with Priyanka—I

Rail Museum, Chanakyapuri
One year before this night

She came thirty minutes late. I had seen the whole museum twice, examined every little train model, stepped inside India's oldest coal engine, understood the modern interactive siren system. I went to the canteen, which was on an island in the middle of an artificial pond. It was impressive landscaping for a museum. I thought of lighting a cigarette, but I caught sight of the sign: 'Only Steam Engines are Allowed to Smoke'. I was cradling a lukewarm Coke in the museum canteen when she arrived.

'Okay. Don't say anything. Sorry, I'm late, I know, I know,' she said and sat down with a thump in front of me.

I didn't say anything. I looked at her tiny nose, I wondered how it allowed in enough oxygen.

'What, say something,' she said after five seconds.

'I thought you told me to be quiet,' I said.

'My mother needs professional help,' Priyanka said. 'She really does.'

'What happened?' I swirled the straw in my coke, making little fizzy drops implode.

'I'll tell you. First, how do you like this place? Cute, isn't it?'

'The Rail Museum?' I said, throwing my hands in the air. 'How old are we, twelve? Anyway, what happened with mom? What was the fuel today?'

'We don't need fuel, just a spark is enough. Just as I was ready to leave to come here, she made a comment on my dress.'

'What did she say?' I asked, looking at her clothes. She wore a blue tie-and-dye skirt, and a T-shirt that had a peace sign on it. It was typical Priyanka stuff. She wore earrings with blue beads, which matched her necklace. She had a hint of kohl in her eyes, which I was crazy about.

'I was almost at the door and then she says, why don't you wear the gold necklace I gave you for your last birthday?' Priyanka said.

'And then?' She obviously wasn't wearing any gold necklace, as my gaze turned to the hollow of her neck, which I felt like touching.

'And I was like, no mom, it won't go with my dress. Yellow metal is totally uncool, only aunties wear it. Boom, next thing we are having this big, long argument. That's what made me late. Sorry,' she said.

'You didn't have to fight. Just wear the chain in front of her and remove it later,' I said as the waiter came to take our order.

'But that's not the point. Anyway,' she said and turned to the waiter, 'get me a plate of samosas, I'm starving. Actually wait, that is so fattening, do you have a salad?'

The waiter gave us a blank look.

'Where do you think you are?' I said. 'This is the Rail Museum canteen, not an Italian bistro. You get what you see.'

'Okay, okay,' she said, eyeing the stalls. 'Get me the potato chips. No, get me the popcorn. Popcorn is lighter, right?' She looked at the waiter as if he was a nutritionist.

'Just get the popcorn,' I said to the waiter.

'So, what else is happening? Met Vroom?' she said.

'Was supposed to, but couldn't. He had a date.'

'With who? New girl?'

'Of course. He never sticks to one. I wonder what girls see in him. All hot ones too,' I said.

'I can't understand the deal with Vroom. He is the most materialistic and unemotional person I have met in my entire life,' Priyanka said as the popcorn arrived at our table.

'No he isn't,' I said, grabbing more popcorn than I could hold.

'Well, look at him—jeans, phones, pizzas and bikes. That is all he lives for. And this whole new girlfriend every three months, c'mon, at some point you've got to stop that, right?'

'Well, I'm happy to stick to the one I have,' I said, my mouth overflowing with popcorn.

'You are so cute,' Priyanka said, as she blushed and smiled. She took some more popcorn and stuffed it into my mouth.

'Thanks,' I said as I munched the popcorn. 'Vroom has changed. He wasn't like this when he first joined from his previous job.'

'The one at the newspaper?'

'Yeah, journalist trainee. He started in current affairs. Do you know what one of his famous pieces was called?'

'No, what? Oh crap,' Priyanka said, looking at someone behind me.

'What happened?'

'Nothing, just don't look back. Some relatives of mine with their painful kids are here. Oh no,' she said, looking down at our table.

Now when someone tells you not to look at something, you always feel an incredible urge to do just that. From the corner of my eye I saw a family with two kids at the corner of the room.

'Who else do you expect to come here but kids?' I said. 'Anyway, they are quite far.'

'Shut up and look down. Anyway, tell me about Vroom's piece,' she said.

'Oh yeah. It was called "*Why Don't Politicians Ever Commit Suicide?*" '

'What? Sounds morbid.'

'Well, the article said all kinds of people—students, housewives, businessmen, employees and even film stars—commit suicide. But politicians never do. That tells you something.'

'What?' she said, still keeping her eyes down.

'Well, Vroom's point was that suicide is a horrible thing and people do it only because they are really hurt. This means they feel something. But politicians don't. So, basically, this country is run by people who don't feel anything.'

'Wow! Can't imagine that going down well with his editor.'

'You bet it didn't. However, Vroom had sneaked it in. The editor only saw it after it was printed and all hell broke loose. Vroom somehow saved his job, but his bosses moved him to Page 3.'

'Our Vroom? Page 3?'

'They told Vroom he was good looking, so he would fit in there. In addition, he had done a photography course. He could click the pictures himself.'

'Cover Page 3 because you are good looking? Now that sounds dumb,' she said.

49

'It is dumb. But Vroom took his revenge there too. He took unflattering pictures of the glitterati—faces stuffed with food, close-ups of cellulite thighs, drunk people throwing up—that sort of stuff showed up in papers the next day.'

'Oh my god,' Priyanka laughed. 'He sounds like an activist. I can't understand his switching to the call center for money.'

'Well, according to him, there is activism in chasing money too.'

'And how does that work?'

'Well, his point is that the only reason Americans have a say in this world is because they have cash. The day we get money, we can screw them. So, the first thing we have to do is get the money.'

'Interesting,' Priyanka said and let out a sigh. 'Well, that is why we slog at night. I could have done my B.Ed right after college. But I wanted to save some money first. Can't open my dream nursery school without cash. So until then, it is two hundred calls a night, night after night.' Priyanka rested her chin on her elbows. I looked at her. I think she would make the cutest nursery school principal ever.

'Western Appliances, Sam speaking, how may I help you? *Please* let me help you? Please...' I said, imitating an American accent.

Priyanka laughed again.

'Priyanka dideeee,' a five-year-old boy's voice startled customers from their samosas.

The boy running towards Priyanka had a model train set and a glass of fountain coke precariously balanced in his hands. He ran without co-ordination: the excitement of seeing his didi was too much for him. He tripped near our table and I lunged to save him. I succeeded, but his fountain coke fell all over my shirt.

'Oh no,' I said even as I saw another three-year-old girl with a huge lollipop in her mouth running towards us. I moved aside from the tornado to save another collision. She landed straight on Priyanka's lap. I went to the restroom to clean my shirt.

'Shyam,' Priyanka said when I returned, 'meet my cousin, Dr Anurag.' The entire family had shifted to our table. Priyanka introduced me to everyone. I forgot their names as soon as I heard them. Priyanka told her doctor cousin I worked at a call center. I think the cousin was less interested in talking to me after that. The kids had eaten half the popcorn and spilt the rest of it. The boy was running his model train set through popcorn fields on the table and screaming a mock siren with his sister.

'Sit, Shyam,' Priyanka said.

'No, actually I have an early shift today,' I said and got up to leave.

'But wait...' Priyanka said.

'No, I have to go,' I said and ran out of the Rail Museum, which had turned as chaotic as a railway station.

# #6

'OUCH,' ESHA'S SCREAM IN THE MIDDLE OF HER CALL BROKE MY train of thought and memories.

'What?' I said.

'I heard loud static. Really bad line...hello, yes madam,' Esha said.

Radhika was knitting something with pink wool while she waited for a call. People were busy, but I could sense that the call volume was lower than usual tonight.

'Eew,' Priyanka said five seconds later.

'Freaking hell,' Vroom said as he pulled off his headset from his ears.

'What's going on?' I said.

'There's shrill static coming every few seconds now. Ask Bakshi to send someone,' Vroom said, rubbing his ear.

'I'll go to his office. You guys cover the calls,' I said and looked at the time. It was 10:51 p.m. The first break was in less than an hour.

I passed by the training room on my way to Bakshi's office. I peeked inside: fresh trainees were attending a session. Some students were snoozing; they were probably still getting used to working at night.

'35=10', the instructor wrote in big bold letters on the blackboard.

I remembered the $35=10$ rule from my training days two years ago. It helped agents adjust to their callers.

'Remember,' the instructor said to the class, 'a thirty-five-year-old American's brain and IQ is the same as a ten-year-old Indian's brain. This will help you understand your clients. You need to be as patient as you are when dealing with a child. Americans are dumb, just accept it. I don't want anyone losing their cool during the calls...'

I dreaded the day when I would have to teach in such classes. My own Delhi accent was impossible to get rid of, and I must have come last in my accent class.

'I have to get out of this,' I said to myself as I went to Bakshi's cabin.

Bakshi was in his oversized office, staring at his computer with his mouth open. As I came in, he rapidly closed the windows. He was probably surfing the Internet for bikini babes or something.

'Good evening Sir,' I said.

'Oh hello, Sam...please come in.' Bakshi liked to call us by our Western names. I hated it.

I walked into his office slowly, to give him time to close his favorite websites.

'Come, come Sam, don't worry. I believe in being an open door manager,' Bakshi said.

I looked at his big square face, unusually large for his 5'6" body. The oversized face resembled the Ravan cut-out at Dusshera. His face shone as usual. It was the first thing you noticed about Bakshi—the oilfields on his face. I think if you could recreate Bakshi's skin as our landscape, you could solve India's oil problems. Priyanka told me once that when she met Bakshi for the first time, she had had an overwhelming urge to take a tissue and wipe it hard across his face. I do not think one tissue would be enough though,

Bakshi was around thirty but looked forty and spoke like he was fifty. He had worked in Connexions for the past three years. Before that, he did an MBA from some unpronounceable university in South India. He thought he was Michael Porter or something (Porter is this big management guru—I didn't know either, but Bakshi told me in an FYI once) and loved to tall in manager's language or Managese, which is another larguage like English and American.

'So, how are the resources doing?' Bakshi said, swiveling on his chair. He never refers to us as people; we are all 'resources'.

'Fine, sir. I actually wanted to talk about a problem. The phone lines are not working properly—lots of static coming in the calls. Can you ask systems...'

'Sam,' Bakshi said, pointing a pen at me.

'Yes?'

'What did I tell you?'

'About what?'

'About how to approach problems.'

'What?'

'Think.'

I thought hard, but nothing came to mind.

'I don't remember sir.... Solve them?'

'No. I said big picture. Always start at the big picture.'

I was puzzled. *What was the big picture here?* There was static coming through on the phones and we had to ask systems to fix it. I could have called them myself, but Bakshi's intervention would get a faster response.

'Sir, it is a specific issue. Customers are hearing disturbance...'

'Sam,' Bakshi sighed and signaled me to sit down, 'what makes a good manager?'

'What?' I sat down in front of him and surreptitiously looked at my watch. It was 10:57 p.m. I hoped the call flow was moderate so the others wouldn't have a tough time with one less person on the desk.

'Wait,' Bakshi said and took out a writing pad and pen. He placed the pad on the middle of the table and then drew a graph that looked like this:

He finished the graph and turned the notebook hundred and eighty degrees to make it face me. He clicked his pen shut with a swagger, as proud as da Vinci finishing the Mona Lisa.

'Sir, systems?' I said, after staying silent for a few seconds.

'Wait. First you tell me. What is this?' Bakshi said and tapped his index finger on the diagram.

I tried to make sense of the chart and any possible connection to the static on the phone lines. I couldn't get it.

I shook my head in defeat.

'Tch-tch, see let me tell you,' Bakshi said. 'This chart is your career. If you want to be more senior, you have to move up this curve.' He put a fat finger on the curve and traced it, guiding me on how I should look at my life.

'Yes sir,' I said, having nothing better to say.

'And do you know how to do that?'

I shook my head. Vroom probably thought I was out smoking. I did feel some smoke coming out of my ears.

'Big Picture. I just told you, focus on the big picture. Learn to identify the strategic variables, Sam.'

Before I could speak, he had pulled out his pen again and was drawing another diagram.

'Maybe I can explain this to you with the help of a 2x2 matrix,' Bakshi said and bent down to write 'High' and 'Low' along the boxes. I had to stop him.

'Sir, please,' I said, placing both my hands down to cover the sheet.

'What?' he said with irritation, as if Einstein had been disturbed at work.

'Sir, this is really interesting to me. I must come back and learn this. But right now my team is waiting and my shift is in progress.'

'So?' Bakshi said.

'The phones, sir. Please tell systems they should check the WASG bay urgently,' I said, without pausing to breathe.

'Huh?' Bakshi said, surprised at how fast I was speaking.

'Just call systems sir,' I said and stood up, 'using that.' I pointed at his telephone and rushed back to my bay.

## 7

'NICE BREAK EH?' VROOM SAID WHEN I RETURNED TO OUR BAY.

'C'mon man, just went to Bakshi's office about the static,' I said.

'Is he sending someone?' Vroom asked as he untangled his phone wires.

'He said I should identify the **strategic variables** first,' I said and sat down on my seat. I rested my face on my hands.

'Strategic variables? What's that?' Vroom said, without looking at me.

'How the hell do I know?' I snorted. 'If I did, I would be team leader. He also made some diagrams.'

Radhika, Esha and Priyanka were busy on calls. Every few seconds, they would turn the phone away from their ears to avoid the loud static. I wished the systems guy would come by soon.

'What diagram?' Vroom said, as he took out some chewing gum from his drawer. He offered one to me.

'Some crap 2x2 matrix or something,' I said, declining Vroom's offer.

'Poor Bakshi, he is just a little silly but a harmless creature. Don't worry about him,' Vroom said.

'Where the hell is the systems guy?' I picked up the telephone and spoke to the systems department. They had not yet received a call from Bakshi. 'Can you please come fast...yes, we have an emergency...yes, our manager knows about it.'

'I can't believe Bakshi hasn't called them yet,' I said, after I had got the systems guys to promise they'd send someone right away.

'Things are bad around here, my friend,' Vroom said. 'Bad news may be coming.'

'What do you mean? Are they cutting jobs?' I asked, now a little worried and anxious, along with being frustrated. It's amazing how all these nasty emotions decide to visit me together.

'I'm trying to find out,' Vroom said, clicking open a window on his screen. 'The Western Computers account is really suffering. If we lose that account, the call center will sink.'

'Crap. I heard something about it from Shefali. I think the website we made was too useful. People have stopped calling us,' I said.

A visitor in our bay interrupted our conversation. I knew he was the systems guy, as he had three pagers on his belt and two memory cards around his neck.

Priyanka told him about the problem and made him listen to the static.

The systems guy asked us to disconnect our lines for ten minutes.

Everyone removed their headsets. I saw Esha adjusting her hair. She does it at least ten times a night. First she will remove the rubber band that's tying up her hair and her hair will all come loose. Then, she assembles it all together and ties it back again.

Her hair was light-colored and intensely curly towards the ends: the result of an expensive hairstyling job, which cost as much as a minor surgery. It didn't even look that nice if you ask me. Naturally curly hair is one thing, but processed curly hair looks like tangled telephone wires.

I saw Vroom stare at Esha. It is never easy for guys to work with a hot girl in office. I mean, what are you supposed to do? Ignore their sexiness and stare at your computer? Sorry, somehow I don't think men were designed to do that.

Radhika took her pink wool out from her bag and started to knit frantically. Military Uncle's system was still working and he stayed glued to his monitor.

'What are you knitting?' Esha turned to Radhika.

'A scarf for my mother-in-law. Damn sweet she is, feels cold at night,' Radhika said.

'She is not sweet—' Vroom began to say but Radhika interrupted him.

'Shh Vroom. She is fine, just traditional.'

'And that sucks, right?' Vroom said.

'Not at all. In fact, I like the cozy family feeling. They are only a little bit old-fashioned,' Radhika said and smiled. I did not think the smile was genuine, but it was none of my business.

'Yeah right. Only a little. As in always cover your head with your sari types,' Vroom said.

'They make you cover your head?' Esha asked, speaking through teeth clenched around her rubber band.

'They don't *make* me do anything, Esha. I am willing to follow their culture. All married women in their h~~ ~~ do it,' Radhika said.

'Still, it is a bit weird,' Esha said doubtfully

'Anyway, I took it as a challenge. I love Anuj and he said he came as a package. But yeah, sometimes I miss wearing low waist jeans like you wore the day before.'

I was amazed Radhika remembered what Esha wore the day before. Only women have this special area in the brain that keeps track of everything they and their friends wore the last fifty times.

'You like those jeans?' Esha said, her eyes lighting up.

'I love them. But I guess you need the right figure for them,' Radhika said. 'Anyway, sorry to change the topic guys, but we're forgetting something here.'

'What? The systems?' I asked, as I looked under the table. The systems guy lurked within, in a jungle of tangled wires. He told me he would need ten more minutes.

I checked my watch. It was 11:20 p.m. I wondered if Bakshi would be coming for his daily rounds soon.

'Not the static,' Radhika said as she kept her knitting aside. 'Miss Priyanka has some big news for us, remember?'

'Oh yes. C'mon Priyanka tell us,' Esha screamed. Military Uncle looked up from his screen for a second, and then went back to work. I wondered if he'd been this quiet when he lived with his son and daughter-in-law.

'Okay I do have something to tell you,' Priyanka said with a sheepish grin, making her two dimples more prominent. She brought out a box of sweets from her large plastic bag.

'Whatever your news is, we do get to eat the sweets, right?' Vroom wanted to know.

'Of course,' Priyanka said, carefully opening the red cellophane wrapping on the box. I hate it when she is so methodical. Just rip the damn wrapping off, I thought. Anyway, it was not my business. I looked under the table for a few seconds, as if to help the systems guy. Of course, my ears were focused on Priyanka's every word.

'So, what's up? Ooh milk cake, my favourite,' Radhika said, even as Vroom jumped to grab the first piece.

'I'll tell you, but you guys have to swear it won't leave WASG,' Priyanka said. She offered the box to Radhika and Esha. Radhika took two pieces, while Esha broke the tiniest piece possible with human fingers. I guess the low-cut jeans figure comes at a price.

'Of course we won't tell anyone. I hardly have any friends outside the WASG. Now tell please,' Esha said and wiped her long fingers with a tissue.

'Well, let's just say, my mom is the happiest person on earth today,' Priyanka said.

'No riddles man. Just tell the story,' Vroom said.

'Well, you know my mom and her obsession for an NRI match for her rebellious daughter.'

'Uh-uh,' Radhika nodded as she ate her milk cake.

'So these family friends of ours brought a proposal for me. It came from one of their relatives in Seattle. I would have said no like always. However, this time, I saw the pictures, which were cute. I spoke to the guy on the phone—he sounded decent. He works in Microsoft—so is doing well. His parents are in Delhi and I met them today. Nice people,' Priyanka said and paused to break a piece for herself. She could have broken a smaller piece, I thought, but it was not really my business.

'And,' Esha said, her eyes opened wide and staring at Priyanka.

'I don't know, just something clicked or what,' Priyanka said, playing with her milk cake rather than eating it. 'They asked for my decision upfront and I said—yes.'

'Waaaoooow! Oh wow!' the girls screamed at their highest pitch possible. The systems guy shook in terror under the table. I told him everything was fine and asked him to continue. At least everything was fine outside. Inside, I had a burning feeling, like someone had tossed a hot coal in my stomach.

Radhika and Esha got up to hug Priyanka as if India had won the World Cup or something. People get married everyday. Did these girls really have to create a scene? I wished the phones would start working again so I did not have to listen to this nonsense.

I looked at my computer screen and saw that Microsoft Word was open. Angrily I closed all windows with the Microsoft logo on it.

'Congratulations, Priyanka,' Vroom said, 'that's big news.'

Even Military Uncle got up and came to shake hands with Priyanka. Grown ups like it when young people decide to get married. Of course, he was back at his desk in twenty seconds.

'This deserves more than milk cake. Where is our treat?' Esha asked. Girls like Esha hardly eat anything, but still jump around asking for treats.

'Treat will come guys,' Priyanka said, her smile taking permanent residence on her face. 'I have only said yes. No ceremonies have happened yet.'

'You've met the guy?' Vroom asked.

'No, he's in Seattle. But we spoke for hours on the phone. And I have seen his picture. He is cute. Want to see the photo?' Priyanka said.

'No thanks,' I blurted out in reflex. Damn, I could not believe I'd said that. By sheer luck, I had not said it loud enough for Priyanka to hear.

'Huh? You said something?' Priyanka asked, looking at me.

I shook my head and pointed under the table. Yes, my only focus was to fix the phones.

'Do you want some milk cake?' Priyanka asked and shunted the box towards me.

'No, thanks,' I said and slid the box back.

'I thought milk cake was your favorite.'

'Not anymore. My tastes have changed,' I said. 'And I'm trying to cut down.'

'Not even a small piece?' she asked and tilted her head. At some stage of my life, I used to find that head-tilt cute, but today I remained adamant.

I shook my head. Our eyes locked. When you have shared relationship with someone, the first change is in how you look into each other's eyes. The gaze becomes more fixed, and it is hard to pull away from it.

'Aren't you going to say anything?' Priyanka said. When girls say that, it's not really a question. It means they *want* you to say something.

'About what? The phone lines? They'll be fixed in ten minutes,' I said.

'Not that. I'm getting married, Shyam.'

'Oh really,' I said, as if this were the first time I had heard the news.

'I just said yes to a proposal today,' she said.

'Good,' I said and turned to my screen.

'Show us the picture!' Esha screamed, as if Priyanka was going to show her Brad Pitt naked or something. Priyanka took out a photograph from her handbag and passed it around. I saw it from a distance: he looked like a regular software geek, similar to the guy under our table, but with better clothes. He stood straight with his stomach pulled in—an old trick any guy with a paunch applies when he gets his picture clicked. He wore glasses, and had a super neat hairstyle as if his mom clutched his cheeks and combed his hair every morning. Actually, she just might have for this 'arranged marriage' picture. He was standing with the Statue of Liberty in the background, perhaps to emphasize that he was an NRI match and thus better than others. His forced smile made him look like a total loser if you ask me—like the kind of guy who never spoke to a girl in college. However, now he was hot, and girls with dimples were ready to marry him without even meeting him.

'He's so cute. Like a little teddy bear,' Esha said and passed the picture to Radhika.

When girls call a guy 'teddy bear', they just mean he is a nice guy but they will never be attracted to him. Girls may say they like such guys, but teddy bears never get to sleep with anyone. Unless of course their moms hunt the neighborhood for them.

Are you okay?' Priyanka said to me. The others were busy analyzing the picture.

'Yeah. Why?'

'No. Just expected a little more reaction. We've known each other for four years, more than anybody else on the desk.'

Radhika, Esha and Vroom turned their heads away from the picture to look at us.

'Reaction?' I said, 'I thought I said *good*.'

'That's all?' Priyanka said. Her smile had left the building.

'What?' I said. 'I'm busy trying to get the system fixed.'

Everyone continued to stare at me.

'Okay,' I said, 'okay, Priyanka. This is *great* news. I am *so* happy for you. *Okay?*'

'You could have used a better tone,' Priyanka said. 'Anyway, I'll just come back,' she mumbled, and walked away quickly towards the ladies room.

'What? Why is everyone staring at me?' I said and everyone turned away.

The systems guy finally came out from under the table.

'Fixed?' I said.

'I need signal testing equipment,' he said, wiping sweat off his forehead. 'The problem could be outside. Builders are digging all over Gurgaon right now, some stupid contractor may have dug over our lines. Just take a break while I come back. Call your manager here as well,' he said and left.

I picked up the telephone to call Bakshi. The line was busy I left a voice mail for him to come to the desk.

Priyanka returned from the restroom. I noticed she had washed her face. Her nose still had a drop of water on top of it.

'Sounds like an easy night. I hope it never gets fixed,' Radhika said, knitting ferociously.

'Nothing better than a call center job if the phones are not working,' Priyanka said and closed the box of sweets.

'So tell us more, what is he like?' Esha said.

'Who? Ganesh?' Priyanka asked.

'His name is Ganesh? Nice,' Esha said and switched on her mobile phone. Everyone else followed suit and several opening tones filled the room. Normally agents could not use cell phones in the bay, but it was okay to do so now as the system was down.

I had two text messages from Shefali: One wishing me goodnight, and another one wishing me sweet dreams and a cuddly night. I cringed.

'Does Ganesh like to talk? Sometimes the software types are real quiet,' Radhika said.

'Oh yes, he talks a lot. In fact, I might get a call from him now because my phone is on,' Priyanka said and smiled. 'We're still getting to know each other, so any communication is good.'

'You sound sooo happy,' Esha said. Her 'so' lasted four seconds.

'I *am* happy. I can see what Radhika says now about getting a new family. Ganesh's mom came home today and gave me a big gold chain. And she was all hugging me and kissing me.'

'Sounds gross,' Vroom said.

'Shut up, Vroom,' Esha said. 'Oh Priyanka, you're so lucky.'

Vroom sensed that I was not exactly jumping with joy at the conversation.

'Cigarette?' he said.

I looked at my watch. It was 11:30, our usual time for taking a smoke. In any case, I preferred burning my lungs to sticking around to find out Ganesh's hobbies.

# #8

VROOM AND I WENT TO THE CALL CENTER PARKING LOT. VROOM leaned against his bike and lit two cigarettes with one matchstick. I looked at his tall and thin frame. If he weren't so skinny, you'd say he was a stud. Still, a cigarette looked out of place on his boyish face. Perhaps conscious of the people who had called him Baby Face before, he always kept a one-day old stubble. He passed an already burning cigarette to me. I took a puff and let it out in the cold night air.

We kept quiet for a minute and I was thankful to Vroom for that. One thing guys do know is when to shut up.

Vroom finally spoke, starting with a neutral topic. 'I need a break man. Good thing I'm going to Manali next weekend.'

'Cool, Manali is really nice,' I said.

'I'm going with my school buddies. We might ride up there on bikes.'

'Bikes? Are you nuts, you'll freeze to death.'

'Two words: leather jackets. Anyway, when did you go there?'

'Last year. We took a bus though,' I said.

'Who all went?' Vroom said as he looked for a place to flick ash. He found none. He stepped to a corner of the parking lot and plucked two large leaves from a tree. We tapped our cigarettes on the improvised ashtray.

'Priyanka and I,' I said and turned silent. Vroom did not respond either for ten seconds.

'Fun?' he finally said.

'Yeah, it was great. Apart from the aches from the bus ride,' I said.

'Why, what happened?'

'We took a bus at four in the morning from ISBT. Priyanka was in her anti-snob phase, so she insisted we take the ordinary slow bus and not the deluxe fast one. She also wanted to enjoy the scenery slowly.'

'And then?'

'Then what? The moment the bus reached the highway, she leaned on my shoulder and slep off. My shoulder cramped and my body turned sore. But apart from that horrible journey, it was great fun.'

'She's a silly girl,' Vroom said, letting out a big puff, his face smiling behind the smoke ring.

'She is. You should have seen her then. She used to wear all these beads and FabIndia stuff all the time. And then she'd sit with the truck drivers and have tea.'

'Wow. Can't imagine Priyanka like that now,' Vroom said.

'Trust me, the girl has a wild side,' I said and paused, as her face came to mind. 'Anyway, it's history now. Girls change.'

'You bet. She's all set now.'

I nodded. I didn't want to talk about Priyanka anymore. At least one part of me didn't. The rest of my parts always wanted to talk about her.

'NRI catch, Microsoft and all. Not bad,' Vroom continued as he lit another cigarette. I narrowed my eyes at him.

'What?' he said. 'It's in my daily quota. It is only my third of five.' He exhaled a giant cloud.

'It's a little too quick, isn't it?' I said.

'What? The cigarette? I need it today.'

'Not that. Priyanka's wedding. Don't you think she is deciding too fast?'

'Fast? C'mon man, you don't get matches like this everyday. He is in freaking Microsoft. As good as they get. He is MSGroom 1.1—deluxe edition.'

'What is the deal with Microsoft? Good job?'

'Dude, I'm sure he packs close to a hundred grand a year.'

'What is that? A hundred thousand US dollars a year?'

Vroom nodded. I tried to convert hundred thousand US dollars to rupees and divide it by twelve to get the monthly salary. There were too many zeros and it was a tough calculation to do in my head. I racked my brain for a few seconds.

'Stop calculating in rupees,' Vroom said and smiled.

'I'm not doing any calculations.'

'Priyanka's got a catch, I'm telling you,' Vroom repeated.

He paused and looked at me. His eyes were wet like a puppy's, brown and kind to look at. I could see why girls flocked to him. It was the eyes.

'I'm going to ask you a question. Will you answer it honestly?' Vroom said.

'Sure.'

'Are you upset she is getting married? I know you have feelings for her.'

'No,' I said and started laughing. 'I just find it a bit strange. But I wouldn't say I'm upset. That is too strong a word. It is not like we're going around now or anything. No sir, I am not *upset* upset.'

Vroom waited while I continued to laugh exaggeratedly. When I'd stopped he said, 'Okay, don't bullshit me. What happened to your re-proposal plans?'

I remained silent.

'It's okay man. You can tell me.'

I sighed, 'Well, of course I feel for her. But they are just vestigial feelings.'

'Vesti what?'

'Like vestigial organs. They serve no purpose or value. But they can give you a pain in the appendix. Same with my feelings for Priyanka. I'm supposed to have moved on, but obviously it hasn't happened. Meanwhile, Mr NRI comes and gives me a kick in the rear end,' I said.

'Talk to her. Don't tell me you're not going to,' Vroom said and exhaled two smoke rings.

'I was planning to real soon. I thought we'd submit the website user manual and hopefully that would have made it easier for Boston to approve my promotion. How did I know there would be milk cake distribution tonight? How was it by the way? I didn't touch it.'

Anyway, screw that. Listen, you still have some time. She has only said yes.'

'I hope so. Though even as team leader, it's hard to compete with Mr Microsoft,' I said.

We remained silent for a few more seconds. Vroom spoke again.

'Yeah man. Girls are strategic. They'll talk about love and romance and all that crap—but when it comes to doing the deal, they will choose the fattest chicken,' he said, and bunched up the leaf ashtray so it became like a bowl.

'I guess I can only become fat, not a fat chicken,' I said.

'Yeah, you need to be fat, fresh and fluffy. Girls know their stuff. That's why you shouldn't feel so upset. We aren't good husband material—just accept it.'

'Thanks Vroom, that really makes my day,' I said. I did agree with Vroom though. It was evolution. Maybe nature wanted dimple-cheeked, software-geek, mini-Ganesh babies. They were of far more value to society than depressed, good-for-nothing junior Shyams.

'And anyway, it's the girl who always gets to choose. Men propose and women accept the proposal or, as in many cases, reject it.'

It's true. Girls go around rejecting men like it is their birthright. They have no idea how much it hurts us. I read once (or maybe saw it during one of my Discovery Channel phases) that the reason for this is that the female of the species has to bear their offspring with a lot of effort. Hence they choose their mates carefully. Meanwhile, men dance around, spend cash,

over. The only species where courting works in reverse ⌐
sea horse. Instead of the females, the male sea horse bea
offspring: they carry baby sea horse eggs in their pockets. ⌐
what? The female sea horses are always hitting on the m ⌐
while the latter pucker their noses and get to pick the cut⌐
female. I wished I were a sea horse. How hard can it be to car⌐
a couple of eggs in a backpack?

Vroom interrupted my thoughts.

‐‘But who knows. Priyanka isn't like other girls, or maybe
she is after all. Either way, don't give up man. Try to get her
back,' Vroom said and patted my shoulder in encouragement.

‘Speaking of back, shouldn't we be heading back to the bay?'
I said and looked at my watch. ‘It's 11:45 p.m.'


We passed the Western Computers main bay as we returned
from the parking lot. The main bay sounded like a noisy school,
except the kids weren t talking to each other, but to customers.
Monitor problems, viruses, strange error messages—there was
nothing Connexions could not help you with.

‘Still looks busy,' I said.

'Not at all. People have told me call traffic is down forty
percent. I think they'll cut a lot of staff, or worst case scenario,
cut all people and shift the client to the Bangalore center.'

‘Bangalore? What will happen here?' I said.

‘They'll close this poorly managed madhouse down. What
else? That is what happens when people like Bakshi spend half
their time playing politics with other managers,' Vroom said.

and pointed her out to me.

'Close down!' I said, after studying the pretty girl for half a second. 'Are you serious, what will happen to the hundreds of jobs here?'

'Like they care. You think Bakshi cares?' Vroom said and shrugged his lanky shoulders.

'Crap happens in life. It could happen tonight,' Vroom said as we reached the WASG.

## 9

THE SYSTEMS GUY WAS UNDER THE TABLE AGAIN.

'No calls yet. They've called for a senior engineer,' Priyanka said.

'It's an external fault. Some cables are damaged I think. Gurgaon is going nuts with constructions,' the systems guy said, as he emerged from under the table.

'Bakshi knows?' I said.

'I don't know,' Priyanka said.

Vroom and I sat down at our desk.

'It's not too bad. Nice break,' Esha said as she filed her nails with a weirdly shaped nail cutter.

Priyanka's cell phone began to ring, startling everyone.

'Who is calling you so late?' Radhika said, still knitting her scarf.

'Long distance I think,' Priyanka said and smiled.

'Ooooh!' Esha squealed, like a two-year-old on a bouncy castle. What is the big deal about a long distance phone call? I thought.

'Hi Ganesh. I just switched my phone on,' Priyanka said. 'I can't believe you called so soon.'

I could not hear Ganesh's response. Thank god.

'Fifteen times? I can't believe you tried my number fifteen times...so sorry,' Priyanka said, looking idiotic with happiness.

'Yes, I'm at work. But it's really chaotic today. Systems are down.... Hello? ... How come you're working on Thanksgiving? Oh, nice of the Indians to offer to work...hello?' Priyanka said.

'What happened?' Esha said.

'There's hardly any network,' Priyanka said, shaking her phone as if that would improve the reception. I felt like shaking her.

'We're in the basement. Nothing comes into this black hole,' Vroom said. He was surfing the Internet, and was on the Formula I website.

'Landline,' Esha said, pointing to the spare phone on our desk. Every team in Connexions had a spare independent landline at their desk for emergency use. 'Tell him to call on the landline.'

'Here?' Priyanka asked, looking to me for permission.

Normally this would be unthinkable, but our systems were down so it did not really matter. Also, I did not want to look like a sore loser preventing a new couple from starting their romance.

I nodded and pretended to be absorbed by my computer screen. As the ad-hoc team leader, I had some powers. I could approve any personal calls. I could also listen in on any line on the desk on my headset. However, I could not listen in on the independent emergency phone. Not unless I went under the table and tapped it.

'Tap the landline,' a faint voice echoed in my head.

'No, it's wrong,' I said and mentally reprimanded myself. I could still hear one side of the conversation though.

'Hello...Ganesh, call the landline...yes, 22463463 and 11 for Delhi.... Call after ten minutes, our boss might come on his rounds soon..... I know ten minutes is six hundred seconds, I'm sure you'll survive,' she laughed uncontrollably and hung up. When women laugh non-stop, they're flirting. I hate Priyanka.

'He sounds so *cute*,' Esha said, stretching the last word to five times its normal length.

'Enough is enough, I'm going to call Bakshi. We need to fix the systems,' I said and stood up. I couldn't bear the systems guy lurking under the table anymore. More than that, I could not bear six-hundred-seconds-without-you survival stories.

I was walking towards Bakshi's office when I noticed him walking towards me.

'Agent Sam, why aren't you on your desk?' Bakshi said.

'I was looking for you sir,' I said.

'I'm all yours,' Bakshi said as his face broke into a smile. He came and placed his arm around my shoulder. I hate it when he does that.

Bakshi and I returned to WASG. Everyone heard the sound of Bakshi's heavy steps. Radhika hid her knitting gear under the table. Esha put her nail file in her bag. Vroom opened his screen to an empty MSWord document.

The systems guy came out from under the table and called his boss, the head of the IT department.

'Looks like we have technology issues here,' Bakshi said and the systems guy nodded his head.

The head of IT came soon after. He and the systems guy discussed geek stuff between themselves in so-called English. When the discussions were over, the IT head ranted out incomprehensible technical details to us. I only understood that the system was under a strain: eighty percent of the WASG capacity was damaged, and the remaining twenty percent could not handle the current load.

'Hmmm,' Bakshi said, his left hand rubbing his chin, 'hmmm...that's really bad, isn't it?'

'So, what do you want us to do?' the IT head asked.

All eyes turned to Bakshi. It was a situation Bakshi hated— to be asked to take a decision or recommend action.

'Hmmm,' Bakshi said and flexed his knees, knee by slow knee, to buy time. 'We really need a methodical game plan here.'

'We can shut down the WASG system tonight. Western Computers main bay is running fine anyway,' the junior IT guy suggested.

'But WASG has not lost all its capacity. Boston won't like it if we shut the bay,' the IT head said, referring to the Western Computers and Appliances headquarters in Boston.

'Hmmm,' Bakshi said again and pressed a sweaty palm on my desk. 'Upsetting Boston will not be good at this time. We are already on a slippery slope at Connexions. Let's try to be proactively oriented here.'

Vroom couldn't resist a snigger at Bakshi's jargon. He looked away and clenched his teeth.

'Sir, can I make a suggestion,' I said, even though I should have kept my trap shut.

'What?' Bakshi said.

'We could take Bangalore's help,' I said, referring to the location of the second Western Appliances and Computers call center in India.

'Bangalore?' Bakshi and the IT head said in unison.

'Yes sir. It is Thanksgiving and call volumes are low. So Bangalore will be running light as well. If we pass most of our calls there, it will get busier for them, but it won't overload them. Meanwhile, we can handle a limited flow here,' I said.

'That makes sense. We can easily switch the flow for a few hours. We can fix the systems here in the morning,' the junior IT guy said.

'That's fine,' I said. 'And people will start their Thanksgiving dinner in the States soon, so call volumes will fall even more.'

Everyone on the desk looked at me and nodded. Secretly they were thrilled at the easy shift tonight. Bakshi, however, had fallen into silent contemplation.

'Sir, you heard what Shyam said. Let's ask Bangalore. That is our only option,' Priyanka said.

Bakshi remained silent and pondered for a few more seconds. I want to know what he actually thinks in these moments.

'See, the thing is,' Bakshi said and paused again, '...aren't we comparing apples to oranges here?'

'What?' Vroom looked at Bakshi with a disgusted expression.

I wondered what Bakshi was talking about. Was I the apple? Was Delhi the orange? What fruit was Bangalore?

'I have an idea. Why don't we use Bangalore?' Bakshi said and snapped his fingers.

'But that is what Shyam—' the junior IT guy began, but Bakshi interrupted him. Poor junior IT guy, he isn't familiar with Bakshi's ways.

'See, it sounds unusual, but sometimes you have to do **out-of-the-box** thinking,' Bakshi said and tapped his head in self-admiration.

'Yes sir,' I said. 'That is a good idea. We have it all sorted now.'

'Good,' the IT guys said and started playing with the computer menus. Bakshi had a smug smile on his face.

Before the IT guys left they told us that the WASG call volume would be super-light, maybe even less than twenty calls an hour. We were overjoyed, but kept a straight face before Bakshi.

'See, problem solved,' Bakshi said and spread his hands. 'That is what I'm here for.'

'Lucky us, Sir,' Priyanka said.

We thought Bakshi would leave, but he had other plans.

'Shyam, as you are free tonight, can you help me with some strategic documents? You know, it will give you some exposure.'

'What is it, Sir?' I said, not happy about sacrificing my night.

'These are ten copies of the monthly data sheets I just printed out,' Bakshi said and held up some documents in his right hand. 'For some reason the sheets didn't come in order. It is ten page ones, then page twos and so on. Can you help fix this?'

'You didn't collate them. You can choose the option when you print,' Vroom said.

'You can choose to collate?' Bakshi asked, as if we'd told him about an option for brain transplants.

'Yes,' Vroom said and took some chewing gum from his drawer. He popped a piece into his mouth. 'Anyway, it is easier to take one printout and photocopy the rest. Comes out stapled too.'

'I need to upgrade my technical skills. Technology changes so fast,' Bakshi said. 'But Shyam, can you help arrange and staple them this time?'

'Sure,' I said. As if I had a choice.

Bakshi dumped the sheets on my table and left the room.

Priyanka looked at me with her mouth open.

'What?' I said.

'I can't believe it,' she shook her head. 'Why do you let him do this to you?'

'C'mon Priyanka, leave Shyam alone. Bakshi runs his life,' Vroom said.

'Exactly. Because he lets him. Why can't people stand up for themselves?'

I don't know why I can't stand up for myself, but I definitely can't stand Priyanka's rhetorical questions. She doesn't understand the point, and then asks the world out aloud.

I tried to ignore her. However, her words had affected me. It was difficult to focus on the sheets. I stacked the first set and was about to staple them when Vroom said, 'He can't take on Bakshi right now. Not at this time, Priyanka, they are in the mood to fire people.'

'Yes, thanks, Vroom. Can someone explain reality? I need to make a living. I don't have Mr Microsoft PowerPoint waiting for me in Seattle,' I said and pressed the stapler hard. I missed and the staple pin pierced my finger.

'Oww!' I screamed loud enough to uproot Military Uncle from his desk.

'What happened?' Priyanka said and stood up.

I lifted my finger to show the streaks of blood. A couple of drops spilt onto Bakshi's document.

The girls squealed 'eews' in rapid succession.

'Symbolism, dude. Giving your life blood to this job,' Vroom said. 'Can someone give this guy a band-aid before he makes me throw up?'

'I have a band-aid,' Esha said as the girls came up and surrounded me. Women love to repair an injury—as long as it is not too gross.

'That's bad,' Esha said, taking out a band-aid from her bag. She had like fifty of them.

'It's nothing. Just a minor cut,' I said. I clenched my teeth hard as it hurt like hell.

Priyanka took out a few tissues from her bag. She held my finger and cleaned the blood around it.

'Ouch!' I screamed.

'Oh, the staple is still in there,' she said. 'We need forceps. Forceps anyone?'

Esha had forceps in her handbag, which I think she uses to rip her eyebrows out. Girls' handbags have enough to make a survival kit for Antarctica.

Priyanka held the forceps and went to work on my finger with a surgeon's concentration.

'Here's the culprit,' she said as she pulled out a staple pin drenched in blood. I swear, ever since I've developed a fear of staples—staplophobia, you can call it.

Priyanka wiped my finger and then stuck the band-aid on it. With no more fun, bloody sights to see, everyone returned to their seats. I went back to collating sheets. Perhaps my abilities really did lie in mindless labor.

Esha and Radhika began talking about Bakshi.

'He had no idea what IT was saying,' Radhika said.

'Yeah, bu. 'd you see his face?' Esha said. 'He looked like he was doing a CBI investigation.'

I looked at Priyanka. The word CBI brought back memories. Even as I collated Bakshi's sheets, my mind drifted to Pandara Road.

# #10:

# My Past Dates with Priyanka—II

Havemore Restaurant, Pandara Road
Nine months before this night

'Shyam,' Priyanka said as she tried to push me away. 'This is not the place to do these things. This is Pandara Road.'

'Oh really,' I said, refusing to move away. We were sitting on a corner table. A carved wooden screen partially hid us. 'What's wrong with Pandara Road?' I said, continuing to kiss her.

'This is a family place,' she said; she spread a palm on my face and pushed me back again, firmly this time.

'So, families get made by doing these things.'

'Very funny. Anyway, you chose this place. I hope the food is as good as you said it was.'

'It's the best in Delhi,' I said. We had come to Havemore Restaurant, one of the half-dozen overpriced but excellent restaurants on Pandara Road. We had done enough museums.

After the Rail Museum, we had gone to the Planetarium (the dark empty theatre with its romantic possibilities was fun, I admit), the Natural History Museum, the Doll Museum and the Science Museum. According to Priyanka, museums offered good privacy, great gardens and cheap canteens.

'A hundred and thirty bucks for daal!' Priyanka exclaimed as she opened the menu. Her kohl-lined eyes turned wide and her nostrils flared again: her face had the expression of a stunned cartoon character. It was embarrassing, especially as the waiter was already at our table to take the order.

'Just order okay?' I said in a hushed voice.

Priyanka took five more minutes to place the order. Here is how she decides. Step one: sort all the dishes on the menu according to price. Step two: re-sort the cheaper ones based on calories.

'One naan, no butter. Yellow daal,' she said as I glared at her.

'Okay, not yellow, black daal,' she said. 'And...'

'And one shahi paneer,' I said.

'You always order the same thing, black daal and shahi paneer,' she made a face.

'Yes, same girl, same food. Why bother experimenting when you already have the best,' I said.

'You are so cute,' she said. Her smile made her eyes crinkle. She pinched my cheeks and fed me a little vinegar-onion from the table. Hardly romantic, but I liked it.

She moved her hand away quickly when she saw a family being led to the table adjacent to us. The family consisted of a young married couple, their two little daughters and an old lady. The daughters were twins, probably four years old.

The entire family had morose faces and no one said a word to each other. I wondered why they had come out when they could be grumpy for free at home.

'Anyway,' Priyanka said, 'what's the news?'

'Not much, Vroom and I are busy with the troubleshooting website.'

'Cool, how's it coming along?'

'Really well. Nothing fancy though: the best websites are simple. Vroom even checked out many sites meant for mentally handicapped people. He said if we can model it on such websites, Americans will surely be able to use it.'

'They're not *that* dumb,' Priyanka laughed. 'Americans invented computers remember?'

The waiter came with our food.

'Yeah, America has like ten smart guys. The rest call us at night,' I said, as I tore a piece of my naan and dipped it in the daal.

'I agree the people who call us are pretty thick. I'm like—figure out where the power button is, hello?' she said.

She put micro-portions of food on her plate.

'Eat properly,' I said. 'Stop dieting all the time like Esha.'

'I am not that hungry,' she said, even as I forcefully gave her human portions of food.

'Hey, did I tell you about Esha? Don't tell anyone,' she said, her voice dipping, eyebrows dancing.

I shook my head. 'You love to gossip. Don't you? Your name should be Miss Gossip F 1 99.5,' I said.

'I *never* gossip,' she said, waving a fork at me solemnly. 'Oh my god, the food is so good here.'

My chest inflated with pride as if I had spent all night cooking the dishes myself.

'Of course you love to gossip. Whenever someone starts with "don't tell anyone", that to me is a juicy tit-bit of gossip coming,' I said.

Priyanka blushed and the tip of her nose turned tomato-red. She looked cute as hell. I would have kissed her right then, but the grumpy family next to us was beginning to argue in murmurs. I did not want to spoil the somber ambience for them.

'Okay so maybe I gossip, but only a little bit,' Priyanka relented. 'But I read somewhere, gossip is good for you.'

'Oh really?' I teased.

'Yes, it's a sign you're interested in people and care for them.'

'That is so lame,' I burst out laughing, pointing my spoon at her. 'Anyway, what about Esha. I know Vroom has the hots for her. But does she like him?'

'No Shyam, that is old news. She has rejected Vroom's proposal before. The latest is that she had signed up for the Femina Miss India contest. Last week she got a rejection letter because she was not tall enough. She is five-five, the minimum is five-six. Radhika saw her cry in the toilet.'

'Oh wow! Miss India?'

'C'mon, she is not that pretty. She should really stop this modeling trip of hers. God, she is so thin though. Okay, I'm not eating anymore.' She pushed her plate away.

'Stupid, eat. You want to be happy or thin?' I said, pushing her plate back towards her.

'Thin.'

'Shut up, eat properly. The name of the restaurant should tell you something. And as for Esha, well too bad Miss India didn't work out. However, trying doesn't hurt,' I said.

'Well, she was crying. So it hurt her. After all, she's come to Delhi against her parent's wishes. It's not easy struggling alone,' she said.

I nodded.

We finished our meal and the waiter reappeared like a genie to clear our plates.

'Dessert?' I said.

'No way. I'm too full,' Priyanka said, placing her hand on her neck to show just how full. She is way too dramatic sometimes, just like her mom. Not that I dare tell her that.

'Okay, one kulfi please,' I said to the waiter.

'No, order gulab jamun, no?' she said.

'Huh? I thought you didn't want...okay, one gulab jamun please.'

The waiter went back into his magic bottle.

'How's your mom?' I said.

'Same. We haven't had a cry fest since last week's showdown, so that alone is a reason to celebrate. Maybe I will have half a gulab jamun.'

'And what happened last week?'

'Last week? Oh yes, my uncles were over for dinner. So picture this: dinner ends and we are all having butterscotch ice cream at the dining table. One uncle mentioned that my cousin was getting married to a doctor, a cardiac surgeon or something,' Priyanka said.

The waiter came and gave us the gulab jamuns. I took a bite.

'Ouch, careful, these are hot,' I said, blowing air out. 'Anyway, what happened then?'

'So I'm eating my ice cream and my mother screams "Priyanka, make sure you marry someone well settled".' The latter phrase was said in falsetto.

'I'm going to be a team leader soon,' I said and fed her a slice of gulab jamun.

'Relax, Shyam,' Priyanka said, as she took a bite and patted my arm. 'It has nothing to do with you. The point is how could she spring it on me in front of everyone. Like, why can't I just have ice cream like the others. Why does my serving have to come with this hot guilt sauce. My younger brother, nobody says anything to him while he stuffs his face.'

I laughed and signaled for the bill.

'So what did you do then?' I said.

'Nothing. I slammed my spoon down on the plate and left the room.'

'Major drama, you are no less,' I said.

'Guess what she says then, to everyone, "This is what I get for bringing her up and loving her so much. She doesn't care. I nearly died in labor when she was born, but she doesn't care".'

I laughed uncontrollably as Priyanka did an outstandi imitation of her mother. The bill arrived and my eyebrows s up for a second as I paid the four hundred and sixty th. bucks.

We stood up to leave and the grumpy family's voices reached us.

'What to do? Since the day this woman came to our house, our family's fortunes have been ruined,' the old woman was saying. 'The Agra girl's side were offering to set up a full clinic. I don't know where our brains were then.'

The daughter-in-law had tears in her eyes. She had not touched her food. The man was eating nonchalantly.

'Look at her now, sitting there with a stiff face. Go, go to hell now. Not only did you not bring anything, now you have dumped these two girls like two curses on me,' the mother-in-law said.

I looked at the little girls. They had identical plaits with cute pink ribbons in them. The girls were holding one hand of their mother each. They looked scared.

Priyanka was staring at them. I noticed they had ordered kulfi and wondered if I should have done the same and at least saved my now scalded tongue.

'Say something now, you silent statue,' the mother-in-law said and shook the daughter-in-law's shoulders.

'Why doesn't she say anything?' Priyanka whispered to me.

'Because she can't,' I said. 'When you have a bad boss, you can't say anything.'

'Who will pay for these two curses? Say something now,' the mother-in-law said. The daughter-in-law's tears came down faster.

'I'll say something,' Priyanka shouted, facing the mother-in-law.

The grumpy family turned to look at us in astonishment. I looked for a deep hole to hide myself from the embarrassment.

'Who are you?' the husband asked, probably his first words during the entire meal.

'We'll worry about that later,' Priyanka said, 'but who the hell are *you*? Her husband I presume?'

'Huh? Yes I am. Madam, this is a family matter,' he said.

'Oh really? You call this a family? Doesn't look like a family to me,' Priyanka said. 'I just see an old shrew and a loser wimp who are troubling these girls. Don't you have any shame? Is this what you married her for?'

'See, here is another one,' the mother-in-law said. 'Look at the girls of today: don't know how to talk—look at her, eyes made up like a heroine.'

'The young girls know how to talk and behave. It is you old ones who need to be taught a lesson. These are your granddaughters, and you are calling them curses?' Priyanka said, her nose a cuter red than before. I wanted to take a picture of that nose.

'Who are you madam? What is your business here?' the husband said, this time in a firmer voice.

'I'll tell you who I am,' Priyanka said and fumbled in her handbag. She took out her call center id card and flashed it for a nanosecond. 'Priyanka Sinha, CBI, Women's Cell.'

'What?' the husband said, in half-disbelief.

'What is your car number?' Priyanka said, talking in a flat voice.

'What? Why?' the bewildered husband asked.

'Or should I go outside to check,' she said and glanced at the keys on the table. 'Santro, isn't it?'

'DGI 463. Why?' the husband said.

Priyanka took out her cell phone and pretended to call a number. 'Hello? Sinha here. Please retrieve records on DGI 463...yes...Santro...thanks.'

'Madam, what is going on?' the husband said, his voice quivering.

'Three years. Harassing women is punishable for three years. Quick trial, no appeal,' Priyanka said and stared at the mother-in-law.

The old woman pulled one of the twin granddaughters onto her lap.

'What? Madam this is just a f-f-f-family affair and...' the husband stammered.

'Don't say family!' Priyanka said, her voice loud.

'Madam,' the mother-in-law said, her tone now sweet, as if someone had soaked her vocal cords in gulab jamuns, 'we are just here to have a meal. I don't even let her cook see, we just had—'

'—Shut up! We have your records now. We will keep track. If you mess around, your son and you can have lots of meals together—in jail.'

'Sorry madam,' the husband said with folded hands. He asked for the bill and fumbled for cash. Within a minute, they had paid and left.

I looked at Priyanka with my mouth open.

'Don't say anything,' she said, 'let's go.'

'CBI?' I said.

'Don't. Let's go.'

We sat in the Qualis I had borrowed from the call center driver.

'Stupid old witch,' Priyanka said. I started to drive. Five minutes later, Priyanka turned to me. 'Okay, you can say what you want now.'

'I love you,' I said.

'What? Why this now?'

'Because, I love it when you stand up for something that you feel for. And that you do such a horrible job of acting like a CBI inspector. I love it when you want to order the cheapest dishes only because I'm paying for them. I love the kohl in your eyes. I love it when your eyes light up when you have gossip for me. I love it that you say you don't want dessert and then ask me to change mine so you can have half. I love your stories about your mother. I love it that you believe in me and are patient with my career. Actually, you know what, Priyanka?' I said.

'What?'

'I may not be a heart surgeon—but the one little heart I have, I have given it to you.'

Priyanka laughed aloud and put her hand on her face.

'Sorry,' she said and shook her head, still laughing. 'Sorry, you were doing so well, but for the heart surgeon line. Now, that is seriously cheesy.'

'You know what,' I said and removed one hand from the steering wheel to tweak her nose. 'They should put you in jail for killing romantic lines.'

# #11

'I CAN'T BELIEVE THIS,' RADHIKA SAID AND THREW HER MOBILE phone on her desk, breaking up my Pandara Road dream.

Everyone turned to look at her. She covered her face with her hands and took a couple of deep breaths.

'What's up,' Priyanka said.

'Nothing,' Radhika said and h aved a sigh. She looked upset, but also younger at the same time. Five years ago, Radhika must have been pretty, I thought.

'Tell no,' Esha said.

'It's Anuj. Sometimes he can be so unreasonable,' she said and showed her phone to Esha. On the screen was an SMS message.

'What is it?' Priyanka said.

'Read it out,' Radhika said as she fumbled through her bag for her anti-migraine pills. 'Damn, I only have one pill left.'

'Really? Okay,' Esha said and started reading the message: 'Show elders respect. Act like a daughter-in-law should. Goodnight.'

'What did I do wrong? I was in a hurry, that is all,' Radhika mumbled to herself as she took her pill with a sip of water.

Esha put a hand on her shoulder.

'What happened?' Esha asked softly. Women do this so well: a few seconds ago she was squealing in excitement over Ganesh, now she was whispering in concern over Anuj.

'Anuj is in Kolkata on tour. He called home and my mother-in-law told him "Radhika made a face when I told her to crush the almonds a bit finer". Can you believe it? I was running to catch the Qualis and still made her milk,' Radhika said and started to press her forehead.

'Is this what mom and son talk about?' Priyanka said.

Radhika continued, 'And then she told him, "I am old, if the pieces are too big they will choke my food pipe. Maybe Radhika is trying to kill me." Why would she say something so horrible?'

'And you're still knitting a scarf for her? Vroom said, pointing at the knitting needles.

'Trust me, being a daughter-in-law is harder than being a model,' Radhika said. The pill was starting to have an effect: her face was looking calm again. 'Anyway, leave my boring life and me. What's up? Ganesh calling soon or what?'

'Are you okay?' Esha said, still holding Radhika's arm.

'Yes, I'm fine. Sorry guys, I overreacted. It's just a little miscommunication between Anuj and me.'

'Looks like your mother-in-law likes melodrama. She should meet my mother,' Priyanka said.

'Really?' Radhika said.

'Oh yes. She is the Miss Universe of melodrama. We cry together at least once a week. Though today, she is on cloud nine,' Priyanka said. She pulled the landline closer to her.

My attention was diverted by a call flashing on my screen.

'I'll take it,' I said, raising my hand. 'Western Appliances, Sam speaking, how may I help you?'

It was one of my weird calls of the night. The caller was from Virginia and was having trouble defrosting his fridge. It took me four long minutes to figure out the reason. Turns out the caller was a 'big person', which is what Americans call fat people. Hence his fingers were too thick to turn the tiny knob in the fridge's compartment that would activate the defrosting mechanism. I suggested that he use a screwdriver or a knife. Fortunately, that solution worked after seven attempts.

'Thank you for calling Western Appliances, sir,' I said and ended the call.

'More politeness, agent Sam. Be more courteous,' I heard Bakshi's voice and felt his heavy bre th on my neck.

'Sir, you again?' I said and turned around. Bakshi's face was as shiny as ever. So oily, he probably slipped off his pillow every night.

'Sorry, I forgot something important,' he said. 'Have you guys done the Western Computers website manual? I am finally sending the project report to Boston.'

'Yes sir. Vroom and I finished it yesterday,' I said and took out a copy from my drawer.

'Hmm,' Bakshi said as he scanned the cover sheet.

*Western Computers Troubleshooting Website*
*User Manual and Project Details*

*Developed by Connexions, Delhi*

*Shyam Mehra and Varun Malhotra*
*(Sam Mason and Victor Mell)*


'Do you have a soft copy that you can email me?' Bakshi said. 'Boston wants it urgently.'

'Yes sir,' Vroom said, pointing to his computer, 'I have it stored here. I'll send it to you.'

'Also, did you do the collation, Sam?'

'Yes sir,' I said and passed him the ten sets.

'Excellent. I empowered you, and you **delivered the output**. Actually, I have another document, the board meeting invite. Can you help?'

'What do I have to do?' I said.

'Here is a copy,' Bakshi said and gave me a five-page document. 'I didn't print more this time. Can you Xerox ten copies for me please? My secretary is off today.'

'Err. Sure Sir, just Xeroxing right?'

Bakshi nodded.

'Sir,' Vroom said, 'what is the board meeting for?'

'Nothing, just routine management issues,' Bakshi said.

'Are people going to get fired?' Vroom asked, his direct question making everyone spring to attention.

'Err...' Bakshi said, at his usual loss for words when asked something meaningful.

'There are rumors in the Western Computers main bay. We just want to know if we will be fine,' Vroom said.

'Western Appliances won't be affected, right?' Esha said.

Bakshi took a deep breath and said, 'I can't say much. All I can say is we are under pressure to right size ourselves.'

'Right size?' Radhika asked in genuine confusion.

'That means people are getting fired, right?' Vroom said. Right size never meant otherwise.

Bakshi did not respond.

'Sir, we need to increase our sales force to get new clients. Firing people is not the answer,' Vroom said, with a boldness that was high even by his standards.

Bakshi had a smirk on his face as he turned to Vroom. He put his hand on Vroom's shoulder. 'I like your excitement Mr Victor,' he said, 'but a seasoned management has to study all underlying variables and come up with an optimal solution. It is not so simple.'

'But sir, we can get more...' Vroom was saying as Bakshi patted his shoulder twice and left.

Vroom waited to ensure that Bakshi was out of the room before he spoke again.

'This is insanity. Bakshi's fucked up the place and they are firing innocent agents,' he said, his voice at shouting levels.

'Stay calm,' I said, and started assembling the sheets.

'Yes stay calm. Like Mr Xerox Boy here—finds acceptance in everything,' Priyanka said.

'Excuse me,' I said looking up. 'Are you talking about me?'

Priyanka kept quiet. I felt agitated inside and just had to respond.

'What is your problem? I come here, make fifteen grand a month and go home. It sucks that people are being fired, and I am trying to do my best to save my job. Overall, yes I accept my situation. And Vroom, before I forget, can you email Bakshi the user manual please?'

'I'm doing it,' Vroom said, as he clicked his mouse, 'though what is happening here is still wrong.'

'Don't worry. We've done the website. We should be safe,' I said.

'I hope so. Damn, it will suck if I lose my fifteen grand a month. If I don't get my pizza thrice a week, I will die,' Vroom said.

'You have pizza that often?' Esha said.

'Isn't it unhealthy?' Radhika asked. Despite the SMS argument, she was back to knitting her scarf. Knitting habits die hard I guess.

'No way. Pizzas are the ultimate balanced diet. Look at the contents: grain in the crust, milk protein in the cheese, vegetables and meat as toppings. It has all the food groups. I read it on the Internet—pizza is good for you.'

'You and your Net,' Esha said. It was true. Vroom got all his information off the Internet—bikes, jobs, politics, dating tips and, as I had just learnt, pizza nutrition as well.

'Pizzas are not healthy. I gain weight so fast if I have a lot of it,' Priyanka said, 'especially with my lifestyle. I hardly get time to exercise. On top of that, I just sit and work in a confined space.'

Priyanka's last two words made my heart skip a beat. 'Confined space' means only one thing to me—that night at the 32nd Milestone disco.

# #12:
# My Past Dates with Priyanka—III

32nd Milestone, Gurgaon Highway
Seven months before this night

I should not really call this one a date, since this time it was a group thing with Vroom and Esha joining us. I argued earlier with Priyanka about going out with work people, but she told me I should be less anti-social. Vroom picked 32nd Milestone and the girls agreed because the disc had no door-bitch. According to Priyanka, a door-bitch is the hostess who stands outside the disco. She screens every girl walking in, and if your waist is more than twenty-four inches, or if you were not wearing something right out of an item number, the door-bitch will raise an eyebrow at you like you are a fifty-year-old aunty.

'Really? I never noticed those door girls before,' I said as we took stools at the bar.

'It's a girl to girl thing. They size you up, and unless you are drop dead gorgeous, you get that mental smirk,' Priyanka said.

'So why should you care? You *are* gorgeous,' I said. She smiled and pinched my cheek.

'Mental smirk? Girls and their coded communication. Anyway, drink anyone?' Vroom said.

'Long Island Ice Tea please,' Esha said and I noticed how stunning she looked with make-up. She wore a black fitted top and black pants. Her pants were so tight, she would probably have to roll them down when removing them.

'Long Island? Want to get drunk quick or what?' I said.

'C'mon. I need to de-stress. I ran around like mad last month chasing modeling agencies. Besides, I have to wash down last week's one thousand calls,' Esha said.

'That's right. Twelve hundred calls for me,' Vroom said. 'Let's all have Long Islands.'

'Vodka cran for me please,' Priyanka said. She wore camel-colored pants and a pistachio-green sequinned kurti. I had given her the kurti as a gift on her last birthday. She had just a hint of eyeliner and a light gloss of lipstick. I preferred it to Esha's Asian Paints job.

'Any luck with modeling assignments?' I idly asked Esha.

'Not much. I did meet a talent agent. He said he would refer me to some designers and fashion show producers. I need to be seen in those circles,' Esha said as she pulled her top down to cover her navel.

Vroom went to the bartender to collect our drinks. I scanned the disc. The place had two levels: a dance floor on the mezzanine and a lounge bar on the first floor. A remixed version of *Dil Chahta Hai* played in the background. As it was Saturday night, the disc had more than three hundred customers. They were all rich, or at least had rich friends who could afford drinks at over Rs 300 a cocktail. Our budget was a lavish thousand bucks each: a treat for making it through the extremely busy summer period at the call center.

I noticed some stick-thin models on the dance floor. Their stomachs were so flat, if they swallowed a pill you would probably see an outline of it when it landed inside. Esha's looks are similar, except she is a bit short.

'Check it out. She is totally anorexic. I can bet on it,' Priyanka said, pointing to a pale-complexioned model on the dance floor. She wore a top without any sleeves or neck or collar. I guess the girls call it 'off-shoulder'. Defying physics, it did not slip off, though most men waited patiently.

The pale-complexioned model turned, displaying a completely bare back.

'Wow, I wish I were that thin. But, oh my god, look at what she is wearing,' Esha said.

'I can't believe she is not wearing a bra, must be totally flat,' Priyanka said.

'Girls!' I said.

'Yes?' Esha and Priyanka turned to me.

'I'm bored. Can you choose more inclusive conversation topics,' I pleaded. I looked for Vroom, he had collected the drinks and was waving maniacally at us for help.

'I'll go,' Esha said and went over to Vroom.

Finally, to my relief, it was only Priyanka and I.

'So,' she said as she leaned forward to peck at my lips. 'You're feeling left out with our irlie talk?'

'Well, this was supposed to be a date. I forced myself to come with them. I haven't caught up with you in ages.'

'I told you, Vroom asked me and I didn't want to be anti-social,' Priyanka said as she ruffled my hair. 'But we'll go out for a walk in a bit. I want to be alone with you too, you know?'

'Please, let's go soon.'

'Sure, but they're here now,' Priyanka said as Vroom and Esha arrived. Vroom passed us our drinks. We said 'cheers', and tried to sound lively and happy, as everyone in a disc always should.

'Congrats on the website guys. I heard it's good,' Esha said as she took a sip.

'The website is cool,' Vroom said. 'The test customers love it. No more dialing. And it's so simple—just right for those spoon-feed-me Americans.'

'So, promotion finally coming for Mr Shyam here,' Priyanka said. I noticed she had finished a third of her drink in just two sips.

'Now Mr Shyam's promotion is another story,' Vroom said. 'Maybe Mr Shyam would like to tell it himself.'

'Please man. Some other time,' I said even as Priyanka looked at me expectantly.

'Okay, well Bakshi said he is talking to Boston to release headcount. But it will take a while.'

'Why can't you just be firm with him?' Priyanka said.

'Like how? How can you be firm with your own boss?' I said, my voice loud with irritation.

'Cool it guys,' Vroom said. 'It's a party night and—'

A big noise interrupted our conversation. We noticed a commotion on the dance floor as the DJ turned off the music.

'What's up?' Vroom said and we all went towards the dance floor.

A fight had broken out on the floor. A gang of drunken friends had thought someone had pawed one of the girls with them. They accused that someone else and grabbed his collar. Soon, Mr Accused's own gang came to his defense. As the dance floor was too noisy for vocal arguments, people expressed themselves only with fists and kicks. The music stopped when someone knocked one guy flat on the floor. Several others were on top of each other. Bouncers finally disentangled everyone and restored peace. A stretcher emerged to carry away the knocked-out guy.

'Man, I wish it had gone on a bit longer,' Vroom said.

It's true. The only thing better than watching beautiful people in a disc is watching a fight. A fight means the party is totally rocking.

Five minutes later the music was back and occupying the floor again was the anorexic girls' brigade.

'That is what happens to kids with rich dads and too much money,' Vroom said.

'C'mon Vroom. I thought you said money is good. That is how we'll beat the Americans, right?' Priyanka said with the confidence that comes after drinking a Long Island Iced Tea in seven minutes.

'Yes, doesn't money pay for your mobile phones, pizzas and discos?' I asked.

'Yes, but the difference is that I've earned it. These rich kids, they have no clue how hard it is to make cash,' Vroom said and held up his glass. 'This drink is three hundred bucks— it takes me almost a full night of two hundred irritating Americans screaming into my ear to earn it. Then I get this drink. Which is full of ice-cubes anyway. These kids can't make that comparison.'

'Oh, I feel so guilty drinking this now,' Priyanka said.

'C'mon, you get good money. Significantly more than the eight grand you made as a journalist trainee,' I said.

'Yes,' Vroom said as he took a big hundred-and-twenty-rupee sip. 'We get paid well, fifteen thousand a month. Fuck, that is almost twelve dollars a day. Wow, I make as much a day as a US burger boy makes in two hours. Not bad for my college degree. Not bad at al  Fucking nearly double of what I made as a journalist anyway.' He pushed his empty glass and it slid to the other end of the table.

Everyone was silent for a minute. Vroom on his temper trip is unbearable.

'Stop being so depressed. Let's dance,' Esha said and tugged at Vroom's hand.

'No,' Vroom said.

'Come for one song,' Esha said and stood up from her stool.

'Okay, but if anyone teases you, I'm not getting into a fight,' Vroom said.

'Don't worry, no one will. There are prettier girls here,' Esha said.

'I don't think so. Anyway, let's go,' Vroom said as they went to the dance floor. The song playing was *Sharara Sharara*, one of Esha's favorites.

Priyanka and I watched them dance from our seats.

'Want to go for a walk now?' Priyanka said after a few minutes.

'Sure,' I said. We held hands and walked out of 32nd Milestone. The bouncer at the door stamped our palms so that we could re-enter the disco. We headed to the parking lot, as the music was softer there. My ears never felt so nice.

'It's so calm here,' Priyanka said. 'I don't like it when Vroom gets all worked up. The boy needs to control his temper. Too much unchecked aggression going on there.'

'He's young and confused. Don't worry, life will slap him into shape. I think he regrets moving to Connexions sometimes. Besides, he has not taken his dad and mom's separation so well. It shows now and then.'

'Still, he should get a grip on himself. Get a steady girlfriend maybe, that will help him relax.'

'I think he likes Esha,' I said.

'I don't know if Esha is interested. She's quite focused on her modeling trip.'

We reached our Qualis. I opened the door to take out a pack of cigarettes.

'No smoking near me,' she said and grabbed the pack from me.

'See, maybe it is not such a good idea to have a steady girlfriend,' I said.

'Really? So Mr Shyam is having second thoughts?' she said, tilting her head.

'No,' I said, and opened the Qualis again. I took out a bottle.

'What's that?' she asked.

'Some Bacardi we keep handy. It's three hundred bucks for a drink inside, the cost of this whole bottle.'

'Cool. You guys are smart,' Priyanka said and pulled at my cheek. Then she took a sip from the bottle.

'Careful. There's no need to get drunk just because it's free.'

'Trust me. There is a need when you a have a psycho parent.'

'What happened now?'

'Nothing. I don't want to talk about her today. Let's do a shot.' The bottle's lid acted as one cup, and I broke the top of a cigarette packet for the other. We poured Bacardi into both and warmth traveled down from my lips to my insides as we tossed down our first shot.

'I'm sorry about the Bakshi comment I made inside,' she said.

'It's alright. Doesn't matter,' I said, and wondered if we should do shot number two now or later.

'I can be a bitch sometimes. But I do make it up to you. I'm a loving person, no?' she said, high from mixing her drinks.

'You're just fine,' I said and looked at her moist eyes. Her nose puckered up a bit and I could have looked at it forever.

'So,' she said.

'So what?' I said, still hypnotized by her nose.

'Why are you looking at me like that?' she said and smiled.

'Like what?'

'The come-hither look. I see mischief in your eyes, mister,' she said playfully, grabbing both my hands.

'There is no mischief—that's just your imagination,' I said.

'We'll see,' she said and came up close. We hugged as she kissed me on my neck.

'Listen,' she said.

'What?' I mumbled.

'When was the last time we made love?'

'Oh, don't even ask. It's really pathetic—over a month ago.'

It was true. The only place we made love was my house when it was empty. However, recently my mom had started staying more at home because of the cold. She had even given up her favorite past time of meeting relatives.

'Have you ever made love in confined spaces?'

'*What?*' I said loudly, right into her ear.

'Ouch!' she said, rubbing her ear. 'Hello? You heard me right?'

'What are you talking about?'

'Well, we have the time, soft music and a desolate spot.'

'So?'

'So, step into the Qualis, my friend,' she said and opened the door. I climbed into the backseat and she followed me.

Our Qualis was parked right behind the disco, and we could hear the music if we were quiet. The song changed to *Mahi Ve* from the movie *Kaante*.

'I love this song,' she said and sat astride my lap, facing me.

'It's a pole dancer song. You know that?' I said.

'Yes. But I like the lyrics. Their love is true, but fate has something else in store.'

'I never focus on the lyrics.'

'You just notice the scantily clad girls in the video,' she said and ran her fingers through my hair.

I stayed silent.

'So, you didn't answer my question—have you made love in confined spaces?' she said.

'Priyanka, are you crazy or are you drunk?'

She unbuttoned the top few buttons of my shirt. 'Both. Okay mister, the thing about confined spaces is that you have to cooperate. Now move your hands out of the way,' she said.

We were quiet, apart from our breathing.

She confirmed that the windows were shut and ordered me to remove my shirt. She took off her kurti first, and then slowly unhooked her bra.

'Be careful with your clothes. We'll need to find them quickly afterwards,' she said.

'Are you mad...' I gasped even as I raised my arms so she could pull my shirt over my head. She moved to keep my shirt aside and her foot landed on my left baby toe.

'Ouch!' I screamed.

'Oops, sorry,' she said in a naughty-apologetic tone. she moved her foot away, her head hit the roof.

'Ouch,' she said. 'Sorry, this isn't as elegant as in th Titanic movie.'

'It's alright. Clumsy sex is better than choreographed sex. And certainly better than no sex,' I said as I pulled her close.

'By the way, do you have a condom?' she said.

'Yes sir. We live in constant hope,' I said as I pulled out my wallet.

We laughed as she embraced me. She started kissing me on my face. I kissed her shoulders. In a few moments, I forgot I was in the company Qualis.

Twenty minutes later we collapsed in each other's arms on the backseat.

'Amazing. That is simply amazing, Ms Priyanka.'

'My pleasure, Sir,' she said and winked at me. 'Can we lie here and talk for a while?'

'Sure,' I said, reaching for my clothes.

She cuddled me again after we had dressed.

'Do you love me?' she asked. Her voice was serious.

'More than anybody else on this planet, and that includes me,' I said, caressing her hair.

'You think I'm a caring person?' she said. Her voice told me she was close to tears.

'Why do you keep asking me that?' I said.

'My mother was looking at our family album today. She stopped at a picture of me when I was three years old: I'm sitting on a tricycle and my mother is pushing me. She saw that picture, and you know what she said?'

'What?'

'She said I was so cute when I was three.'

'You're cute now,' I said and pressed her nose like a button.

'And she said I was so loving and caring then and that I wasn't so loving anymore. She said she always wondered what had made me so heartless...' Priyanka said and burst into tears.

I held her tight and felt her body shake. I thought hard about what I could say. Guys can never figure out what to say in such emotional moments and always end up saying something stupid.

'Your mother is crazy...'

'Don't say anything about my mother. I love her. Can you just listen to me for five minutes?' Priyanka said.

'Of course. Sorry...' I said as her sobs grew louder. I swore to myself to stay quiet for the next five minutes. I started counting my breath to pass time. Sixteen a minute is my average; eighty breaths would mean I had listened to her for five minutes.

'We weren't always like this. My mom and I were best friends. Until class eight I think. Then as I became older, she became crazier,' she said.

I wondered if I should point out that she had just told me not to call her mum crazy. However, I had promised myself I would keep quiet.

'She had different rules for me and my brother. And that began to bother me. She would comment on everything I wore, everywhere I went, whereas my brother...she would never say anything to him. I tried to explain it to her, but she just became more irritating, and by the time I reached college, I couldn't wait to get away from her.'

'Uh-uh,' I said, calculating that almost half my time must have passed. My leg was cramping. When sex is over, confined spaces are a pain.

'All through college I ignored her and did what I wanted. In fact, this whole don't-care phase was born out of that.

But at one level, I felt so guilty. I tried again to connect with her after college. But she had a problem with everything—my thinking, my friends, my boyfriend.'

The last word caught my attention. I had to speak, even though only fifty-seven breaths had passed.

'Sorry, but did you say boyfriend?'

'Well yeah. She knows I'm with you. And she has this thing about me finding someone settled.'

*Settled*? The words rewound and repeated itself in my head several times. *What does that mean anyway?* Just someone rich, or someone who gets predictable cash flows at the end of every month. Except parents do not say it that way because then it really sounds like they're trading their daughter to the highest bidder. But in some ways, they are. They do not give a damn about love or feelings or crap like that. 'Show me the money and keep our daughter for the rest of your life.' That is the arrangement in an arranged marriage.

'What are you thinking about?' she said.

'I'm a loser according to your mom, isn't it?' I said.

'That is not what I said.'

'Don't you bring up Bakshi and my promotion every time we have a conversation?' I said, moving away.

'Why do you get so defensive? Anyway, if Bakshi doesn't promote you, you can look for another job.'

'I'm tired of job hunting. There is nothing good out there. And I'm tired of rejections. Moreover, what is the point of joining another call center? I'll just have to start as a junior agent all over again—without you, without my friends. And let me tell you this, I may not be team leader, but I am happy. I am content. You realize that? And tell your drama queen mom to come say it to my face that I am a loser. And she can send you off with whichever fucking settled annuity income earner she likes. I am what I am...' I said, my face beetroot-red.

'Shyam, please can you try and understand?'

'Understand what? Your mother? No, I can't. And you can't either, but I suspect deep down you might agree with her. Like, what am I doing with this loser,' I said.

'Stop talking nonsense,' Priyanka shouted. 'I just made love to you for god's sake. And stop using that loser word,' she said and broke into tears again.

Two brief knocks on the window disturbed our conversation. It was Vroom; Esha was standing next to him.

'Hello? I thought we came together. You love birds are inseparable, eh?' he said.

# #13

T HE LOUD RING OF THE LANDLINE TELEPHONE BROUGHT ME
back from 32nd Milestone. Priyanka grabbed the phone. 'Hiiiii
Ganesh,' she said, her stretched tone too flirty, if you ask me.
But then, who the hell cares for my opinion anyway.

I wondered what *his* tone was like. '*Get under the table. Tap
the phone, Shyam,*' a voice told me. I immediately scolded myself
for the horrible thought.

'Of course I knew it was you. No one else calls on this
emergency line,' Priyanka said and ran her fingers through her
hair. Women playing with their hair while talking to a guy is
an automatic female preening gesture; I saw it once on Discovery
Channel.

'Yeah,' Priyanka said after a few seconds, 'I like cars. Which
one are you planning to buy?...Lexus?'

'Lexus! The dude is buying a Lexus,' Vroom screamed, loud
enough for me to understand that this was an expensive car.

'Ask him which model, ask him please,' Vroom said and Priyanka looked at him startled. She shook her head at Vroom.

'Let them talk, Vroom. They've got better things to discuss than car models,' Esha said.

'What colour? C'mon, it's your car. How can I decide for you?' Priyanka said as her fingers started playing with the curled telephone wire. Over the next five minutes Ganesh did most of the talking, while Priyanka kept saying monosyllabic 'yes' or equivalents.

'*Tap the phone,*' the voice kept banging in my head. I hated myself for it, but I knew I would to do it. I wondered when Priyanka would step away from the desk.

'No, no, Ganesh, it's fine, go for your meeting. I'm here only, call me later,' Priyanka said as she ended her call. I guess Mr Microsoft did have some work to do after all.

'Vroom, is Lexus a nice car?' Priyanka said.

Vroom was already on the Net, surfing Lexus pictures. He turned his monitor to Priyanka. 'Check this out. Lexus is one of the coolest cars. The guy must be loaded.'

Priyanka looked at Vroom's screen for a few seconds and then turned to the girls. 'He wants me to choose the colour. Can you believe that? I don't think I should though,' she said.

Vroom pushed himself back in his swivel chair. 'Go for black or silver. Nothing is as cool as the classic colors. But I'll check out some more for you,' he said. 'And tell him the interiors have to be dark leather.'

Meanwhile, my interiors were on fire. I felt like throwing up.

I wondered when I could tap the phone. It was totally wrong, and Priyanka and the rest of the girls would probably kill me if they found out. But I had to do it. It was masochistic, but I just had to hear that ass woo my ex-girlfriend away with the promise of expensive cars.

I tried to set the stage so I had some excuse to get beneath the table.

'Why have there been no calls in the last ten minutes?' I said. 'I should check if the connections are fine.'

'Let it be,' Esha said. 'I'm enjoying the break.'

'Yes me too,' Radhika said. 'And the connection is okay. Bangalore is just over-eager and picking up all the calls.'

'Bio?' Priyanka said to Esha. It was their code word to go the toilet toge  . for a private conversation.

'Sure.' Esha sensed the need for gossip and got up from her chair.

'I'll come too,' Radhika said and stood up. She turned to me: 'The girls want a bio break  eam leader.'

'You're *all* going?' I said, pretending to be reluctant, but secretly thrilled. This was my chance. 'Well, okay, since nothing much is happening right now.'


As soon as the girls were out of sight I dived under the table.

'What are you doing?' Vroom said.

'Nothing. I don't think the connections are firm,' I said.

'And what the hell do you know about the connections,' Vroom said. He bent down to look under the table. 'Tell me honestly what you're doing.'

I told him about my uncontrollable urge to tap the phone. Vroom scolded me for five seconds, but then got excited by the challenge and joined me under the table.

'I can't believe I'm helping you with this. The girls will kill us if they find out,' Vroom said.

'They won't have a clue,' I said, and connected the wires. 'Look, it's almost done.'

Vroom picked up the landline and we tested the arrangement. I could select an option on my computer and listen in on the landline via my headset. Mr Microsoft was in the bag.

'Why are you doing this?' Vroom said.

'I don't know. Don't ask me that.'

'And why are the girls taking so long?'

'You know them, they have their girl talk in the toilet.'

'And you don't want to hear what they're saying? I'm sure they're discussing Mr Microsoft there.'

'Oh no,' I said, worried about what I could be missing. 'Although how would we be able to eavesdrop?'

'From the corner stall of the men's toilet,' Vroom said. 'It shares a wall with the girl's toilet. If you press your ear hard against the wall, you can hear them.'

'Really?' I said, my eyes lighting up.

Vroom nodded.

'It'll be wrong though, eavesdropping through a stall,' I said.

'Yes it will.'

'But who cares. Let's go,' I said and Vroom and I jumped off our chairs.


Vroom and I squeezed in and bolted the door in the corner stall of the WASG men's toilet. We pressed our ears against the wall. I could hear Radhika's voice.

'Yes, he sounds like a really nice guy,' she was saying.

'But I shouldn't tell him the color, no? It's his car and it is so expensive. But you know what he said?' Priyanka said.

'What?' Radhika said.

'He said "no, it is *our* car", and then he said "you have brought color to my life, so you get to choose the color".'

'Oh, he sounds so romantic,' Esha said.

'That is such a lame loser line. Color of my life, my ass,' I said to Vroom.

'Shh. They'll hear us, stupid. Keep quiet,' Vroom said and put his hand on my mouth.

'Anyway, how s Anuj?' Priyanka said. I could hear the jingle of her bangles. She was probably brushing her hair.

'Anuj is fine,' Radhika said. 'He is at a dealer conference in Kolkata. I think he has to be up late as some dealers can't seem to have enough to drink.'

'Sales jobs are tough,' Esha said. 'Okay, excuse me, but I have to change this...ouch!'

'What's happening?' I said.

Vroom shrugged his shoulders.

'Esha, your wound has not healed for days. Just a band-aid is not enough,' Priyanka said. I guessed Esha was changing the band-aid on her shin.

'No, I'm fine. As long as it heals before the Lakme fashion week,' Esha said.

'Let's go back girls, it is almost 1:00 a.m.,' Radhika said. 'Otherwise the boys will grumble.'

'The boys always grumble. Like they never have their cigarette breaks,' Esha said.

'But today they are extra grumbly. At least *someone* is,' Radhika said.

Vroom pointed a finger at me. Yes, the girls were talking about me.

I grumbled in lip sync.

'You think Shyam is not taking the news well?' Priyanka said, her voice becoming fainter as they walked towards the toilet's exit.

'You tell us. You know him better than we do,' Esha said.

'I wish I knew him now. I don't know why he sulks and acts so childish sometimes,' Priyanka said as they left the toilet.

'Childish? Me? I am childish?' I said to Vroom, jumping up and down in the stall. 'What the hell. Mr Microsoft gives these cheesy lines and he is cute and romantic. I say nothing and I am childish,' I banged a fist on the stall door.

'Shyam, don't behave like a kid,' Vroom said.

We came out of the stall. I jumped back a step as I saw Bakshi by the sink.

Through the mirror, Bakshi saw both of us. His jaw dropped as he turned towards us.

'Hello Sir,' Vroom said and went up to the sink next to him.

'Sir, it is not what you think…' I said, pointing back at the stall.

'I am not thinking anything. What you do in your personal lives is up to you. But why aren't you at the desk?' Bakshi said.

'Sir, we just took a short break. Call traffic is very low today,' I said.

'Did you log your break? The girls are missing from the bay as well,' Bakshi said. His face was turning from a shiny pink to a shiny red.

'Really? Where did the girls go?' Vroom said.

Bakshi turned away from us and walked to the urinal stalls. I went to the stall adjacent to him.

'Didn't you just use the toilet?' Bakshi said.

'Sir,' I said and hesitated. 'Sir, that was different, with Vroom.'

'Please. I don't want to know,' Bakshi said.

'Sir, no,' I said.

Now this is something women never have to deal with: standing next to your boss in the toilet as he pees is one of the world's most awkward situations. What are you supposed to do? Leave him alone or give him company and entertain him? Is it okay to talk to him while he is doing his business or not?

'Sir, how come you are using this restroom?' I said, as I had not seen him there before.

'Didn't mean to. I always use the executive toilet,' Bakshi said, emphasizing his superior position to me.

'Yes sir,' I said and nodded my head. I had acknowledged his magnanimous gesture of pee ng in the same bay as us. *But why was he here?*

'Anyway, I came to your desk to drop off a courier for Esha.'

'Courier?' Vroom said from his position at the sink. 'At this time?'

'I've kept the parcel on her desk. Just tell her,' Bakshi said as he zipped up.

'Also, Shyam, can you tell the voice agents to come to my office for a team meeting later, say 2:30 a.m., okay?' Bakshi said.

'What's up sir?' Vroom said.

'Nothing. I want to share some pertinent insights with the resources. Anyway, can I ask you a couple of questions on the website? You know it well, right?'

'Yes sir. And most questions will be answered in the FAQ section of the user manual we sent you,' Vroom said.

'FAQ?'

'Frequently asked questions.'

'Good. Boston may have some queries. I will rely on you smart people to answer them. For instance, how do you update the site for new computer models?'

'It's easy, Sir. Any systems person can modify the website backend and change the queries to suit the model,' Vroom said.

Bakshi asked us a few more questions. They were simple enough for Vroom or me to answer them, especially as we had built the website from scratch.

'Good, good. I am impressed by your knowledge. Anyway, thanks for the user manual, I have already sent it to Boston,' Bakshi said and shook his hands dry. I moved away to avoid any droplets falling on me.

'You did?' both of us said in unison.

'Sir, if you could have copied us on the email...we would like to be in the loop,' Vroom said. Good one, he was using Bakshi's phrases back at him.

'Oh, i didn't? I am so sorry. I am not good with emails anyway. I'll just forward it to you. But you guys man the bay now, okay?'

'Of course, Sir,' I said.

'And have you finished the **ad-hoc task** I gave you,' Bakshi said.

'What, Sir?' I said, and then realized he meant the photocopying of the board meeting invite. 'Almost done, Sir. I will send it to you.'

Bakshi nodded and left us behind in the restroom. I felt weird that Bakshi had not copied us on the email sending out the website proposal. However, it did not surprise me.

'Is he a total moron or what? Can't cc people on an email?' Vroom said.

'Easy man. Let's get back to the bay,' I said.

# #14

WE RETURNED FROM THE MEN'S ROOM. CALL FLOW HAD resumed at the WASG. Radhika explained to a caller how to open his vacuum cleaner. Priyanka advised a lady not to put hot pans in the dishwasher. Esha taught an old man to pre-heat an oven and simultaneously dodged his telephonic 'your-voice-is-so-sexy' pass.

Another call flashed on my screen.

'I know this guy. Can I take this call?' Vroom said.

'Who is it?' I raised my eyebrows.

'A prick called William Fox. Listen in if you want,' Vroom said.

I selected the option on my computer.

'Good afternoon, Western Appliances, Victor speaking. How may I help you today, Mr Fox,' Vroom said.

'You bloody well help me smart ass,' the man on the phone said. He had a rough voice, with a heavy southern American accent; he sounded like he was in his mid-thirties. I could guess he was drunk.

'Who is he,' I whispered, but Vroom shushed me.

'Sir, if I may confirm, I am speaking to Mr William Fox'

'You bet you are. You think just 'cos you know my name it's okay to sell me crap hoovers?'

'What is the problem with your vacuum cleaner, Sir? It's a VX-100?'

'It doesn't suck dust anymore. It just doesn't.'

'Sir, do you remember when you last changed the dust bags?' Vroom said.

'Like fuck I remember when I changed the dust bags. It's just a crap machine you dumbass.'

Vroom took three deep breaths. He remembered the suggested line in such a situation. 'Sir, I request you to not use that language.'

'Oh really? Then make your fucking hoover work.'

Vroom pressed a button on his phone before he spoke again. 'Fuck you first you sorofabitch prickhead...' he said.

'What are you doing?' I said, panicking.

'Just venting, don't worry it is on mute,' Vroom smirked. 'Back to normal now.' He pressed the button again and, trying his best to keep his tone calm, said, 'Sir, you need to change the dust bags when they are full.'

'Who am I speaking to?' the voice on the phone became agitated.

'Victor, sir.'

'Tell me your fucking name. You're some kid in India, isn't it?'

'Sir, I am afraid I can't disclose my location.'

'You're from India. Tell me, boy.'

'Yes sir. I am in India,' Vroom gave in.

'So what did you have to do to get this job? Fucking degree in nuclear physics?'

'Sir, do you need help with your cleaner or not?' Vroom said.

'C'mon son, answer me. I don't need your help. Yeah, I'll change the dust bag. What about you guys? When will you change your dusty country?'

'Excuse me, sir, but I want you to stop talking like that,' Vroom said.

'Oh really, now some brown kid will tell me what to do—' William Fox's voice stopped abruptly as I cut off the call.

Vroom didn't move for a few seconds. His whole body trembled and he was breathing heavily. Then he placed his elbows on the table and covered his face with his hands.

'You don't have to talk to those people. You know that,' I said to Vroom.

The girls glanced at us while still on their calls.

'Vroom, I'm talking to you,' I said.

He raised his face and slowly turned to look at me. Then he banged a fist on the table. 'Damn,' he screamed and kicked hard under the table.

'What the...' Priyanka said. 'My call just got cut.'

Vroom's kick had dislodged the power wires, disconnecting all our calls. I wanted to check the wires, but had to check on Vroom first. Vroom stood up and his six-foot-plus frame towered above us.

'Guys, there are two things I cannot stand,' he said and showed us two fingers. 'Racists. And Americans.'

Priyanka started laughing.

'What is there to laugh?' I said.

'Because there is a contradiction. Doesn't like racists, can't stand Americans,' Priyanka said.

'Why?' Vroom said, ignoring Priyanka. 'Why do some fat ass, dim-witted Americans get to act superior to us? Do you know why?'

Nobody answered.

Vroom continued, 'I'll tell you why. Not because they are smarter. Not because they are better people. But because their country is rich and ours is poor. That is the only damn reason. Because the losers who have run our country for the last fifty years couldn't do better than make India one of the poorest countries on earth. Great job, thank you, dear great fucking leaders.'

'Stop overreacting Vroom. Some stupid guy calls and...' Radhika said.

'Screw Americans,' I said and gave him a bottle of water. 'Look, you've broken down the entire system.' I pointed to the blank call screens.

'Someone kicked the Americans a bit too hard. No more calls for now,' Priyanka said, rolling her eyes.

'Let me take a look,' I said and went under the table. I was more worried about the wires tapping the emergency phone. However, they were intact.

'Shyam, wait,' Esha said, 'we have a great excuse for not taking calls. Let it be for a while.'

Everyone agreed with her. We decided to call systems after twenty minutes.

'Why was Bakshi here? I saw him come out of the men's toilet,' Priyanka said.

'To deliver a courier for Esha,' I said. 'And he said there is a team meeting at 2:30 a.m. Oh man, I still have to Xerox the board meeting invite.'

I assembled Bakshi's sheets again.

'What courier,' Esha said. 'This?'

She lifted a brown packet that was lying near her computer.

'Must be,' Vroom said, 'though which courier delivers stuff at this time?'

Esha opened the packet. She took out two bundles of hundred rupee notes. One bundle had a small yellow post-it note on it. She read the post-it and her face went pale.

'Wow, someone's rich,' Vroom said.

'Not bad. What's the money for?' Radhika said.

'It's nothing. Just a friend returning money she borrowed from me,' Esha said.

She dumped the packet in her drawer and took out her mobile phone. Her face was pensive, as if she was debating whether or not to make a call. I collected my sheets to go to the Xerox room.

'Want to help?' I called out to Vroom.

'No thanks. People I worked with are becoming national TV reporters, but look at me. Taking calls from losers and being asked to help with loser jobs,' Vroom said and looked away from me.

# #15

I SWITCHED ON THE XEROX MACHINE IN THE SUPPLIES ROOM and put Bakshi's stack in the document feeder. I had just pressed the 'start' button on the agenda document when the copier creaked and groaned to a halt. 'Paper Jam: Tray 2' appeared in big, bold letters on the screen.

The copier in our supplies room is not a machine. It is a person. A person with a psychotic soul and a grumpy attitude towards life. Whenever you copy more than two sheets, there is a paper jam. After that, the machine teases you: it gives you systematic instructions on how to un-jam it—*open cover, remove tray, pull lever.* Now if it knows this much, why doesn't it fix itself?

'Damn,' I mumbled to myself as I bent down to open the paper trays. I turned a few levers, and pulled out whatever paper was in sight.

I stood up and rearranged the documents on the feeder tray. I pressed 'start' again, not realizing that my ID was resting on

Bakshi's original document. As the machine re-started, it sucked in the ID along with the paper. The ID pulled at my strap, which tightened around my neck.

'Aaargh,' I said as I choked. The ID went inside the machine's guts, and the strap curled tighter around my neck. I screamed loudly and pulled at my ID. However, the machine had more strength. I was sure it wanted to kill me—and probably making a copy of my ID for my obituary while it was at it. I started kicking the machine hard.

Vroom came running into the room. 'What the...' he appeared nonplussed. He saw A4 sheets spread all over the room, a groaning Xerox machine, and me lying down on top of the photocopier, desperately tugging at my strap.

'Do something,' I said in a muffled voice.

'Like what?' he said and bent over to look at the machine. The screen was flashing the poetic words 'Paper Jam'. My ID strap ran right into the machine.

Vroom looked around the supplies room and found a pair of scissors.

'Should I?' he said and smiled at me. 'I really want the others to see this.'

'Shut...up...and...cut,' I said.

Snap! In one snap, my breath came back.

'Okay now?' Vroom asked as he threw the scissors back in the supplies tray.

I nodded as I rubbed my neck and took wheezing breaths. I rested my head down on the warm, soothing glass of the photocopy machine. I must have rested it too hard, or maybe my head is too heavy. I heard a crack.

'Fuck,' Vroom said, 'you broke the glass.'

'What?' I said as I lifted my head.

'Get off,' Vroom said and pulled me off the machine. 'What is with you man? Having a bad office supplies day?'

'Who knows?' I said, collecting Bakshi's document. 'I really am good for nothing. Cannot even do these loser jobs. I almost died. Can you imagine the headline—"Copier decapitates man, duplicates document".'

Vroom laughed and put his arm around my shoulder.

'Don't take tension dude. And I apologize.'

'For what,' I said. Nobody has ever apologized to me in the past twenty-six years of my life.

'I'm sorry I was rude and didn't come and help you. First these rumors about the call center closing down. Then Boontoo makes it to NDTV. And Bakshi sends the document without copying us. Meanwhile, some psycho caller screams curses at me. Just gets to you sometimes.'

'What gets to you?' I asked. I was trying to copy Bakshi's document again, but the Xerox machine was hurling abusive messages on the screen every time I pressed a button. Soon it self-detected a crack in the glass and switched itself off. I think it committed suicide.

'Life,' Vroom said, sitting down on one of the stools in the supplies room, 'life gets to you. You think you are perfectly happy—you know, good salary, nice friends, life is a party—but all of a sudden, in one little snap, everything can crack, like this stupid glass pane of the Xerox machine.'

I did not fully understand Vroom's glass pane theory of life, but his face told me he was upset. I decided to soothe the man who had just saved my life.

'Vroom, you know what your problem is?'

'What?'

'You don't have real love in your life. You need to fall in love, be in love and stay in love. That is the gap you are facing,' I said firmly, as if I really knew what I was talking about.

'You think so?' Vroom said. 'I've had girlfriends. I'll make another one soon—you know that.'

'Not those kind of girls. Someone you really care about. And I think we all know who that is.'

'Esha?' he said.

I kept quiet.

'Esha is not interested. I have asked her. She has her modeling and says she has no time for a relationship. Besides, she has other issues with me,' Vroom said.

'What issues?' I said.

'She says I don't know what love is. I care for cars and bikes more than girls.'

I laughed. 'You do.'

'That is such an unfair comparison. It's like asking women what they care for more, nice shoes or men. There is no easy answer.'

'Really? So we are benchmarked to footwear?'

'Trust me, women can ignore men for sexy shoes. But come to the point—Esha.'

'Do you think you love her?' I said.

'Can't say. But I've felt something for her for over a year now.'

'But you dated other girls last year.'

'Those girls were never important. They were like TV channels you surf while looking for the real program you want to see. You are with that Curly Wurly chick, and you still have feelings for Priyanka,' Vroom said.

The statement startled me.

'Shefali is there to help me move on,' I said.

'Screw moving on. That chick can put you off women forever. Maybe that will help you get over Priyanka,' Vroom said.

'Don't change the topic. We're talking about you. I think you should ask Esha again for a real relationship. Do it man.'

Vroom looked at me for a few seconds. 'Will you help me?' he said.

'Me? You're the expert with girls,' I said.

'This one is different. The stakes are higher. Can you be around when I talk to her? Just listen to our conversation. Maybe we can analyze it late

'Okay, sure. So, let's do it now.'

'Now?'

'Why not? We have free time. Afterwards calls will begin and we'll be busy again. Worst case, management may fire us. Better act fast, right?' I said.

'Okay. Where do we do it?' Vroom said as he put his hand on his forehead to think. 'The dining room?'

The dining room made sense. I could be nearby, but inconspicuous.

## 16

'EVERYTHING OKAY? I HEARD NOISES,' ESHA SAID, AS WE returned from the supplies room. She stretched back on her chair. Her top slid up and the navel ring twinkled.

'The Xerox machine died. Anyway, anyone for a snack?' I said.

'Yes, let's go. I need a walk. Come, Priyanka,' Esha said and tried to pull Priyanka up by her upper arm.

'No, I'll stay here,' Priyanka said and smiled. 'Ganesh might call.'

A scoop of hot molten lead entered through my head and left from my toes. *Try to move on,* I reminded myself. At the same time, I had the urge to pick up that landline and smash it to fifty pieces.

Radhika was about to get up when I stopped her.

'Actually Radhika, can you stay back? If Bakshi walks by, at least he'll see some people on the desk,' I said.

Radhika sat back puzzled as we left the room.

The dining area at Connexions is a cross between a restaurant and a college hostel mess. There are three rows of long granite-covered tables, with seating on both sides. The chairs are plush; they're upholstered in black leather in an attempt to give them a hip designer look. The tables have a small vase every three feet. Management recently renovated the place when some overpriced consulting firm (full of MBAs) recommended that a bright dining room would be good for employee motivation. A much cheaper option would have just been to fire Bakshi, if you ask me.

Vroom took a cheese sandwich and chips (we don't serve Indian food—again for motivation reasons) in his tray and sat at one of the tables. Esha just took soda water and sat opposite Vroom. I think she eats once every three days. I took an unhealthy sized slice of chocolate cake. I shouldn't have, but justified it as a well-deserved reward for helping a friend.

I sat at the adjacent table, took out my phone, and started typing fake SMS messages.

'Why isn't Shyam sitting with us?' Esha said to Vroom, twisting on her seat to look at me.

'Private SMSing,' Vroom said. Esha rolled her eyes and nodded.

'Actually Esha, I wanted to tell you something,' Vroom said, fingering the chips on his plate. I had already finished half my cake. I was probably a pig with a reverse eating disorder in my previous life.

'Yeah?' Esha said to Vroom, dragging the word as an eyebrow rose in suspicion. The invisible female antennae were out and suggesting caution. 'Talk about what?'

'Esha,' Vroom said, clearing his throat. 'I've been thinking about you a lot lately.'

'Really?' she said and looked sideways to see if I was eavesdropping. Of course I was, but I made an extra effort to display a facial expression that showed I was really focusing on my cake. She watched as I joyfully consumed what was probably her weekly calorific consumption in a few seconds.

'Yes really, Esha. I may have met a lot of girls, but no one is like you.'

She giggled and, taking a flower out from the vase, began plucking out its petals.

'Yes,' Vroom continued, 'and I think rather than fool around, I could do with a real relationship. So, I'm asking you again—will you go out with me?'

Esha was quiet for a few minutes. 'What do you expect me to say?'

'I don't know. How about a yes?'

'Really? Well unfortunately that word did not occur to me,' Esha said, her expression serious.

'Why?' Vroom said. I could tell he thought it was over already. He had told me once, if a girl hints she is not interested, it's time to cut losses and quit. Never try the persuasion game.

'I've told you before. I have to focus on my modeling career. I can't afford the luxury of making a boyfriend,' she said, her voice unusually cold.

'What is with you, Esha? Don't you want someone to support you...' Vroom said.

'That's right, with three different girlfriends last year, I am sure you will always be there for me,' Esha said.

'The other girls were just for fun. They meant nothing, they're like pizza or movies or something. They are channel surfing, you are more serious,' Vroom said.

'So what serious channel am I? The BBC?' Esha said.

'I have known you for more than a year. We have spent hundreds of nights together...'

I thought Vroom's last phrase came out odd, but Esha was too preoccupied to notice.

'Just drop it, Vroom,' Esha said and put the flower back in the vase. Her voice was breaking, though she was not crying yet.

'Are you okay?' Vroom said and extended his hand to hold hers. She sensed the move and pulled her hand away nanoseconds before he reached it.

'Not really,' Esha said.

'I thought we were friends. I just wanted to take it to the next level...' Vroom said.

'Please stop it,' Esha said, and covered her eyes with her hands. 'You chose the worst time to talk about this.'

'What's wrong Esha? Can I help?' Vroom said, his voice now held more concern than the nervousness of romance.

She shook her head frantically.

I knew Vroom had failed miserably. This girl was not interested and was in a strange mood tonight anyway. I finished my thousand-calorie chocolate cake, and went to the counter to get water. By the time I returned, they had left the dining room.

# #17

I RETURNED TO THE WASG BAY WITH THE TASTE OF chocolate cake lingering in my mouth. I sat down at my desk and began surfing irrelevant websites. Radhika was giving Priyanka recommendations on the best shops in Delhi for bridal dresses. Esha and Vroom were silent. My guilt for eating the chocolate cake combined with my guilt for not reporting the systems failure. When guilt combines, it multiplies manifold. I finally called IT to fix our desk. They were busy, but promised to come in ten minutes.

The spare landline's ring startled us all.

'Ganesh,' Priyanka said as she scrambled to pick up the phone. I kept a calm face while I selected the option to listen in on the call.

'Mom,' Priyanka said, 'why aren't you sleeping? Who gave you this number?'

'What sleeping? No one has slept a wink today,' her mother said in an excited voice. I had never met her. However, through Priyanka's stories, I felt I knew her intimately.

The tapped line had exceptional clarity. Her mother sounded elated, which was unusual for a woman who (according to Priyanka) had spent most of her life in self-imposed, obsessive-compulsive depression.

Priyanka's mother explained how Ganesh had just called her and given her the emergency line number. Ganesh's family in India had also not slept; they had been calling Priyanka's parents at least once an hour. Ganesh had told Priyanka's family that he was 'on top of the world'. I guess the sad dude really had no other life.

'I am so happy today. Look how God sent such a perfect match right to our door. And I used to worry about you so much,' Priyanka's mother said.

'That's great mom, but what's up?' Priyanka said. 'I'll be home in a few hours. How come you called here?'

'Just like that Can't a mother call her daughter?' Priyanka's mom said. 'Can't a mother' is one of her classic lines.

'No mom, I just wondered. Anyway, Ganesh and I spoke a few times today.'

'And?'

'And what?'

'Did he tell you his plans?'

'What plans?'

'He is coming to India next month. Originally he'd planned the trip so he could see girls. But now that he has made his choice, he wants to get married on that trip,' Priyanka's mom said, her voice turning breathless with excitement.

'What?' Priyanka said, 'next month?' and looked around at all of us with a shocked expression. Everyone returned puzzled looks, as they did not know what was going on. Of course, I also pretended to look confused.

'Mom, no!' Priyanka wailed. 'How can I get married next month? That is less than five weeks.'

'Oh you don't have to worry about that. I am there to organize everything. You wait and see, I will work day and night to make it a grand event.'

'Mom I'm not worried about organizing a party. I have to be ready to get married. I hardly know Ganesh,' Priyanka said, entwining her fingers nervously in the telephone wire.

'Huh? Of course, you are ready for it. When the families have fixed the match, bride and groom are happy, why delay? And the boy can't come again and again. He is in an important position after all.'

Yeah right, I thought. He was probably one of the thousands of Indian geeks coding away in Microsoft. But to his in-laws, he was Mr Bill Gates himself.

'Mom please. I cannot do it next month. Sorry—but no,' Priyanka said, 'and I have to keep the phone down now.'

'What do you mean no? This is too much. You have to disagree with me always or what?'

'Mom, how does this have anything to do with disagreeing with you? In fact, how does it have anything to do with you? It is my life, and sorry, I can't marry anyone I have only known for five weeks.'

Priyanka's mother stayed silent for a while. I thought she would retaliate, but then I figured out: this silence was working more effectively than words. She knows how to put an emotion slasher knife right at Priyanka's neck.

'Mom, are you there?' Priyanka asked after ten seconds.

'Yes, I am still here. Will be dead soon, but unfortunately still here.'

'Mom c'mon now...'

'Don't even make me happy by mistake,' Priyanka's mother said. What a killer line, I thought. I almost applauded.

Priyanka threw a hand up in the air in exasperation. She grabbed a stress ball lying near Vroom's computer across the table and squeezed it hard. I tugged the headset closer to my ear as Priyanka's voice turned softer.

'Mom, please. Don't do this.'

'You know I prayed for one hour today...praying you stay happy...forever,' Priyanka's mother said as she broke into tears. Whoever starts crying first always has an advantage in an argument. This works for Priyanka's mother, who at least has obedient tear glands, if not an obedient daughter.

'Mom, don't create a scene. I'm at work. What do you want from me? I have agreed to the boy. Now why is everyone pushing me?'

'Isn't Ganesh nice? What is the problem?' her mother said in a tragic tone that could put any Bollywood hero's mother to shame.

'Mom, I didn't say he isn't nice or there is a problem. I just need time.'

'You aren't distracted, are you? Are you still talking to that useless call center chap, what is his name...Shyam.'

I jumped when I heard my name.

'No mom. That is over. I have told you so many times. I have agreed to Ganesh right?'

'So, why can't you agree for next month—for everyone's happiness? Can't a mother beg her daughter for this?'

There you go: 'can't-a-mother...' Number II for the night.

Priyanka closed her eyes to compose herself. She spoke slowly, 'Can I think about it?'

'Of course. Think about it. But think for all of us. Not just yourself.'

'Okay. I will. Just...just give me some time.'

Priyanka hung up the phone and kept still. The girls asked her for details.

She looked around and threw the stress ball at her monitor.

'Can you believe this? She wants me to get married next month. Next month!' Priyanka said and stood up. 'They brought me up for twenty five years, and now they can't wait more than twenty-five days to get rid of me. What is with these people—am I such a burden?'

Priyanka repeated her conversation to Esha and Radhika. Vroom checked his computer to see if Bakshi had sent us any emails.

'It doesn't matter right? You have to marry him anyway. Why drag it out?' Radhika said to Priyanka.

'Yes, you get to drive the Lexus sooner too,' Vroom said, without looking up from his screen. Screw Vroom. I gave him a firm glare out of the corner of my eye.

'What will I wear?' Esha said. Her somber mood had lightened with the new announcement. Give her a chance to dress up and she will ignore people dying around her. 'This is too short a notice,' she continued, 'I need a new dress for every ceremony.'

'Get your *designer friends* to lend you a few dresses,' Vroom said to Esha, with a hint of sarcasm in his voice.

Esha's face dropped again. Only I saw it, but her eyes became wet. She took a tissue from her purse. She pretended to fix her lipstick and casually wiped her tears.

'I'm so not ready for this. In one month I'll be someone's wife. Gosh, little kids will call me auntie,' Priyanka said.

Everyone discussed the pros and cons of Priyanka getting married in four weeks. Most of them felt getting married so quickly wasn't such a big deal once she had chosen the guy. Of course, most people don't give a damn about me as well.

In the midst of the discussions the systems guy returned to our desk.

'What happened here?' he said from under the table. 'Looks like someone ripped these wires apart.'

'I don't know,' I said. 'See if we can get some traffic again.'

Priyanka's mother and her words—'the useless call center boy'—resounded in my mind. I remembered the time when Priyanka told me her mother's views on me. It was not long ago: it was one of our last dates at Mocha Café.

# #18:
## My Past Dates with Priyanka—IV

Mocha Café, Greater Kailash I
Five months before this night

We promised to meet on one condition—we would not fight. No blame games, no sarcastic comments and no judgmental remarks. She was late again. I fiddled with the menu as I looked around me. Mocha's décor had a Middle Eastern twist, with hookahs, velvet cushions and colored glass lamps everywhere. Many of the tables were occupied by couples, sitting with intertwined fingers, obviously deeply in love. The girls laughed at whatever the guys said. The guys ordered the most expensive items on the menu. Every now and then their eyes met and giggles broke out. It was perfect—like all they needed to be happy was each other. The silly delusions in the initial stage of a relationship: aren't they amazing?

My life was nowhere near perfect, of course. For starters, my girlfriend, if I could still call her that, was late. Plus, I could sense she was itching to dump me. Priyanka and I had ended eight of our last ten calls with someone hanging up the phone on the other.

I had not slept the entire day, which is not a big deal for most people, but considering I work all night, it had not left me feeling too good. My job was going nowhere, with Bakshi bent on sucking every last drop of my blood. Maybe he was right—I just did not have the strategic vision or managerial leadership or whatever crap things you are supposed to have to do well in life. Maybe Priyanka's mom was right too—her daughter was stuck with a loser.

These thoughts enveloped me as she came in. She had just had a haircut. Her waist-length hair was now just a few inches below her shoulders. I liked her with long hair, but she never listened to me. I told you, I didn't have the leadership skills to influence *anyone*. Anyway, her hair still looked nice. She wore a white linen top and a flowing lavender skirt with lots of crinkly edges. She had on a thin silver necklace, with the world's tiniest diamond pendant hanging from it. I stared at my watch as a sign of protest.

'Sorry, Shyam,' she said as she put a giant brown bag on the table, 'that ass hairdresser took so long. I told him I had to leave early.'

'No big deal. A haircut has to be more important than me,' I said, without any emotion in my voice.

'I thought we said no sarcasm,' she said, 'and I did say sorry.'

'That's right. One sorry for half an hour seems fair. In fact, go get a two-hour facial done as well. You can come back and say sorry four times.'

'Shyam, please. I know I'm late. We promised not to fight. Saturday is the only day I get time for a haircut.'

'I told you to keep your hair long,' I said.

'I did for a long time. But it's so hard to maintain it, Shyam. I'm sorry, but you need to understand sometimes. I had the most boring hair in the world and I could do nothing with it. And it took one hour to oil the damn thing. And it feels so hot in the Delhi heat.'

'Whatever,' I said in a bored voice, looking at the menu. 'What do you want?'

'I want my Shyam to be in a good mood,' she said and held my hand. We didn't intertwine fingers though.

'My' Shyam. I guess I still count, I thought. Girls sure know how to sweet talk.

'Hmm...' I said and let out a big sigh. If she was trying to make peace, I guess I had to do my bit. 'We can have their special Maggi noodles.'

'Maggi? You've come all this way to eat Maggi?' she said, and took the menu from me. 'And check this out: ninety bucks for Maggi?' She said the last phrase so loudly that the tables and a few waiters next to us heard us.

'Priyanka, we earn now. We can afford it,' I said.

'Order chocolate brownies and ice cream,' she said. 'At least something you don't get at home.'

'I thought you said you'll have whatever I want,' I said.

'Yes, but Maggi?' she said and made a quirky face. Her nostrils contracted for a second. I had seen that face before, and I could not help but smile. I saved myself time by ordering the brownie.

The waiter brought the chocolate brownie and placed it in front of Priyanka. Half a liter of chocolate sauce dripping over a blob of vanilla ice cream placed precariously over a huge slice of rich chocolate cake. It was a heart attack served on a plate. Priyanka had two spoons and slid the dish towards me.

'Look at me, eating away like a cow,' she said.

'Did you have a heart to heart with your mom?' I said.

Priyanka wiped her chocolate-lined lips with tissue. I felt like kissing her right then. However, I hesitated. When you hesitate in love, you know something is wrong.

'Me and my mom,' she said, 'are incapable of having a rational, sane conversation. I tried to talk to her—about you and my plans to study further. It sounds like a simple conversation, right?'

'What happened?'

'We were crying in seven minutes. Can you believe it?'

'With your mother, I can. What exactly did she say?'

'You don't want to know.'

'But I have to know,' I insisted.

'She said she has never liked you. Because you are not settled, and because since the day I started dating you I have changed and become an unaffectionate and cold person.'

'Unaffectionate? What the...?' I shouted, my face turning red. 'How the hell have I changed you?'

The second comment cut me into thin slices. Sure, I hated the 'not settled' tag too, but there was some truth to that. How could she accuse me of turning Priyanka into a cold person, though?

She did not say anything. Her face softened and I heard tiny sobs. It was so unfair, I was the one being insulted: I should be the one getting to cry. However, I guess only girls look nice crying on dates.

'Listen Priyanka, your mom is a psycho...' I said.

'No she is not. It is not because of you, but I *have* changed. Maybe it is because of my age—and she confuses it with my being with you. We used to be so close, and now she doesn't like anything I do,' she said and broke down into full-on crying. Everyone in the café must have thought I had cheated on my girlfriend and was dumping her or something. I got some 'you-horrible-men' looks from girls at other tables.

'Calm down, Priyanka. What does she want? And tell me honestly, what do you want?' I said.

Priyanka shook her head and remained silent.

It drives me nuts. The effort it sometimes takes to make women speak up is harder than interrogating terrorists.

'Please, talk to me,' I said, looking at the brownie. The ice cream had melted to a gooey mess.

She finally spoke. 'She wants me to show that I love her. She wants me to make her happy and marry someone she chooses for me.'

'And what do you want?' I said.

'I don't know,' she told the tablecloth.

*What the hell?* I thought. All I get for four years of togetherness is an '*I don't know*'?

'You want to dump me, don't you? I am just not good enough for your family.'

'It isn't like that Shyam. She married my dad who was just a government employee only because he seemed like a decent human being. But her sisters waited to marry better-qualified boys and they are richer today. Her concern for me comes from there. She is my mother. It is not as if she does not know what is good for me. I want someone doing well in his career as well.'

'So your mother is not the only cause for the strain in our relationship. It is you as well.'

'A relationship never flounders for one reason alone. There are many issues. You don't take feedback. You are sarcastic. You don't understand my ambitions. Don't I always tell you to focus on your career?'

'Just get lost okay,' I said.

My loud voice attracted the attention of the neighboring tables. All the girls at Mocha were probably convinced I was the worst possible male chauvinist pig ever.

Her tears were back. However, she noticed people watching us and composed herself. A few wipes with a tissue and she was normal again.

'Shyam, it is this attitude of yours. At home, my mother doesn't understand. Over here, you don't. Why have you become like this? You have changed Shyam, you are not the same happy person I first met,' she said, her voice restrained but calm.

'Nothing has happened to *me*. It is you who finds new faults in me everyday. I have a bad boss and I am trying to manage as happily as possible. What has happened to you? You used to eat at truck drivers' dhabas. Now all of a sudden you need an NRI cardiac surgeon to make ends meet?'

We stared at each other for two seconds.

'Okay, it's my fault. That is what you want to prove, right? I am a confused, selfish, mean person right?' she said.

I looked at her. I couldn't believe I had loved her and those flared nostrils for four years. And now it was difficult to say four sentences without disagreeing.

I sighed. 'I thought there was to be no arguing, blaming and sarcasm. But we have done it all.'

'I care a lot for you,' she said and held my hand.

'Me too,' I said, 'but I think we need to take care of other things in our life as well.'

We asked for the bill and made cursory conversation about the weather, traffic and the decor of the café. We were talking a lot, but we weren't communicating at all.

'Call me in the evening if you're free,' I said as I paid the bill and got up to leave.

It had come to this: we had to tell each other to call. Previously, not a waking hour passed without one of us SMS-ing or calling the other.

'Okay, or I will SMS you,' she said. An SMS seemed simpler than dealing with another conversation.

We did a basic hug, without really touching. A kiss was out of the question.

'Sure,' I said, 'it's always nice to get your messages.'

Sarcasm. Man, will I never learn?

## #19

MOCHA CAFÉ AND ITS COLORED ARABIAN LIGHTS FADED AWAY from my mind as it returned to WASG's tube light-lit interiors. I checked the time: it was close to 2:00 a.m. I got up to take a short walk. I did not know what was more disgusting—thinking about Priyanka's mother or hearing the girls obsess about Priyanka's marri ge. I went to the corner of the room where Military Uncle sat. We nodded to each other. I looked at his screen and saw pictures of animals—chimps, rhinos, lions and deer.

'Are those your customers?' I said and laughed at my own non-funny joke.

Military Uncle smiled back. He was in one of his rare good moods.

'These are pictures I took at the zoo. I scanned them to send to my grandson.'

'Cool. He likes animals?' I said and bent over to take a closer look at the chimp. It bore an uncanny resemblance to Bakshi.

'Yes, I'm sending it by email to my son. But I'm having trouble as our emails do not allow more than four megabyte attachments.'

I decided to help Uncle, if only to avoid going back to the bay until the systems guy had fixed the phones.

'Hmm...these are large files,' I said, as I took over his mouse. 'I could try to zip them—though that won't compress images much. The other way is to make the pictures low resolution. Otherwise, you can leave a few animals out.'

Military Uncle wanted to keep them high resolution. We agreed to leave out the deer and the hippos as those were not his grandson's favorite animals.

'Thanks so much, Shyam,' Military Uncle said, as I successfully pressed 'send' on his email. I looked at his face: there was genuine gratitude. It was hard to believe he had been booted out because he was too bossy with his daughter-in-law—a piece of gossip Radhika had once passed on to me.

'You're welcome,' I said. I noticed Vroom signal to me to come back. Hoping that the topic of Priyanka's wedding was over, I returned to the desk.


'Bakshi has sent us a copy of the proposal,' Vroom said.

I sat at my desk and opened my inbox. There was a message from Bakshi.

The calls had not resumed; the systems guy had gone back to his department again to get new wires.

'Let's see which white bozos he sucked up to. Who has he sent it to?' Vroom's voice was excited.

I opened the mail to see who had been the original recipients. It was the who's who of Western Computers and Appliances in Boston: the sales manager, the IT manager, the operations head and several others. Bakshi had sent it to the entire directory of people in our client base. I have to say, he is better at being a mass-suck-up than a gangbang porn star.

'He has copied everyone. Senior management in Boston in the "to" field, and then India senior management in the "cc" field,' I said.

'And yet somehow he forgot to copy us. Bakshi the great,' Vroom said.

I read out the contents of his short mail:

'Dear All,

Attached please find the much-awaited user manual of the customer service website that changed the parameters of customer service at Western Appliances. I just wrapped this up today. I would love to discuss this more when I'm in Boston...'

I let out a silent whistle.

'Boston? How is that ass going to Boston,' Vroom said. The girls heard us.

'What are you talking about?' Priyanka said.

'Bakshi's going to Boston,' Vroom said. 'Any of you ladies want to tag along?'

'What?' Esha said. 'What is he going to Boston for?'

'To talk about our website. Must have swung a trip for himself,' I said.

'What the hell is going on here anyway? On one hand we are downsizing to save costs, on the other hand there is cash to send idiots on trips to the US?' Vroom said and threw his stress ball on the table. It hit the pen stand and the contents fell out.

'Careful,' Esha said, sounding irritated, as a few pens rolled towards her. She had her mobile phone in her hand, probably still trying to call someone.

'Madness. That is what this Connexions is. Boston!' Priyanka said and shook her head. She was surfing the Internet. I wondered which sites she was looking at—wedding dresses, life in the US, or the Lexus official website.

I was about to close Bakshi's message when Vroom stopped me.

'Open the document,' Vroom said, 'just open the file he sent.

'It's the same file we sent him. The user manual,' I said.

'Did you open it?'

'No, what is the need...'

'Just open it,' he said so loudly that Esha looked at us. I wondered whom she was calling this late, but Vroom's voice was battering into me.

I opened the file, which was our user manual.

'Here, it is the same,' I said, and scrolled down. As I reached the bottom of the first page, my jaw grew lax, partly in horror and partly in reflex preparation to voice some major curse words.

*Western Computers Troubleshooting Website*
*Project Details and User Manual*

*Developed by Connexions, Delhi*

*Subhash Bakshi*
*Manager, Connexions*

'Like fuck it is the same,' Vroom said and threw the pens he had collected back on the table. One landed on Esha's lap, who by this time had tried to connect to a number at least twenty times. She threw an angry look at Vroom and hurled the pen back at him. He ignored her as his eyes were on my screen.

'It says it is by fucking Subhash Bakshi,' Vroom said, tapping his finger hard on my monitor. 'Check this out. Mr Moron, who can't tell a computer from a piano, has done this website and this manual. Like crap he has.'

Vroom banged his fists on the table. In a mini-fit, he violently swept the table with his hands. All the pens fell on the floor.

'What is wrong with you?' Esha said and pulled her chair away to avoid the shower of pens. Desperately shaking the phone to get a connection, she got up and went to the conference room.

'He passed off our work as his, Shyam. Do you realize that?' he said and shook my shoulder hard.

I was numb as I stared at the first page of our, or rather Bakshi's, manual. This time Bakshi had bypassed himself in stealing credit. My head felt dizzy and I fought to breathe.

'This is so crap. Six months of work on this manual alone,' I said and closed the file. 'I never thought he would stoop this low.'

'And?' Vroom said.

'And what? I don't really know what to do. I'm in shock. Plus, right now there is this fear he may downsize us...' I said.

'Downsize us?' Vroom said and stood up. 'We worked on it for six months man. And all you can say is we can't do anything as he may downsize us? This fucking loser Baskhi is turning you into a loser. Mr Shyam, you are turning into a mousepad, people are rolling over you everyday. Priyanka tell him to say something. Go to Bakshi's office and hold his damn collar.'

Priyanka looked up at us, and for the second time that night, our eyes met bang on. She had that look; that same gaze that had made me feel small before. Like what was the point of even shouting at me.

She shook her head and gave a wry smile. I knew that wry smile by heart, too. Like she had known this was coming all along. I had the urge to go shake her by the collar. It is freaking easy to give those looks when you have a Lexus waiting for you. I wanted to say. But I didn't say anything. Bakshi's move had hurt me—it wasn't just the six months of effort, but also that the prospects for my promotion were gone. And that meant—poof!—Priyanka was going too. But right now the people around me just wanted me to express anger. People see you as weak if you express hurt. They always want to see you strong, meaning in a raging temper. Maybe I do not have it in me. That is why I am not a team leader. That is why no girls distribute sweets in the office for me.

'Are you there, Mr Shyam?' Vroom said. 'Let's email all the people this was sent to and tell them what is going on.'

'Just cool down Vroom. There is no need to act like a hero,' I snapped.

'Oh really? So, what should we act like? Losers? Tell us Shyam, you should be the expert on that,' Vroom said.

A surge of anger choked me. 'Just shut up and sit down,' I said. 'What do you want to do? Send another mail to the whites? And tell them there's in-fighting going on here? And whom are they going to believe: somebody who is going to Boston to meet them or some frustrated agent who claims he did all the work? Get real Mr Varun. You'll get fired and nothing else. Bakshi is management—he manages, yes, he does. But only his own career. Not us.' I was so caught up in the argument I did not even notice Radhika. She was standing next to me with a bottle of water in her hand.

'Thanks,' I said and took a few noisy sips.

'Feeling better?' Radhika said.

I raised my hand to stop her from saying more. 'I don't want to talk about this anymore. It is between us and Bakshi. And I don't want some random people, whose life is one big party, to give their opinion on it. Yes, my boss sucks. Most bosses suck. It isn't such a big deal,' I said and sat down. I glared at Vroom. He sat down as well.

Vroom opened a notepad and drew a 2x2 matrix.

'What the fuck is that?' I said.

'I think I've finally figured Bakshi out. Let me explain with the help of a diagram,' Vroom said.

'Don't mess with me. I don't want any diagrams,' I said.

'Just hear me,' Vroom said as he labeled the matrix.

On the horizontal axis he wrote 'good' and 'evil' next to each box. On the vertical axis, he wrote 'smart' and 'stupid.'

'Okay, here is my theory about people like Bakshi,' Vroom said and pointed with his pen to the matrix. 'There are four kinds of bosses in this world based on two dimensions: a) how smart or stupid they are, and b) whether they are good or evil. Only with extreme good luck do you get a boss who is smart *and* a good human being. However, Bakshi is the most dangerous but common category. He is stupid, as we all know. But more than that—he is evil,' Vroom said, tapping his pen in the relevant quadrant of the matrix.

'Stupid-evil,' I echoed.

'Yes, we underestimated him. He is a scary one. He is like a blind snake: you feel sorry for it, but it still has a poisonous bite. You can see it—he is stupid, hence the call center is so mismanaged. But he is also evil, so he will make sure all of us go down instead of him.'

I shook my head.

'Forget it. Destiny has put an asshole in my path. What can I say,' I said and smirked.

Radhika took the bottle from my desk. 'Sorry to interrupt your discussion guys, but I hope you weren't talking about me when you said people whose life is a party. My life is not a party, my friend. It really isn't—'

'—It wasn't you, Radhika. Shyam most clearly meant me,' Priyanka interrupted Radhika.

'Oh forget it,' I said and stood up. I moved from the desk, just to get away from these nagging people. As I left, I could hear Vroom's words: 'If I could just once have the opportunity to fuck this Bakshi's happiness, I'd consider myself the luckiest person on earth.'

## 20

I WALKED AWAY FROM THE WASG DESK. MY MIND WAS STILL messed up. I felt like cutting Bakshi into little bits and feeding those bits to every street dog in Delhi. I approached the conference room. The door was shut. I knocked and waited for a few seconds. Everything seemed quiet inside.

'Esha?' I said and turned the knob to open the door.

Esha was sitting on one of the conference room chairs. Her right leg was bent and resting on another chair. She was examining the wound on her shin.

She held a blood-tipped box cutter in her hand. I noticed a used band-aid on the table. There was fresh blood coming out of the wound on her shin.

'Are you okay?' I said, moving close to her.

Esha turned to look at me with a blank expression.

'Oh hi Shyam,' she said in a calm tone.

'What are you doing here? Everyone's looking for you.'

'Why? Why would anyone look for me?'

'No particular reason. What are you doing here anywa
And your wound is bleeding, do you want some lotion or
bandage?' I said and looked away. The sight of blood nausea
me. I don't know how doctors show up to work everyday.

'No Shyam, I like it like this. With lotion, it may stop
hurting,' Esha said.

'What?' I said. 'Isn't that the idea? You want the pain to
end, right?'

'No,' Esha smiled sadly. She pointed to the wound with the
box cutter. 'This pain takes my mind away from the real pain.
Do you know what real pain is, Shyam?'

I really had no idea what this girl was saying. But I knew
if she didn't cover the wound soon, I'd throw up my recently
consumed chocolate cake.

'Listen, I'll get the first-aid kit from the supplies room.'

'You didn't answer my question. What is real pain, Shyam?'

'I don't know…what is it?' I said, shifting anxiously as I saw
fresh drops of blood trickle down her smooth leg.

'Real pain is mental pain,' Esha said.

'Right,' I said, trying to sound intelligent. I sat down on a
chair next to her.

'Ever felt mental pain, Shyam?'

'I don't know if I have. I'm a shallow guy, you see. I don't
feel a lot of things,' I said.

'Everyone feels pain, because everyone has a dark side to
their life.'

'Dark side?'

'Yes, dark side—something you don't like about yourself, something that makes you angry or something that you fear: all this makes up our dark side. Do you have a dark side, Shyam?'

'Oh let's not go there. I have so many—like half a dozen dark sides. I am like dark-sided hexagon,' I said.

'Ever felt guilt, Shyam? Real hard, painful guilt?' she said as her voice became weak.

'What happened, Esha?' I said, as I finally found a position that allowed me to look at her face but avoid a view of her wound.

'Can you promise not to judge me if I tell you something?'

'Of course,' I said. 'I'm a terrible judge of people anyway.'

'I slept with someone,' she said and let out a sigh, 'to win a modeling contract.'

'What?' I said, as it took me a second to figure out what 'slept' meant. It didn't mean 'zzzs'.

'Yes, my agent said this man was connected. I just had to sleep with him once to get a break in a major fashion show. Nobody forced me. I chose to do it. But ever since, I feel this awful guilt. Every single moment. I thought it would pass, bu it hasn't. And that pain is so bad, this wound in my leg feels like a tickle,' she said and took the box cutter to her shin. She started scraping skin around the wound.

'Stop it Esha, what are you doing?' I said and snatched the box cutter from her. 'Are you insane? You'll get tetanus or gangrene or whatever other horrible things they show on TV in those vaccination ads.'

'This is tame. I'll tell you what is dangerous. Your own fucked up brain, the delusional voice in you that says you have it in you to become a model. You know what this man said afterwards?'

'Which man?' I said as I shoved the box cutter to the other side of the table.

'The guy I slept with—a forty-year-old designer. He told my agent later I was too short to be a ramp model,' Esha said, her voice rising as anger mingled with sadness. 'Like the bastard didn't know that when he slept with me.' She began crying. I don't know what is worse—a shouting girl or a crying one. I'm awful at handling either. I placed my hands on Esha's shoulders, ready for a hug in case she needed it.

'And that son of a bitch sends some cash as compensation afterwards,' she said, now sobbing. 'And my agent tells me, this is part of life. Sure it is part of life—part of Esha the failed model's fucked-up life. Give me my box cutter back, Shyam,' she said, spreading a palm.

'No, I won't. Listen, now I am not really sure what to do in this situation, but just take it easy,' I said. It was true; nobody would ever demand to have sex with me. Therefore, feeling-guilty-after-demanded-sex was completely unfamiliar territory.

'I hate myself, Shyam. I just hate myself. And I hate my face, and the stupid mirror that shows me this face. I hate myself for believing people who told me I could be a model. Can I get my face altered?'

I did not know of any plastic surgeons who specialized in turning pretty girls ugly, so I kept quiet. She stopped crying after ninety seconds, around the time any girl would stop crying if you ignored her. She took a tissue from her bag and wiped her eyes.

'Shall we go? They must be waiting,' I said. She held my hand to stand up.

'Thanks for listening to me,' Esha said. Only women think there is a reason to thank people if they listen to them.

# #21

To MY DISGUST, PRIYANKA'S WEDDING WAS STILL THE TOPIC OF discussion when Esha and I returned to the bay.

Esha sat down quietly.

'Now where were you?' Priyanka asked Esha.

'Here only. Wanted to make a private call,' Esha said.

'I'm taking mother-in-law tips from Radhika,' Priyanka said. 'I'm so not looking forward to that part. She seems nice now, but who knows how she will turn out.'

'C'mon, you are getting so much more in return. Ganesh is such a nice guy,' Radhika said.

'Anyway I'd take three mothers-in-law for a Lexus. Bring it on man,' Vroom said.

Radhika and Priyanka started laughing.

'I'll miss you Vroom,' Priyanka said, still laughing, 'I really will.'

'Who else will you miss?' Vroom said and all of us fell silent.

Priyanka shifted on her seat: Vroom had caught her on the spot. She did not want to say my name, I knew it.

'Oh I'll miss all of you,' she said, diplomacy queen that she can be when she wants to. She thinks she can outsmart the world with her boring replies.

'Whatever,' Vroom said.

'Anyway, don't wish for three mothers-in-law, Vroom. It can be like asking for three Bakshis. Well, at least it can be for women,' Radhika said.

'So your mother-in-law is evil?' Vroom said.

'I never said she is bad. But she did say those things to Anuj. What will he think?'

'Nothing. He won't think anything. He knows how lucky he is to have you,' Priyanka said firmly.

'It is hard sometimes. She isn't my mom, after all.'

'Oh, don't go there. I can get along with anyone else's mom better than my own. My mom's neurosis has made me mother-in-law proof,' Priyanka said, and everyone on the desk laughed. I did not, as there is nothing funny about Priyanka's mom to me. Emotional manipulators like her should be put in jail and made to watch sappy TV serials all day.

'Anuj should be okay, right? Tell me guys: he won't hate me?' Radhika said

'No,' Priyanka got up and went to Radhika. 'He loves you and he will be fine.'

'You want to check if he is okay?' Vroom said. 'I have an idea.'

'What?' Radhika said.

I looked at Vroom. What the hell did he have to say about Anuj and Radhika?

'Let's play radio jockey,' Vroom said. 'It's really fun.'

'What is radio jockey?' Radhika was baffled.

'Well, I call Anuj and pretend I am calling from a radio show. Then I tell him he has won a prize, a large bouquet of roses and a box of Swiss chocolates that he can send to anyone he loves, anywhere in India, with a loving message. So then, we all get to hear what romantic lines he says to you.'

'C'mon, it will never work,' Priyanka said. 'You can't sound like an RJ.'

'Trust me. I am a call center agent. I can make a convincing RJ,' Vroom said.

I was curious to see how Vroom would do his RJ act.

'Okay,' Vroom said as he got ready, 'It's show time, folks. Take line five everyone. And no noise: breathe away from the mouthpiece, okay?'

Radhika gave him the number as we took line five. Vroom dialed Anuj's mobile phone.

We glued the earpiece to our ears. The telephone rang five times.

'He's sleeping,' Priyanka whispered.

'Shhh,' Vroom went, as we heard someone pick up.

'Hello?' Anuj said in a sleepy voice.

'Hello there, my friend, is this 98101-46301?' Vroom said in an insanely cheerful, radio jockey voice.

'Yes, who is it?' Anuj said.

'It is your lucky call for tonight. This is RJ Max calling from Radio City 98.5 FM, and you my friend have just won a prize.'

'Radio City? Are you trying to sell me something?' Anuj said. I guess being a salesperson himself, he was skeptical.

'No my friend, I am not selling anything—no credit cards, no insurance policies and no phone plans. I am just going to offer you a small prize from our sponsor Interflora and you can request a song if you want to. Man, people doubt me so much these days,' Vroom said.

'Sorry, I was just not sure,' Anuj said.

'Max is the name. What's yours?' Vroom said.

'Anuj.'

'Nice talking to you Anuj. Where are you right now?'

'Kolkata.'

'Oh, the land of sweets, excellent. Anyway, Anuj, you get to send a dozen red roses with your message to anyone in India. This service is brought to you by Interflora, one of the world's largest flower delivery companies.'

Vroom was like a pro, I must admit.

'And I don't have to pay anything? Thanks Interflora,' Anuj said with suitable gratitude.

All of us had our mouths shut tight and the headset mouthpiece covered with our hands.

'No my friend, o payment at all. So are you ready with your special person's name and address?'

'Yes sure. I'd like to send it to my girlfriend Payal.'

I think the earth shook beneath us. I looked at Vroom's face: his jaw had dropped wide open. He waved a hand in confusion.

'Payal?' Vroom said, his voice dropping to more normal levels, less exuberant than that of a hyperactive RJ.

'Yes, she is my girlfriend. She lives in Delhi. She is a modern type of girl, so please make the bouquet trendy...' Anuj said.

Radhika could not stay silent any longer

'Payal? What did you just say, Anuj? Your girlfriend Payal?' Radhika said.

'Who is that?...Radhika...?'

'Yes, Radhika. Your fucking wife Radhika.'

'What is going on here? Who is this Max guy, hey Max?' Anuj said.

I think the Max guy just died. Vroom put his hand on his head, wondering what to say next.

'You talk to me, you asshole,' Radhika said, probably cursing for the first time since she got married. 'What message were you going to send this Payal?'

'Radhika, honey, listen this is a prank. Max? Max?'

'There is no Max. It is Vroom here,' Vroom said in a blank voice.

'You bastar—' Anuj began before Radhika stood up and cut the line. She sat back down on her chair, stunned. A few seconds later, she broke into tears.

Vroom looked at Radhika. 'Damn, Radhika I am so sorry,' he said.

Radhika did not answer. She just cried and cried. In between, she lifted the half-knit scarf to wipe her tears. Something told me Radhika would never finish the scarf.

Esha held Radhika's hand tight. Maybe the tear bug passed through hands because Esha started crying as well. Priyanka went and brought back water. Radhika poured out a glassful of tears, and drank the glass of water.

'Take it easy. It's probably a misunderstanding,' Priyanka said. She looked at Esha, puzzled about why Esha was so upset over Payal. I guess Esha's 'real pain' was back.

Radhika rifled through her bag looking for her headache pills. She only found an empty blister pack. She mouthed some curses and threw it aside.

'Radhika?' Priyanka said.

'Just leave me alone for a few minutes,' Radhika said.

'Girls, I really need to talk,' Esha said, as she wiped her tears.

'What's up?' Priyanka said as she looked at Esha. They xchanged glances: Esha used the female telepathic network to ask Priyanka to come to the toilet. Priyanka tapped Radhika's shoulder and the girls stood up.

'Now where are you girls going?' Vroom said. 'I caused this situation. Can't you talk here?'

'We have our private stuff to discuss,' Priyanka said firmly to Vroom and left the desk.

'What's up? What's the deal with Esha?' Vroom said to me after the girls were out of sight.

'Nothing,' I said.

'C'mon tell me, she must have told you in the conference room.'

'I can't tell you,' I said and looked at my screen. I tried to change the topic. 'Do you think Bakshi expects us to prepare for his team meeting?'

'I think Esha is sad because she regrets saying no to me,' Vroom said.

I smirked.

'If not that, then what is it?' Vroom said, looking at me with a puzzled expression. I shrugged my shoulders.

'Fine. I'll use our earlier technique. I am going to the toilet to find out,' Vroom said.

'No Vroom, no,' I said. I tried to grab his shirt, but he pulled away and went to the men's room.

I did not chase after him. I did not care if he found out. I figured he ought to know what his love interest was up to anyway. I called systems and told them the calls had not resumed yet. They promised to come to my desk with the new cable within 'five minutes maximum'. I guess systems guys are busy. Computers are supposed to help men—but enough computers need help from men as well.

— With no one at the desk and systems down, I decided to take a walk around the room. I passed by Military Uncle's station and noticed him slouched on his desk. This was atypical of him. I went closer. His head was resting on his desk.

'Everything okay?' I said. There were already enough things messed up tonight. Military Uncle raised his head. I looked at his face: his wrinkles seemed more pronounced, making him look older.

'My son replied to the mail I sent,' he said. 'I think the file was too big.'

'Really? What did he say?' I said.

Military Uncle shook his head and put his head back on the desk. The message on his screen caught my eye. It was an email from his son.

Dad... You have cluttered my life enough, now stop cluttering my mailbox. I do not know what came over me that I allowed communication between you and my son. I don't want your shadow on him. Please stay away and do not send him any more emails. For literally or otherwise, we don't want your attachments.

'It's nothing,' Uncle said, as he closed all the windows on his screen. 'I should get back to work. What happened? Your systems are down again?'

'A lot is down tonight, not just the systems,' I said and returned to my seat.

# #22

'DID YOU KNOW?' VROOM WHISPERED TO ME AS HE RETURNED from the men's toilet.

'What?' I said.

'Esha's big bad story.'

'I'd rather not discuss it. It's her private matter.'

'No wonder she won't go out with me. She needs to romp her way to the ramp doesn't she? Bitch.'

'Mind your language,' I said, 'and where are the girls?'

'Coming back soon. Your chick was consoling Radhika when I left.'

'Priyanka is not my chick Vroom. Will you just shut up?' I said.

'Okay, I will shut up. That is what a good call center agent does right? Crap happens around him and he just smiles and says how can I help you? Like, someone just slept with the one girl I care for. But it is okay right? Pass me the next dumb customer.'

'The girls are coming,' I said as I saw them return. 'Pretend you know nothing about Esha.'

The desk was silent as the girls took their seats. Vroom was about to say something, but I signaled him to be quiet. The systems guy finally showed up with new kick-proof wires and re-installed our systems. I was relieved as calls began to trickle in. Sorting Americans' oven and fridge problems was easier than solving our life's problems.

I looked at Priyanka once; she was busy with a caller. 'My chick,' I smirked to myself at Vroom's comment. She was no longer my chick. She was going to marry a rich, successful guy—someone who had no competition from a loser like me. Certainly not after Bakshi backstabbed me with his website, I thought. But had I given up? *Did I still feel for her?* I shook my head at the irrelevant questions. How did it matter if I still felt for her? I did not deserve her, and I was not going to get her. That was reality, and as is often the case with me, reality sucks.

Esha was still quite subdued after returning from the toilet. Priyanka was trying to cheer her up.

'Get a flowing lehnga for the engagement. But what will you wear for the wedding? A sari?' Priyanka asked Esha between calls.

'My navel ring will show,' Esha said.

I am constantly amazed at the ability of women to calm down. All they need to do is talk, hug and cry it out for ten minutes—and then they can face any of life's crap. Esha's 'real pain' was obviously much better, or she was at least distracted from it, given she could discuss her dress plans for Priyanka's big day.

'Don't do anything elaborate,' Priyanka said, 'I'm going to tell my mother I want a simple sari. Of course, she will freak out. Hey Radhika, are you okay?' Priyanka said, as she noticed Radhika massaging her forehead.

'I'll be fine. I am just out of migraine pills,' Radhika said as she picked up a call. 'Western Appliances, Regina speaking. How may I help you?'

The landline telephone's ring caught everyone's attention.

'This is my call. Guys I know system is live, but can I take this call?' Priyanka said.

'Sure. Call flow is so light anyway,' Vroom said as the landline continued to ring.

Priyanka's hand reached for the telephone. I casually switched the option on my screen to listen in to the conversation.

'By the way, dark blue mica is also a good colour,' Vroom said as Priyanka lifted the receiver.

'What?' Priyanka said.

'I saw the Lexus website, dark blue mica is their best colour,' Vroom said.

I threw Vroom a disgusted glance.

'At least that is what I think,' Vroom's voice dropped as he intercepted my look.

'Hello, my center of attention,' Ganesh's beaming voice came over Priyanka and my phones.

'Hi Ganesh,' Priyanka said sedately.

'What's up, Priya? You sound serious,' Ganesh said.

Priyanka hates it when people shorten her name to Priya. This moron did not know that.

'Nothing. Just having a rough day...sorry night. And please call me Priyanka,' she said.

'Well, I am having a rocking day here. Everyone in office is so excited for me. They keep asking me "so when is the date?", "where is the honeymoon?" '

'Yeah Ganesh, about the date,' Priyanka said, 'my mom just called.'

'She did. Oh no. I thought I'd give you the good news myself.'

'What good news?'

'That I am coming to India next month. We should get married then only. What say, honeymoon straight from there? People said the Bahamas is amazing. But I've always wanted to go to Paris. Because what could be more romantic than Paris.'

'Ganesh,' Priyanka said, her voice frantic.

'What?'

'Can I say something?'

'Sure. But first tell me, Paris or Bahamas?'

'Ganesh.'

'Please tell me where you'd rather go.'

'Paris. Now can I say something?' Priyanka said.

Esha and Radhika raised their eyebrows when they heard the word Paris. It was not difficult to guess that honeymoon planning was in progress.

'Sure. What do you want to say?' Ganesh said.

'Don't you think it is a little rushed?'

'What?'

'Our marriage. We have only talked to each other for a week. I know, we spoke quite a bit, but still.'

'You've said yes to me right?' Ganesh said.

'Yes, but…'

'Then why wait? I don't get much leave here. And considering I now spend my every living moment thinking about you, I rather get you here at the earliest.'

'But, this is marriage Ganesh. Not just a vacation. We h to give each other time to get ready for this,' Priyanka said a twirled a strand of hair with her finger. I used to love playing with her hair when we were together.

'But,' Ganesh said, 'you spoke to your mother, right? You heard how happy she is about us getting married next month. My family is excited as well. Marriage is a family occasion too, right?'

'I know. Listen, maybe I am just having a rough night. Let me sleep over it.'

'Sure. Take your time. But did you think of a color?'

'For what? The car?'

'Yeah, I am going to pay the deposit tomorrow. So it is there when you arrive—assuming you agree to next month, of course.'

'I can't say. Wait. I heard dark blue mica is nice.'

'Really? I kind of like black,' Ganesh said.

'Well then take black. Don't let me...' Priyanka said.

'No, dark blue mica it is. I like that colour. I'll tell the dealer it is my wife's choice.'

The words *my wife* sizzled my insides the way they fry French fries at McDonald's. I closed my eyes for a few seconds. I could not bear to hear another man talk like this to Priyanka.

'Hey Ganesh, it is 2:25 a.m. here. I have to get ready for a 2:30 meeting with the boss. Can we talk later?' Priyanka said.

'Sure. I might leave work early today. Maybe see some new tiles for the pool. But I'll call you when I get home okay?'

'Pool?' Priyanka said, as she took the bait.

'Yes, we have a small swimming pool in our house.'

'Our house? You mean you have a private pool?'

'Of course. You know how to swim?'

'I have never stepped inside a pool in my life,' Priyanka said.

'Well, I can teach you. I am sure there are many interesting possibilities in the pool.'

The French fries were burnt charcoal-black from being over fried.

'Bye Ganesh,' Priyanka smiled and shook her head. 'You guys are all the same.'

She hung up the phone.

'What's up,' Esha said as she filed her nails.

'Nothing, same stuff. First tell me, you okay?' Priyanka said.

'I am fine. Please keep me distracted. I heard Paris.'

'Yes, honeymoon destination. And of course, more pressure to get married next month. I don't want to, but I just might have to give in.'

'Well, if it means seeing Paris sooner rather than later...' Esha said and looked over at us. 'Right guys?'

'Sure,' Vroom said. 'What do you think Shyam?'

Stupid ass, I hate Vroom.

'Me?' I said as everyone continued to look at me. Esha kept staring at me for five seconds non-stop. I did not want to come across as sulking (or childish, my new tag for the night), so I responded.

'Sure, might as well get it done. Then go to Paris or Bahamas or whatever.'

Damn. I kicked myself as the words left my mouth. Priyanka heard me and looked at me. Her nose twitched as she thought hard.

'What did you just say Shyam?' Priyanka said slowly, looking straight at me, her nostrils flaring big-time.

'Nothing,' I said, avoiding eye contact. 'I just said get married and go to Paris sooner.'

'No, you also said Bahamas. How did you know Ganesh mentioned Bahamas?' Priyanka said.

— I kept quiet.

'Answer me, Shyam. Ganesh also suggested Bahamas, but I didn't tell you guys. How did you know he'd said that?'

'I don't know anything. I just randomly said it,' I said, trying to be convincing, but my shaking voice was giving me away.

'Were you...listening to my conversation? Shyam, have you played around with the phone?' Priyanka said and got up. She lifted the landline phone and pulled it away from the table. The wire followed her. She looked down under the table and tugged at the wires again. A little wire tensed up all the way back to my seat. *Damn, busted*, I thought.

'Shyam,' Priyanka screamed at the top of her voice and banged the landline instrument on the table.

'Yes,' I said, as calmly as possible.

'What is going on here? I cannot believe you could sink so low. This is the height of indecency,' she said.

At least I had achieved the heights in something, I thought.

Radhika and Esha looked at me. I threw up my hands, pretending to be ignorant of the situation.

Vroom stood and went up to Priyanka. He put his arm around her shoulder, 'C'mon Priyanka, take it easy. We are all having a rough night here.'

'Shut up. This is insane,' she said and turned to me. 'How could you tap into my personal calls? I can complain about this and get you fired.'

'Then do it,' I said, 'what are you waiting for? Get me fired. Do whatever.'

Vroom looked at Priyanka and then at me. Realizing he could not do too much to help, he returned to his seat.

Esha pulled Priyanka's hand, making her sit down again.

'What the...he...' Priyanka said, anger and impending tears showing in her voice. 'Can't one expect just a little decency from their colleagues?'

I guess I was just a colleague now. An indecent colleague at that.

'Say something,' Priyanka said to me.

I stayed silent and disconnected the tapped wire. I showed her the unhooked cable and threw it on the table.

Our eyes met. Even though we were silent, our eyes communicated.

My eyes said to her: Why are you humiliating me?

Her eyes said to me: Why are you doing this Shyam?

I think eye-talk is more effective than word-talk. Every now and then, human beings should shut up and let their eyes speak. But Priyanka was in no mood to be silent.

'Why Shyam, why? Why do you do such childish, immature things? I thought we were going to make this amicable. We agreed to some terms and conditions, didn't we?'

I did not want to discuss our terms and conditions in public. I wanted her to shut up and for me to scream instead. However, I was in the wrong, like the car driver who hits a bicycle. I had no choice but to stay quiet. I had to pay for my 'childishness'.

'We said we could continue to work together. And that even if we have ended our relationship, we do not have to end our friendship. But this?' she said and lifted the wire on the table. Then she threw it down again.

'Sorry,' I said, or rather whispered.

'What?' she said.

'Sorry,' I said, this time loud and clear. I hate it when she does this to humiliate me. Fuck it, if you have heard an apology—just accept it.

'Do me a huge favor. Stay out of my life please. Will you?' Priyanka said, her voice heavy with the sarcasm she had picked up from me.

I looked up at her and nodded. I felt like putting her and Ganesh in their dark blue nica Lexus, wrapping it with the landline wire and drowning it in Ganesh's new pool.

Vroom sniggered, even as he continued clicking his mouse. A smile rippled over Esha and Radhika as well.

'What's so funny?' Priyanka said, her face still red.

'It's okay, Priyanka. C'mon, can't you take it in a bit of good humor?' Vroom said.

'Your humor,' Priyanka said and paused, 'has a tumor. It isn't funny to me at all.'

'It's 2:30 guys,' Esha said and clapped her hands, 'time to go to Bakshi's office.'

Priyanka and I gave each other one final glare before we got up to leave.

'Is Military Uncle required?' Esha said.

'No. Just the voice agents,' I said. I looked at Military Uncle at the end of the room. I could see he was busy at the chat helpline.

'Let's go Radhika,' Vroom said.

'Do you think he loves her? Or is it just sex? Some good, wild sex that they share?' Radhika said.

'You okay Radhika?' I said.

'Yes, I am fine. I am surprised that I am, actually. I think I must be in shock. Or maybe nobody has taught me an appropriate reaction for this situation. My husband is cheating on me. What am I supposed to do? Scream? Cry? What?'

'Nothing for now. Let's just attend Bakshi's meeting,' Vroom said as we turned to go to Bakshi's room.

My brain was still fumbling at Priyanka's words—'we had terms and conditions'. Like our break-up was a business contract. Every moment of our last date replayed itself as I walked to Bakshi's office. We had gone to Pizza Hut, and pizzas have never tasted as good ever since.

# #23:
# My Past Dates with
# Priyanka—V

Pizza Hut, Sahara Mall, Gurgaon
Four months before this night

She came on time that day. After all, she was coming with
a purpose. This was not a date—we were meeting to formally
break up. Actually, there was nothing left in our relationship
to break anymore. Still, I had agreed, if only to see her face
as she told me. She also wanted to discuss how we were
to interact with each other and move forward. Discuss,
interact, move forward—when you start using words like that,
you know the relationship is dead.

We chose Pizza Hut only because it was, well, convenient.
For break-ups, location takes priority over ambience. She had
come to shop in Sahara Mall, where half of Delhi descends
whenever there is a public holiday.

'Hi,' she said and looked at her watch. 'Wow! Look, I have actually come on time today. How are you?' She held her shirt collar and shook it for ventilation. 'I can't believe it is so hot in July.'

Priyanka cannot tolerate awkward silences; she will say anything to fill in the gaps. *Cut the bullshit*, I wanted to say, but did not.

'It's Delhi. What else do you expect?' I said.

'I think most people who come to malls just come for the air-conditioning—'

'Can we do this quickly?' I said, interrupting her. Consumer motives of mall visitors did not interest me.

'Huh?' she said, startled by my tone.

The waiter came and took our order. I ordered two separate small cheese 'n mushroom pizzas. I did not want to share a large pizza with her, even though, on a per square inch of pizza basis, the large one worked out way cheaper.

'I am not good at this break-up stuff, so let's not drag this out,' I said. 'We've met for a purpose. So now what? Is there a break-up line that I'm supposed to say?'

She stared at me for two seconds. I avoided looking at her nose. Her nose, I had always felt, belonged to me.

'Well I just thought we could do it in a pleasant manner. We can still be friends, right?' she said.

What is with women wanting to be friends forever? Why can't they make a clear decision between a boyfriend and no-friend?

'I don't think so. Both of us have enough friends.'

'See, this is what I don't like about you. That tone of voice...' she said.

'I thought we decided not to discuss each other's flaws today. I have come here to break up, not to make a friend or get an in-depth analysis of my behavior.'

She kept silent until the pizzas arrived on our table. I started eating a slice.

'Perhaps you forget that we work together. That makes it a little more complicated,' Priyanka said.

'Like how?'

'Like if there is tension between us, it will make it difficult to focus on work—for us and for the others,' she said.

'So what do you suggest? I have broken up already, now should I resign as well?' I said.

'I didn't say that. Anyway, I am going to be in this job only nine more months. By next year I would have saved enough to fund my B.Ed. Therefore the situation will automatically correct itself. But if we can agree to certain terms and conditions—like if we can remain friendly in the interim...'

'I can't force myself to be friendly,' I interrupted her, 'my approach to rel. tionships is different. Sorry if it is not practical enough for you. But I can't fake it.'

'I'm not telling you to fake it,' she said.

'Good. Because you are past the stage of telling me what to do. Now, let us just get this over with. What are we supposed to say? I now pronounce ourselves broken up? Then we say, I do, I do?'

I pushed my plate away. I had completely lost my appetite. I felt like tossing the pizza like a frisbee to the end of the room.

'What, say something,' I said, after she had remained silent for ten seconds.

'I don't know what to say,' she said, her voice cracking..

'Really? No words of advice, no last minute preaching, no moral high ground in these final moments for your good-for-nothing unsettled boyfriend? C'mon Priyanka, don't lose your chance of slamming the loser.'

She collected her bag and stood up. She took out a hundred-rupee note and put it on the table—her contribution for the pizza.

'Okay, she leaves in silence again. Once again I get to be the prick,' I mumbled, loud enough for her to hear.

'Shyam,' she said, slinging her bag on to her shoulder.

'Yes?' I said.

'You know how you always say you are not good at anything? I don't think that's true. Because there is something you are quite good at,' she said.

'What?' I said. Perhaps she wanted to give me some last-minute praise to make me feel better, I thought.

'You are damn good at hurting people. Keep it up.'

With that, my ex-girlfriend turned around and left.

# #24

WE REACHED BAKSHI'S OFFICE AT 2:30 A.M. THE SIZE OF A ONE-bedroom flat, it is probably the largest unproductive office in the world. His desk, on which he has a swank flat screen PC, is at one corner. Behind the desk is a bookshelf full of management books of a scary thickness. Some of them are so heavy you can use them as assault weapons. The thought of slamming one hard on Bakshi's head had often crossed my mind during previous team meetings. Apart from blonde threesomes, I think hitting your boss is the ultimate Indian male fantasy.

At another corner of the room is a conference table and six chairs. In the center of the table is a speakerphone for multi-party calls with other offices.

Bakshi was not in his office when we reached his room.

'Where the hell is he?' Vroom said.

'Maybe he's in the toilet?' I said.

'Executive toilet, it is a different feeling,' Vroom said as I nodded in agreement.

We sat around Bakshi's conference table. All of us had brought notebooks to the meeting. We never really used them, but it always seems necessary to sit in meetings with an open notebook.

'Where is he?' Priyanka said.

'I don't know. Who cares,' Vroom said and stood up. 'Hey Shyam, want to check out Bakshi's computer?' He walked over to Bakshi's desk.

'What?' I said. 'Are you crazy? He will come any minute. What can you see so fast anyway?'

'Just for fun. Do you want to know what websites Bakshi visits?' Vroom said and leaned over so he could reach Bakshi's keyboard. He opened up Internet Explorer and pressed Ctrl+H to pull out the history of visited websites.

'Have you gone nuts? You'll get in trouble,' I said.

'Come back Vroom,' Esha said.

'Okay, I've just fired a printout,' Vroom said and sprinted across the room to Bakshi's printer. He fetched the printout and leaped back to the conference table.

'Are you stupid?' I said.

'Okay guys check this out,' Vroom said as he held the A4 sheet in front of him. 'Timesofindia.com, rediff.com, and then we have, Harvard business review website, Boston weather website, Boston places to see, Boston real estate—'

'—What's with him and Boston?' Esha said.

'He is going there on a business trip soon,' Radhika reminded her.

'And what other websites?' I said.

'There is more. Aha, here is what I was looking for: awesomeindia.com—the best porn site for Indian girls, adultfriendfinder.com—a sex personals site, cabaretlounge.com—a strip club in Boston, porninspector.com...hello, the list goes on in this department.'

'What's with him and Boston?' I repeated Esha's words.

'Who knows?' Vroom said and laughed. 'Hey check this out: the official website for Viagra, visited six hours ago.'

'I'll try and ask him about Boston,' Priyanka said.

We heard Bakshi's footsteps and Vroom quickly folded the sheet. We turned quiet and opened our notebooks to fresh blank pages.

Bakshi took fast steps as he entered his office.

'Sorry team. I had to visit the computers bay team leaders for some pertinent managerial affairs. So, how is everyone doing tonight?' Bakshi said as he took the last empty seat at his conference table.

No one responded. I nodded my head to show I was doing fine, but Bakshi was not looking at me.

'Team, I have called you today to tell you about a few changes that may happen at Connexions. We need to right size pe...'

'So, people are getting fired. It wasn't a rumor' Vroom said

Radhika's face turned white. Priyanka and Esha had a shocked expression.

'We never want to fire people Mr Victor Bush have to right size sometime.'

'Why? Why are we firing people when clearly there are other things we can do,' Vroom said.

'We have carefully evaluated all the plausible and feasible alternatives, I am afraid,' Bakshi said and took out a pen. Everyone moved back nervously. The last thing we needed was another Bakshi diagram.

'Cost-cutting is the only alternative,' Bakshi said and began to draw something. However, the pen did not work. He tried to shake it into action, a pointless thing to do with a ball pen. The pen refused to cooperate, perhaps sick of Bakshi's abuse.

I was going to offer my own pen but Esha, who was sitting at my side, sensed the movement and quickly pulled at my elbow to stop me. Bakshi continued to lecture us. He spoke non-stop for six minutes (or ninety-six breaths). He went into various management philosophies, schools of thought, corporate governance methods and other deeply complicated stuff that I know nothing about. His point was that we should make the company more efficient. He just did not have an efficient way to say it.

Vroom had promised me he would not mention the website to Bakshi tonight, at least until the lay-offs were over. However, this did not stop him from taking on Bakshi.

'Sir, but cost-cutting is useless if we have no sales growth. We need more clients, not non-stop cuts until there is no company left,' Vroom said, after Bakshi had finished his speech. I guess somewhere within him was a die-hard optimist who really thought Bakshi would listen to him.

'We have thought of every alternative,' Bakshi said. 'A sales force is too expensive.'

'Sir, we can create a sales force. We have thousands of agents. I am sure some of them are good at sales. We talk to customers every day, so we know what they want...'

'But our clients are in the US, we have to sell there.'

'So what? Why don't we send some agents to the US to try and increase our client base. Why not guys?' Vroom said an looked at us, as if we would furiously nod our heads in approv. I was the only one listening, but remained quiet.

Radhika was doodling on her pad, drawing a pattern that looked like this:

Priyanka was making a table of numbers on her notepad. I think she was making a calendar to figure out the day she was getting married. I felt like ripping her notebook to shreds. Esha was digging her pen's ni deep into her notepad so that it came out at the other end.

'Send agents to the US? Move them to Boston?' Bakshi said and laughed.

'Well a few of them, at least on a trial basis. Some of them are really smart. Who knows, they may get that one client that could save a hundred jobs. Right Shyam?' Vroom said.

'Huh?' I said startled to hear my name.

'Mr Victor, as a **feedback-oriented** manager I appreciate your inputs. However, I do not think it is such a good idea,' Bakshi said.

'Why not?' Vroom demanded with the innocence of a primary school kid.

'Because if it was such a good idea, someone would have thought of it before. Why didn't it strike me for instance?' Bakshi said.

'Huh?' Vroom said, completely flabbergasted. I had heard it all before so it did not move me. I was aware of every red, white, and black blood cell in Bakshi's body.

'What's the plan sir, when do we find out who gets fir...I mean right-sized?' I said.

'Soon. We are finalizing the list, but we will let you know by this morning or early tomorrow night,' Bakshi said, his forehead showing relief as I had not challenged him.

'How many people will lose their job, Sir? What percentage?' Radhika said, her first words in the meeting.

'Thirty to forty is the plan as of now,' Bakshi said in a practiced, calm voice as if he was announcing the temperature outside.

'That's hundreds of people,' Vroom said. As if it was such a difficult calculation.

'Such is corporate life, my friend,' Bakshi said and got up, indicating that the meeting was over. 'You know what they say. It is a jungle out there.' I don't know who said that, but when I looked at Bakshi, I realized there are buffoons in that jungle as well.

The girls collected their notebooks primly and stood up. Vroom sat there for a few more seconds. He crushed the printout of websites visited by Bakshi and put it in his pocket.

'Thank you, Sir,' Esha said.

'You're welcome. As you know, I am an ever-approachable manager. Here or Boston, you can reach me anytime.'

We were at the door when Priyanka asked a question.

'Sir, are you going to Boston soon?'

Bakshi was back at his desk. He had picked up the telephone but paused when he heard Priyanka's question. 'Oh yes, I need to tell you about that. Not that it's very important. I am transferring to Boston soon. Maybe in a month or so.'

'Transferring to Boston?' Vroom, Radhika, Esha, Priyanka and I all spoke together.

'Yes. You see I do not like to blow my own trumpet. But looks like they recognized my contributions in the value-addition cycle of the company,' Bakshi said, a smug smile sliming across his shiny face. I thought of toppling the entire bookshelf on his head.

'But details will come later. Anyway, if you do not mind, I need to make a call. I'll keep you posted later if we have more news.'

Bakshi signaled us to shut the door as we left. As I closed the door, I felt like someone had slapped my face. In slow motion, we walked away from his office.

# #25

WE RETURNED TO WASG AFTER OUR MEETING WITH BAKSHI. Calls flashed on the screen, but no one attended to them. I sat at my seat and opened my email. I could not read anything as my mind was having a systems overload.

I looked at the time, it was 2.45 a.m.

Vroom sat at his desk and mumbled inaudible curses. He opened the internal web page of Connexions on his computer. It had the map of the US on it. He held up a pen and tapped at a point on the US east coast.

'This, this is Boston,' he said and clenched his fist tight around the pen. 'This is where our boss will be while we are on the road looking for jobs.'

Everyone stayed quiet.

'Can I ask why everyone is so bloody quiet?' Vroom said.

'I think we should start picking up some calls,' I said and started fumbling with the controls on the telephone.

'Like fuck we should,' Vroom said and jabbed his pen hard on the monitor. A loud ping startled everyone on the desk. Shattered glass made a nine-inch wide, spider-web pattern on Vroom's monitor. The rest of his screen worked as if nothing had happened.

'What happened,' the girls said and came around to Vroom's computer.

'Damn it,' Vroom said and threw his pen hard on the ground. It broke into two pieces. Some people break into tears when they are upset. Some break whatever is around them.

'Oh no. The monitor is totally gone,' Esha said. She put her hand on Vroom's shoulder, 'Are you okay?'

'Don't you dare touch me, you slut,' Vroom said and pushed her hand away.

'What?' Esha said. 'What did you just say?'

'Nothing. Just leave me alone, all right? Go pray for your jobs or whatever. Bloody bitch on her way to becoming a hooker,' Vroom said and moved his chair away from Esha.

For a few seconds the girls stood there, stunned. Then, slowly, they walked back to their seats.

'What's wrong with him?' Priyanka asked Esha in a whisper, which was audible to us.

'I told you he proposed again. Maybe he's not taking my rejection so well,' Esha said to Priyanka.

'Oh really?' Vroom shouted and stood up. 'You think this is about the proposal? Like I do not know about your escapades. Everyone here knows it—Shyam, Radhika and Priyanka. You thought I would not find out? I wish I'd known before I proposed to a certified slut who'll bang for bucks. I feel sick.'

Esha looked at all of us, shocked. Tears appeared in her eyes. She started shaking, and Radhika helped her sit down. It is way more elegant to cry sitting down than standing up.

Priyanka went up to Vroom's seat. She stared at him, her face red. Slap! She deposited a hard slap across Vroom's face.

'Learn how to talk to women. You say one more nasty thing and I'll screw your happiness, understand?' Priyanka said.

Vroom stared at Priyanka, his hand over his cheek. He was too stunned to retaliate. I inserted myself between the two of them. 'Guys, can we have some peace here,' I said. 'Things are already quite messed up. Please let's sit down and do some work.'

'I can't work. I don't know if I'll still have a job in a few hours,' Priyanka said and moved back to her seat. She continued to glare at Vroom.

'At least sit down,' I said.

'I want him to apologize to Esha. The idiot has to watch what he is saying,' Priyanka said.

Esha continued to cry as Radhika tried to console her.

'What do you care about a job? You are getting married. Women have it easy,' Vroom said.

'What? Don't you start that with me now,' Priyanka said. She had reached her seat but refused to sit down. 'You think this is easy?' She pointed a finger to Esha and Radhika.

Vroom kept quiet and looked down.

'Radhika found out her husband is cheating on her. This when she works for him and his family day and night. And Esha can't get a fair break unless she sleeps past creepy men. But they are not breaking monitors and shouting curses, Vroom. Just because we don't make a noise doesn't mean it is easy,' she said, shouting loud enough so you could call it noise.

'Can we not talk for two minutes. Do not take calls. But at least keep quiet,' I pleaded.

Esha stopped crying as Radhika gave her a glass of water. Priyanka sat down and opened her handmade calendar. Vroom became quiet as he looked at the shattered bits of glass on his desk.

The silence gave me a chance to reflect on Bakshi's meeting. *If I lost my job, what would I do? Become an agent again?* I could probably forget about being a team leader.

'I'm sorry,' Vroom mumbled.

'What?' Esha said.

'I'm sorry, Esha,' Vroom said, clearing his throat. 'I said horrible and hurtful things. I was disturbed myself. Please forgive me.'

'It's okay Vroom. It only hurts because there is a bit of truth in it,' Esha said with a wry smile.

'I meant to say those horrible things to myself. Because,' Vroom said and banged two fists simultaneously on the table, 'because the real hooker is me, not you.'

'What?' I said.

'Yes, this salary has hooked me. Every night I come here and let people fuck me,' Vroom said and picked up the telephone headset. 'The Americans fuck me with this, in my ears hundreds of times a night. Bakshi fucks me with his management theories, backstabbing and threats to fire us. And the funny thing is, I let them do it. For money, for security—I let it happen. Come fuck me some more,' Vroom said and threw the headset on the table.

'Do you want water?' Radhika said and handed him a glass of water.

Vroom took the glass and drank the water in one gulp. I wondered if he would throw the empty glass on the floor and shatter it to pieces. Luckily, he just banged it on the table.

'Thanks,' Vroom said. 'I needed that. In fact, I need a break. Otherwise I'll go mad. I can't take this right now.'

'I need a break too,' Priyanka said. 'It's all right Vroom. Only a few more hours left for the shift to get over.'

'No. I want a break now. I want to go for a drive. C'mon people, let's all go for a drive. I'll get the Qualis,' Vroom said and stood up.

'Now? It is close to 3 a.m.,' I said.

'Yes, now. Who gives a damn about the calls? You may not even have a job. Get up.'

'Actually, if someone is going, can you please get some pills for me from the 24-hour chemist?' Radhika said.

'No, all of us are going,' Vroom said. 'Get up Shyam. If you come, everyone will come.'

'I'm game,' Esha said.

'Okay, I'll come too. Just for a bit of fresh air,' Priyanka said.

I looked at them. Everyone wanted to get out of his or her miseries, if only for a few moments. I wanted to get away from Bakshi, Ganesh and Connexions.

'Okay, we can go. But we have to be back soon,' I said.

'Where are we going?' Esha said, 'I heard the new lounge bar Bed is close by.'

'No way, we're just going for a drive...' I said, but Vroom interrupted me.

'Great idea. We are going to Bed—damn cool place.'

'I need a real bed to sleep,' Radhika said and stretched her arms.

All of us got up. We decided to leave individually to prevent suspicion.

'Get up, Military Uncle,' Vroom said, as he went to his desk.

'Huh?' Uncle said getting up. Normally he would have scoffed at Vroom, but I guess he was in too much pain over his son's email to give a conscious reaction.

'We're all going for a drive. The others will tell you everything. I'll get the Qualis,' Vroom said and switched off Uncle's monitor.

## 26

At 3:00 A.M. SHARP, WE WERE OUTSIDE THE MAIN ENTRANCE of Connexions. A white Qualis came up and halted near us.

'Get in,' Vroom said, reaching over to open the doors.

'It's so cold. What took you so long,' Esha said, getting into the front.

'You try shifting a sound-asleep driver to another Qualis,' Vroom said.

Radhika, Priyanka and I took the middle row; Military Uncle preferred to sit by himself at the back. He looked slightly dazed. May be we all did.

Vroom drove past the executive parking area as we left Connexions. We saw Bakshi's white Mitsubishi Lancer.

'Bakshi's got a flash car,' Esha said.

'Company paid, of course,' Priyanka sighed.

Vroom inched the Qualis forward and stopped close to the Lancer. He switched on the Qualis headlights. Bakshi's car shone bright.

'Can I ask a question? What's the punishment for running people over?' Vroom said.

'Excuse me?' I said.

'What if we ran this Qualis over Bakshi? We could do it when he comes to pick up his car in the morning. How many years of jail are we talking?' Vroom said.

It was a silly conversation, but Priyanka led him on anyway.

'Depends on how the court sees it. If they see it as an accident and not as homicide or murder, about two years,' she said.

Vroom restarted the car and turned towards the exit gate.

'Two years is . . . a lot. Can we divide it among the six of us? Four months each?' Vroom said.

'I don't know. Ask a lawyer,' Priyanka shrugged.

'Four months is like nothing to get rid of Bakshi from this earth,' Esha blew a strand of hair that had fallen against her lips.

'Just sixteen weekends of sacrifice. Weekdays are like jail anyway,' Vroom said. 'What say we do it?'

By now we had left the call center and were now on the highway. Apart from a few trucks, the roads were empty. India has a billion people, but at night, ninety-nine percent of them are fast asleep. This land then belongs to a chosen few: truck drivers, late shift workers, doctors, hotel staff and call center agents. We, the nocturnal, rule the roads and the country. Vroom accelerated the Qualis to eighty kilometers an hour.

'I doubt you can split the punishment. The driver gets the full deal,' Priyanka said, still on the stupid Bakshi-homicide topic, 'plus if they know it's premeditated, you are talking ten years plus.'

'Hmmm. Now ten years is a totally different equation. What say Shyam, still not too bad to get rid of Bakshi?'

'Okay, enough of this stupidity,' I said. 'I thought you were taking us out for a drink.'

'I'm just...' Vroom said, raising one hand from the steering wheel.

'Shut up and drive. I need a drink,' I said

'Chemist first please. Can we please stop at a chemist,' Radhika said, giving herself a head massage.

We dropped the topic of killing Bakshi. Though if the law allowed me one free murder in my life, I am quite clear who will top the list. No wait, I am forgetting my ex-girlfriend's mom here. I really wouldn't know whom to kill first, that's the truth. Perhaps the law would see me as a special case and allow me two murders.

Vroom took a sharp right turn on to a road that led to a 24-hour chemist.

Radhika was quiet as she waited. I guess Payal occupied half her mind; the other half had migraine.

'There it is,' Esha said as we sighted a neon red cross.

'Trust me. I know this area,' Vroom said and accelerated the Qualis to a hundred. 'Man, roads and girls are so much more fun at night.'

'That's sick,' Priyanka said.

'Sorry, couldn't help it,' Vroom said and grinned.

Vroom parked the Qualis near the chemist. A sleepy boy, no more than seventeen, manned the medicine shop. A few medical entrance exam guides lay on the counter in front of him. A fly swatter served the function of a bookmark. He looked bored and grateful to see us, more for the company, probably, than the business.

Vroom and Radhika got out of the Qualis. I stepped out to stretch my legs as well.

Radhika walked quickly upto the boy.

'What do you want, Radhika? Saridon?' Vroom said as we reached the counter.

'No,' she shook her head. Turning to the boy, she said, 'Three strips of Fluoxetine, and five strips each of Sertraline and Paroxetine. Make it fast please.' She began to tap on the counter anxiously. Her red bangles jingled a little.

The boy gaped at Radhika. Then he turned around and started rifling through the shelves.

Vroom and I moved a few steps away to escape the smell of medicine. Vroom lit a cigarette and we shared a few puffs.

The boy returned with a stack of tablets and placed them on the counter. Radhika reached out to grab them, but he put his right hand on top of the pile of medicines and slid them away from her. 'This is pretty strong stuff, madam. You have a prescription?' he asked.

'It's three in the morning,' Radhika said in an irritated voice. 'I ran out of pills at work. Where the hell do you expect me to find a prescription?'

'Sorry madam. Just that sometimes these young kids come here to pick up strange medicines before going to '

'Look at me,' Radhika said, pointing to her face, 'do I look like a teenager in a mood to party?'

No, Radhika did not look like a teenager out to party to me—she looked ill, with dark circles under her eyes. I wished the boy would give her the medicines soon.

'But these are still a lot of strong medicines, madam. What do you need these for? I mean, what is wrong with you?' the boy said.

'Fuck you,' Radhika said and banged her fist hard on the glass counter. The glass shook but survived the impact. However two of Radhika's red bangles broke into a million pieces. Shattered bits of bright glass scattered along the counter.

The noise scared the boy; he jumped back two steps. Vroom crushed his cigarette and we joined them at the counter.

'Excuse me, madam,' the boy said.

'Fuck you. You want to know what is wrong with me? You little punk, you want to know what is wrong with *me*?'

'What's up Radhika, everything okay?' Vroom said.

'This dumbass wants to know what is wrong with me,' Radhika said, pointing her finger at the boy. 'Who the hell is he? What does he know about me?'

'Calm down Radhika,' I said, but she probably did not even hear me. That is the story of my life; half the things I say go unnoticed.

'What does he know about wrong and right? Everything is wrong with me you moron—my husband is banging some bitch while I slog my guts out. Happy now?' Radhika said, her face more red than her broken bangles. She held her head for a few seconds. Then she removed her hands from her head and grabbed the medicines. The boy at the counter did not protest this time.

'Water. Can I have some water?' Radhika said.

The boy ran inside his shop and returned with a glass of water.

Radhika tore a few pills out of her new stack. One, two, three—I think she popped in three of them. Some migraine cure this was, I thought.

'Four hundred sixty three rupees, madam,' the boy said, his voice trembling with fear.

'I am alive because of this stuff. I need it to survive, not to party,' Radhika said.

She paid for the medicines and walked back to the Qualis. Vroom and I followed a few steps behind her.

'What medicine is that?' I said.

'What the hell do I know? I am no doctor,' Vroom said.

'You sure she has a prescription for those?' I said.

'Ask her, if you have the guts,' Vroom said.

'No way. Let's get to the lounge bar soon.'

'Everything okay?' Esha said as we got into the Qualis. 'We heard arguments.'

'Nothing. As Bakshi would say, we just had some communication issues. But now, let's put them to Bed,' Vroom said and turned the Qualis around.

Radhika put the medicines in her bag. Her face was calmer as the three pills started to kick in.

Vroom pushed the Qualis to one hundred and ten, the maximum it would go without the engine crying for mercy.

'Slow down Vroom,' Esha said.

'Don't use the words slow and Vroom in one sentence,' Vroom said.

'Dialogue,' I said, 'should we clap?'

A truck stuffed with bags of hay loped past us like an g nt elephant. Our headligh s made the gunn	
n the dark.

'See, even that truck was going faster than us. I am a safe driver,' Vroom said.

'Sorry guys,' Radhika said, her voice becoming more normal as the drugs took effect. 'I apologize for creating a scene there.'

'What did you buy Radhika? Why did the chemist make a fuss?' I said, unable to control my curiosity.

'Anti-depressants. Chemists ask questions, as they're prescription drugs. But most of the time they don't care.'

'Wow!' Vroom said. 'You mean happy drugs like Prozac and stuff.'

'Yes, Fluoxetine is Prozac. Except it is the Indian version, so a lot cheaper.'

'Like all of us,' Vroom said and laughed at his own joke.

'But it's dangerous to take it without medical supervision,' Priyanka said. 'Isn't it addictive?'

'It's legal addiction. I can't live without it and, yes, it is really bad for you. But it is still better than having to face my life,' Radhika said.

'Leave it Radhika—they will harm you,' Military Uncle spoke for the first time on our drive.

'I had cut down, Military Uncle. But sometimes one needs a bigger dose. Can everyone please switch to another topic? How far is this Bed?'

'Just two kilometers from here. Ninety seconds if I am driving, a lot more if Shyam is,' Vroom said without looking at us. I ignored his comment, as I preferred for him to keep his eyes on the road. Some inebriated truckies drove past as Vroom dodged them.

'I heard the Bed is really snooty,' Priyanka said. 'I'm n
dressed at all.' She adjusted her salwar kameez. I noticed
border of glittering stone-work on her dark green chiffon dup

'You look fine,' Esha reassured her, 'the chiffon look is re
in. I should be worried. I look so grungy.'

'Don't worry Esha. Anyone with a navel ring is never denie
entry in a disco,' Vroom said.

'Well, if you girls are in doubt, they definitely won't let in
a boring housewife like me,' Radhika said.

'Don't worry. As long as we're ready to spend cash, we will
be welcome. Plus, the DJ at Bed is my classmate from school,'
Vroom said.

'All your school classmates have such funky jobs,' I said.

'Well, that is the problem. They all have rich dads. I have
to work hard to match their lifestyle. If only my rich dad didn't
have to leave us,' Vroom said. 'Anyway guys, welcome to Bed.
And courtesy your humble driver, it is just 3:23 a.m. He flashed
the headlights at a sign. It said 'Bed Lounge and Bar: Your
Personal Space'.

'Oh no, didn't realize we're there already,' Esha said. She
fished out a mirror from her purse and examined her lips. *How
did women manage before mirrors were invented?*

'How is my hair? Is it awful as usual?' Priyanka said to
Radhika.

I looked at her long curly hair. Priyanka always said how she
had the 'most boring hair in the world', and how she could 'do
nothing with it'. I never quite understood it, as I liked her hair;
loved it actually. I felt the urge to run my fingers through it
just as I had done a hundreds times before. But I couldn't, as

someone called Ganesh would be doing it for me in a few weeks
time. The oil for the McDonald's French fries started simmering
again in my gut. What is the oil they use at McDonald's anyway
It burns like hell.

'Your hair is perfect. Anyway, it'll be dark inside. Let's go,'
Radhika said. 'C'mon Military Uncle, we're going inside.'

# #27

WE FOLLOWED VROOM TO A HUGE BLACK DOOR, THE ENTRANCE of Bed. The door was painted so that it merged with the wall. An ultra beefy bouncer and a malnourished woman stood beside it.

'Are you a member, sir?' the malnourished woman addressed Vroom. She was the hostess (or door-bitch, according to Priyanka) and wore a black dress. She was about five feet four inches, but looked way taller because of her thin frame and heels the size of a coke bottle.

'No, we've just come for a quick drink,' Vroom said and took out his credit card. 'Here, you can open the tab on this.'

'I'm sorry sir, tonight is for members only,' she said. The beefy bouncer looked at us with a blank, daft glare. Like Bakshi, he belonged to the non-human species of mankind.

'How do you become a member?' I said.

'You have to fill a form and pay the annual membership fee of fifty thousand,' the hostess said, as calmly as if she'd asked us for small change.

'What? Fifty grand for this place in the middle of nowhere?' Priyanka said and pointed her finger to the door. She had draped her dupatta in reverse, in an attempt to look hip.

'I suggest you go somewhere else then,' the hostess said. She looked at Priyanka scornfully. A fully-clad female is a no-no at discos.

'Don't you look at me like that,' Priyanka said.

'Hey cool it, Priyanka,' Vroom said and turned to the bouncer. 'What's the deal, dude. Is DJ Jas inside? I know him.'

'Huh…what…' the bouncer said with a dumb, nervous expression. It was the most challenging question anyone had asked him in months.

'You know Jas?' the hostess said, her voice warmer now.

'School buddy of seven years. Tell him Vroom is here,' Vroom said.

'Cool. Why didn't you tell me that before, Vroom?' the hostess said and gave Vroom a flirtatious smile. She bent over to release the velvet ropes. The skeletal structure of her upper torso was visible. If she broke a bone, she wouldn't need an x-ray.

'Can we go in now?' Esha asked the hostess with a bored expression.

'Yes. Though Vroom, next time, please tell your friends to dress up for Bed,' the hostess said and glanced meaningfully at Priyanka and Radhika.

'I could wring her tiny neck, just like that. One twist and it will snap like a chicken bone,' Priyanka said.

As we went in, the bouncer frisked Vroom and me. I finally understood the purpose of his existence. After us, he went towards Priyanka.

'What?' I said to the bouncer.

'I need to check this lady,' he said. 'She acts like she could cause trouble.' He towered over Priyanka, who just froze.

And then, I don't know how, but the words came to me.

'You're not touching her, you understand,' I said.

The bouncer was startled. He turned to me. He had biceps the size of my thighs, and deep inside I shuddered to think how much it would hurt if he delivered a punch across my face.

'What's up now?' the hostess came towards us.

'Nothing, just teach your Mr Tarzan out here how to behave with women,' I said and pulled at Priyanka's hand. In a second we were inside Bed.

The interior design of Bed was a cross between Star Trek and a debauched king's harem. Ultraviolet bulbs and candles were the only sources of light. As my eyes adjusted to the semi-darkness, I noticed two rows of six beds each. Only five beds were occupied, so I could not understand the big fuss at the entrance. I guess it is never easy to get people into bed.

We chose a corner bed, which had two hookahs next to it.

'Why is the hostess so mean?' Esha said, as she hoisted herself onto the bed. She took two cushions to rest her elbows. 'Did you hear her? "Go somewhere else". Is that how you treat customers?'

'It's their job. They're paid to be mean. It gives the place attitude,' Vroom said carelessly as he lit up a hookah. I looked at the hot, smoldering coals and thought of Ganesh. I don't know why, but I thought it would be fun to drop some down his pants.

'I want a job that pays me to be mean. All they tell us in the call center is "be nice, be polite, be helpful"—being mean is so much more fun,' Radhika said and reclined along a long cushion. For someone who had just had a really tough night she looked nice; although I'm not sure anyone can look ugly in ultraviolet-candlelight anyway. I wondered how a moron called Anuj could leave her.

Only Esha and Radhika got to lie down. The rest of us sat cross-legged on the bed.

Vroom went to say hi to DJ Jas, who was playing some incomprehensible French-African-Indian fusion music. He returned with twelve kamikaze shots. Military Uncle declined, and we didn't protest as it meant more alcohol for us. Vroom took Uncle's extra shots and drank them in quick succession.

We had barely finished our kamikazes when another thin woman (a Bed specialty) came up to us with another six drinks.

'Long Island Ice Teas,' she said, 'courtesy DJ Jas.'

'Nice. You have your friends in the right places,' Radhika said as she started gulping her Long Island like it was a glass of water. When you don't get to drink on a regular basis, you go crazy at the chance.

'These Long Islands are very stiff,' I said after a few sips. I could feel my head spin. 'Easy guys,' I said, 'our shift isn't over. We said one quick drink, so let's go back soon.'

'Cool it man. Just one last drink,' Vroom said as he ordered another set of cocktails.

'I'm getting high,' Priyanka said. 'I'm going to miss this. I am going to miss you guys.'

'Yeah right. We'll see when you move to Seattle. Here guys, try this—it is apple flavor,' Vroom said as he took a big drag from the hookah. He passed it around, and everyone (except Military Uncle, whose expression was growing more resigned by the minute) took turns smoking it. DJ Jas' music was mellow, which went well with the long drags we were taking from the hookah.

There were two flat LCD screens in front of our bed, one tuned to MTV, and the other to CNN. A Bollywood item number was being played on MTV, as part of its 'Youth Special' program. A girl stripped off successive items of her clothing as the song progressed. The breaking news on CNN was that the US was considering going to war with Iraq again. I noticed Vroom staring at the TV showing CNN.

'Americans are sick,' Vroom said, as he pointed to a US politician who had spoken out in support of the war. 'Look at him. He would nuke the whole world if he could have his way.'

'No, not the whole world. I don't think they'd blow up China,' Priyanka said, sounding high. 'They need the cheap labor.'

'Then I guess they won't blow up Gurgaon either. They need the call centers,' Radhika said.

'So we are safe,' Esha said, 'that's good. Welcome to Gurgaon, the safest city on earth.'

The girls started laughing. Even Military Uncle smiled.

'It's not funny girls. Our government doesn't realize this, but Americans are using us. We are sacrificing an entire generation to service their call centers,' Vroom said, convincing me that one day he could be a politician.

Nobody responded.

'Don't you agree?' Vroom said.

'Can you please stop this trip…'. I began. As usual, I was put on mute.

'C'mon Vroom. Call centers are useful to us too,' Esha said. 'You know how hard it is to make fifteen grand a month outside. And here we are, sitting in an air-conditioned office, talking on the phone, collecting our pay and going home. And it is the same for hundreds and thousands of young people. What's wrong with that?'

'An air-conditioned sweatshop is still a sweatshop. In fact, it is worse, because nobody sees the sweat. Nobody sees your brain getting rammed,' Vroom said.

'Then why don't you quit? Why are you still here?' I said. I hate it when he ruins my high with his high ground.

'Because I need the money. My friends have a lifestyle that I have to keep up with. Money lets me come to places like this,' Vroom said.

'It's just Bakshi. You are worked up about him and now you are blaming it on the call center,' I said.

'Screw Bakshi, he is not the only bad boss around. C'mon, the whole world is being run by a bad, stupid-evil boss,' he said, pointing to CNN. 'Look at them, scared out of their guts, ready to bomb everyone. Meanwhile, all we do is talk on the phone all night. While the world snores away,' Vroom said.

'Stop complaining about working at night. Doctors do it, hotel people do it, airplane pilots do it, factory workers—hell, even that door bitch works at night,' Priyanka said.

'There is nothing wrong with working at night. And I agree the money is good. But the difference is, we don't have jobs that make us work to our potential. Look at our country, we are still so behind these Americans. Even when we know we are no less than them,' Vroom said, gesturing wildly at the TV screen.

'So? What other kinds of jobs can there be,' Esha said with a hairclip in her mouth. She had begun the ritual of untying and retying her hair.

'So like, there is so much to do. We should be building roads, power plants, airports, phone networks and metro trains in every city like madness. And if the government moves its rear-end and does that, the young people in this country will find jobs there. Hell, I would work days and nights for that—as long as I know that what I am doing is helping build something for my country, for its future. But the government doesn't believe in doing any real work, so they allow these BPOs to be opened and think they have taken care of the youth. Just as this stupid MTV thinks showing a demented chick do a dance in her underwear will make the program a youth special. Do you think they really care?'

'Who?' I said. 'The government or MTV?' I got up and signaled for the check (in bars you always ask for the 'check'— never the 'bill'). It was 3:50 a.m., and I had had enough of Vroom's lecture. I wanted to get back to the call center soon.

Vroom paid for the bill with his credit card and we promised to split the costs later.

'Both. Both of them don't give a fuck,' Vroom said as we left Bed.

The door bitch and the bouncer gave us a puzzled look as we walked out.

## 28

Vroom DROVE US OUT OF BED AND WE WERE SOON BACK ON the highway. Every now and then the Qualis swayed to the left or right of the road.

'Careful,' Esha said, 'you okay Vroom?'

'I'm fine. Man, I love driving,' Vroom said dreamily.

'I can drive if you...' I said.

'I said I'm fine,' Vroom said in a firm voice. A few minutes later, we passed by Sahara Mall, the biggest shopping mall in Gurgaon. Abruptly, Vroom brought the Qualis to a halt.

'I feel nauseous,' Vroom said. I think we were all feeling a little nauseous after Vroom's erratic driving.

'Whatever you do, don't throw up in the Qualis. The driver will kill you,' Esha said.

Vroom rested his head on the steering wheel. The horn blew loud enough to wake up the street dogs.

'Let's take a walk Vroom,' I said and tapped his shoulder. We got out of the Qualis.

I made Vroom walk around the perimeter of the Sahara Mall. We passed by several advertising hoardings showing all kinds of people: a couple all smiles because they had just bought a toothbrush; a group of friends giggling over their mobile phones; a family happily feeding their kid junk food; a young graduate jumping with joy, clutching a credit card; a girl holding seven shopping bags and beaming. All the ads had one thing in common. Everyone looked incredibly happy.

'What the hell are they so happy about?' Vroom said. 'Look at that toothbrush couple. My mom and dad, they are never that happy.'

'Just take deep breaths and walk in a straight line Vroom. You're drunk,' I said.

'I'm fine,' he said, 'but mom and dad… Shyam, why do they hate each other so much?'

'Grown ups man, they are way more complicated than we are. Don't even try figuring them out,' I said.

Vroom stopped walking and straightened up. He told me to pause as well, and continued: 'Think about this. The people who gave birth to me can't stop hating each other enough. What does that tell you about me? Half my genes must be fighting with the other half. No wonder I am so fucking messed up.'

'We are all messed up man, let's go,' I said and prodded his shoulders.

He walked faster to get a few steps ahead of me.

At the corner of Sahara Mall we passed by a Pizza Hut. It was closed. Vroom went up and stood in front of it. I wondered if he had really gone crazy; was he expecting pizza at this time?

We stood near the entrance. On our right, there was a thirty foot wide metal hoarding of a cola company. A top Bollywood actress held a drink bottle and looked at us with inviting eyes. Like a fizzy drink was all it took to seduce her into bed.

Vroom walked close to the actress's face.

'What's up dude?' I said.

'You see her?' Vroom said, pointing to the actress.

I nodded.

'There she is, looking at us like she is our best friend. Do you think she cares for us?'

'I don't know. She is a youth icon man,' I shrugged my shoulders.

'Yes, youth icon. This airhead chick is supposed to be our role model. Like she knows a fuck about life and gives a fuck about us. All she cares about is cash. She doesn't care about you or me. She just wants you to buy this black piss,' Vroom said, pointing to the cola bottle.

'Black piss?' I said and smiled. I sat down on some steps nearby.

'Do you know how much sugar there is in one of these drinks?' Vroom said.

I shook my head.

'Eight spoons of sugar in every bottle—and nothing else. And yet, they convince us this is important. It isn't.'

Vroom looked around and noticed a pile of bricks. He lifted one and threw it hard at the cola hoarding. Bang! It hit the actress's cheek, creating a dimple you would almost think was natural. She still kept smiling.

'Careful, for fuck's sake. Let's go back. Someone will see us and get us arrested.'

'Like I care. Nobody cares,' Vroom said and staggered towards me. I looked at his lanky outline in the streetlights. 'The government doesn't care for anybody,' he continued. 'Even that "youth special" channel, they don't care either. They say youth because they want the damn Pizza Huts and Cokes and Pepsis of the world to come and give their ads to them. Ads that say if we spend our salary to have pizza and coke, we will be happy. Like young people don't have a fucking brain. Tell us what crap to have and we'll have it.'

Vroom sat down in front of the Pizza Hut steps. 'Shyam,' he said. 'I'm going to throw up.'

'Oh no,' I said and moved three feet away from him.

'Unnh…' Vroom said as he threw up. Puke spread around like a 12"-thin crust pizza with gross toppings outside the entrance.

'Feeling better?' I said as I carefully helped him up. Vroom nodded his head.

He stood up and jerked his shoulders free from me. He lifted another brick. He hurled it high, and with one wide swing smashed it into the Pizza Hut restaurant. Crash! A window shattered, and bits of glass fell down like a beautiful ice fountain. An alarm began to ring.

'Damn, Vroom have you gone mad? Let's get the hell out of here,' I said.

Vroom was startled by the alarm as well, and his body sprang to attention.

'Fuck, let's run,' Vroom said and we sprinted towards the Qualis.

'I thought you liked pizza,' I said when we reached the Qualis.
'I like pizza. Damn well I do. I like jeans, mobiles and pizzas.
I earn, I eat, I buy shit and I die. That is all the fuck there is
to Vroom. It is all bullshit man,' Vroom said, panting and
holding his stomach. He didn't look too good, but at least the
run seemed to have sobered him down.

'Seriously dude, can I drive now?' I said, as Vroom opened
the front door of the Qualis. He was taking noisy, heavy breaths.

'No way man,' Vroom said and pushed me away.

The car jerked ahead as Vroom turned on the ignition while
in gear.

'Are you okay?' Esha said.

Vroom nodded and raised his hand in apology. He waited
for a few seconds, and then started the engine carefully. He
promised to drive slow and soon we were on the road again.

'You liked Bed?' Vroom said, more to change the topic from
his inebriated state.

'Great place,' Esha said, 'just the kind of high I needed. Hey
Vroom, have you kept any music in the Qualis?'

'Of course. Let me see, Vroom said and shuffled through
the glove box. He took out a tape and held it up. 'Musafir
lounge?' he said.

'Cool.' Esha and Radhika said.

'No,' Priyanka and I said at the same time.

'C'mon guys. You two not only hate each other, you hate the
same things too?' Vroom said and smiled. He put the tape in and
turned on the music. A song called *Rabba* started playing.

We sat in the same order as before, except this time I sat
next to Priyanka. With every beat of the song, I could feel her

body along my entire right side, like soft electric sparks. I had the urge to grab her hand again, but restrained myself. I opened the window for some fresh air.

'Don't open the window,' Esha said, 'it is so cold.'

'Just for a minute,' I said and let the breeze in.

I focused on the lyrics of the song. The singer spoke of why no beloved should ever enter his life. That if one did, she should damn well stay and never leave. Somehow the lyrics were too close to heart. However, I was more worried about the next song. It was *Mahi Ve*—which would bring back memories of the 32nd Milestone parking lot.

I saw Priyanka's face change from the corner of my eye. She looked nervous in anticipation too. Yes, this was going to be hard.

'I love this song,' Vroom declared, as the song I was dreading filled the Qualis.

The lyrics hit my ears and I pressed the rewind-and-play button in the privacy of my head. Every moment of 32nd Milestone replayed itself. I remembered how Priyanka sat on my lap, stubbed my toe and hit her head on the roof. I recalled every little second of her careful, slow and yet amazing lovemaking. I missed her breath on my stubble, her eyes when they looked into mine, the pleasurable pain when she bit my ears. *What is it about music that it makes you remember things you prefer to forget?* I wished I had got promoted. I wished Priyanka had never left me. I wished my world were a happier place.

I turned my face to look outside. The breeze felt cold, particularly along two lines on my cheeks. I touched my face. Damn, I couldn't believe I was crying.

'Can we please close the window now? It's ruining my hair,' Esha said.

I slid the window shut. I tried to keep my eyes shut as well, but I couldn't as tears wanted to come out. I didn't know I was such an embarrassing wuss.

I looked at Priyanka. Maybe it was my imagination, but her eyes seemed wet too. She turned towards me and then quickly looked away. I couldn't bear to meet her eyes right now. And I certainly could not look at that nose.

Vroom pulled out two tissues from the tissue box in front and swung his arm back to hand them over to us.

'What?' I said.

'There is a rear-view mirror. I can see,' he said.

'We all can see,' Radhika and Esha said together and burst out laughing.

'You keep driving alright,' I said. I took the tissue, and on the pretext of wiping my nose, wiped my eyes. Priyanka took one and swabbed her eyes as well.

Esha reached behind from her seat and rubbed Priyanka's arm.

'You guys are funny. Remind me again how you met in college?' Vroom said.

'Forget it,' I said.

'C'mon Shyam, just tell. You guys never told me,' Radhika said.

'At the campus fair,' Priyanka and I spoke at the same time. I looked at her. We gave each other a formal smile.

'You tell,' Priyanka said.

'No, it's okay. You say it better,' I said.

Priyanka sat up straight to tell a story we had told a hundred times, but never got tired of repeating.

'We met at the campus fair in second year. Both of us had stalls. Mine was on female empowerment. It showed slides of problems faced by rural women in India. Shyam had a video games counter. However, nobody was coming to visit either of us—everyone just wanted to go to the food stalls.'

'Then?' Esha said, her eyes focused on Priyanka.

'Then Shyam and I made a deal that we would visit each other's stalls six times a day. Shyam would come and see slides on hardworking farm women and female education programs. I would go and play Doom II on the Playstation at his stall. By the end of the fair I was so good, I could beat him,' Priyanka said.

'No way,' I said. 'I can take you on at Doom II any day.'

'Well, anyway—so over three days we visited each other's stalls three dozen times. And by the end of it, we felt...' Priyanka said and paused.

'What?' Radhika said.

'We felt that both the stalls belonged to us. And that as long as we were together, we didn't need anyone else to visit,' Priyanka said and her voice choked up.

My throat already had a lump the size of an orange, and I just nodded to keep a straight expression.

We kept silent. I was hoping Priyanka would cry big time now.

'Well, things change. Life goes on—move on to better things. It is like Playstation to X-box,' Vroom said.

I hate Vroom. Just when Priyanka was all mellow, Vroom's wise words brought her back to reality. She composed herself and changed the topic.

'How far are we?' Priyanka said.

I looked at my watch.

'Damn Vroom, it is past 4 a.m. How much further?'

'Around five kilometers from the call center. I am driving slower now. You want me to drive faster?'

'No,' all of us cried.

'We're going to get late. Bakshi will flip out,' I said.

'I can take a shortcut,' Vroom said.

'Shortcut?' I said.

'Next left there is an un-tarred road. It was made for construction projects. It cuts through some fields—saves us about two kilometers.'

'Is the road lit up?' Esha said.

'No, but we have headlights. I've used that way before. Let's take it,' Vroom said.

Vroom took a sharp left after a kilometer.

'Ouch,' Esha said, 'you didn't tell us this road will be so bumpy.'

'Just a few minutes,' Vroom said, 'actually the ground is wet today from the rains yesterday. That is why the ride is not smooth.'

We plunged on into the darkness, even as the headlights tried hard to show us the way. We passed fields and construction sites filled with materials like cement, bricks and iron rods. In a few places, there were deep holes, as builders constructed the foundation for super-high rise apartments. I think the whole of Delhi had decided to move to Gurgaon, and people were growing homes along with the crops.

'There, just one final cut and we are back on the highway,' Vroom said taking a sharp right.

Suddenly the Qualis skidded. The vehicle rattled and down an inclined path.

'Careful,' everyone shouted and held on to anything they could find around them. The Qualis went off the road in a slushy downhill patch. Vroom desperately tried to control the steering but the wheels couldn't grip the ground. Like a drunk tramp, the Qualis staggered down and into the site of a high-rise construction project.

## 29

The slope ended but the Qualis still kept rolling forward. It slowed down as it slid onto a mesh of iron construction rods. Vroom braked hard, and the Qualis halted on the rods with a metallic clang, bounced twice and came to a stop.

'Damn,' Vroom said.

Everyone sat in shocked silence.

'Don't worry guys,' Vroom said and started the ignition. The Qualis shook with wild vibrations.

'Shut...the...ignition...Vroom...' I said. I looked under the Qualis. There was a floor of iron below us that was trembling violently.

Vroom's hands trembled too as he turned the engine off. I think any remaining alcohol in his body had evaporated in seconds.

'Where are we?' Esha said and opened the window. She looked out and screamed, 'Oh no!'

'What?' I said and looked out again. This time I looked around more carefully. What I saw was scary: we had landed in the foundation hole of a building, which had a frame of exposed metal rods covering it. The foundation was a pit, probably fifty-feet deep and had a frame of reinforced cement concrete rods above it. The rods were parallel to the Qualis and jutting out at the other end—and they were all that supported us. Every time we moved, the Qualis bounced, as the rods acted as springs. I could see fear in everyone's face, including Military Uncle's.

'We're hanging above a hole, supported only by toothpicks. We're screwed,' Radhika said, summing up the situation for all of us.

'What are we going to do?' Esha said. The contagious panic in her voice made everyone nervous.

'Whatever you do, don't move,' Vroom said.

A few minutes passed. The heavy breathing of six people was the only sound.

'Should we call for help? The police? Fire brigade? Call center?' Esha said as she took out her mobile phone from her bag.

Vroom nodded. His face had the nakedness of fear.

'Damn, no reception,' Esha said. 'Does anyone else have a mobile that works?'

Priyanka and Radhika's cell phones did not work as well. Military Uncle didn't have a mobile. Vroom took out his phone.

'No network,' he said.

I took out my phone from my pocket and gave it to Esha.

'Your phone is also not working, Shyam,' Esha said and placed it on the dashboard.

'So we can't reach anyone in this world?' Radhika said.

A rod snapped under us. The Qualis tilted a few degrees to the right. Radhika fell towards me; Vroom held the steering wheel tight to keep his balance. He froze in the driver's seat, unable to think of what else to do. Another rod snapped, and then another like feeble twigs under us. The Qualis tilted around thirty degrees and came to a halt.

All of us were too scared to scream.

'Does anyone have any ideas?' Vroom said.

I closed my eyes for a second. I visualized my death. My life could end, just like this in oblivion. I wondered when and how people would find us. Maybe laborers tomorrow or even after a couple of days.

'Six irresponsible agents found dead, alcohol in body' would be the headline.

'Try to open the door, Vroom,' Military Uncle said.

Vroom opened his door. The Qualis wobbled and Vroom shut it immediately.

'Can't,' Vroom said. 'Messes up the balance. And what's the point? We can't step out, we would fall right through.'

I turned around to look out from the rear window. I noticed bushes a few feet behind us.

'Move towards the left. No weight on the right. We have to stay balanced until someone spots us in the morning,' Vroom said.

I checked my watch. It was only 4:14 a.m. Morning was three hours away. A lifetime. And people could show up even later.

'Otherwise?' Esha said.

'Otherwise we die,' Vroom said.

We stayed quiet for a minute.

'Everyone dies one day,' I said, just to break the silence.

'Maybe it is simpler this way. Just end life rather than deal with it,' Vroom said.

I nodded. I was nervous and I was glad Vroom was making small talk.

'My main question is—what if no one finds us even after we die. What happens then?' Vroom said.

'The vultures will find us. They always do. I saw it on Discovery Channel,' I said.

'See, that makes me uncomfortable. I don't like the idea of sharp beaks tearing my muscles, cracking my bones and ripping me to shreds. Plus, my body will be smelling like hell. I'd rather be burnt in a dignified manner and go up in that one last ultimate puff of smoke.'

'Can you guys stop this nonsense. At least be silent,' Esha said and folded her arms.

Vroom smiled at her. Then he turned to me. 'I don't think Esha will smell too much. Her Calvin Klein perfume will keep her carcass fresh for days.'

Beneath us, there were two sharp 'pings' as two more rods snapped.

'Oh no,' Priyanka said as we heard another ping right below her. A flicker of light appeared at the dashboard.

Everyone sprang to attention as my cell phone began vibrating.

'That's my phone,' I said.

The phone started ringing. Everyone's mouth hung open.

'How did this ring without a network?' Esha said, her voice nervous.

'Who is it,' Radhika said.

'Pick it up,' I said with my hand stretched out, unable to reach the dashboard and unwilling to move too much.

Esha lifted the phone. She looked at the screen and gasped.

'Who is it?' I said.

'Do you know someone called...God? It says...God calling, Esha said.

# #30

ESHA'S FINGERS TREMBLED. SHE PRESSED THE BUTTON TO TAKE the call on speaker mode.

'Hi everyone. Sorry to call so late,' a cheerful voice came from the phone.

'Err. Who is it?' Esha said.

'It's God,' the voice said.

'God? God as in...' Radhika said as all of us looked at the brightly-lit phone in fright.

'As in God. I noticed an unusual situation here, so I thought I would just check on you guys.'

'Who is this? Is this a joke?' Vroom asked in a stronger voice.

'Why? Am I being funny? I just said I am God,' the voice said.

I narrowed my eyes. Apart from the fact that God using a cell phone was unusual, I never thought my life was important enough for God to call me.

'God doesn't normally call. Prove that you are God. Otherwise, can you please get us some help,' Vroom said.

'How do I prove I am God? Do I make this cell phone float? Or do I create rain and lightning on demand? Or do you prefer magic tricks? Special effects maybe?' God said.

'Well, I don't know. But yeah, something like that,' Vroom said.

'So, to impress you I have to break the same laws of physics that I made? I'm sorry, I'm not into that these days. And I have plenty of believers. I thought I could help, but I can hang up. See you then...' God said.

'No, no wait. Do help us...G...God,' Esha said and turned slightly so she could hold the cell phone between all of us.

Radhika put a finger on her lips to signal Vroom to be quiet.

'Okay, I'll stay,' God said in a cheerful voice. 'Tell me, how is it going?'

'Help us get out. A few more rods break and we are going to die,' I said.

'Not that, how is it going otherwise? How is life?' God said.

I am really bad at tough, open-ended questions like that. I hate to admit the extent to which my life is screwed up.

'But right now we're trapped...' I said and God interrupted me.

'Don't worry. The Qualis isn't going anywhere. Just relax.

I let out a deep sigh. Everyone was silent.

'So back to the question, how is life going? You want to go first, Radhika?' God said.

'You are God. Obviously you must already know everything. Life is miserable,' Radhika said.

'Actually, I *do* know,' God said. 'I just want to find out how you feel about it.'

'I'll tell you how we feel. Life suc...sorry,' Vroom said, and checked himself, 'It's awful. Like what did we do wrong? Why is our life in the pits—literally and figuratively? That pretty much sums it up for all of us I think.'

Everyone made concurring sounds. God sighed.

'Let me ask you a question. How many phone calls do you take every day?' God said.

'A hundred, on busy days two hundred,' Vroom said.

'Okay. Now do you know which is the most important call in the world?'

'No,' Vroom said. Everyone else shook their heads.

'The inner call,' God said.

'The inner call?' everyone said in unison.

'Yes, the little voice inside that wants to talk to you. But you can only hear it when you are at peace—and then too it is hard to hear it. Because in modern life, the networks are too busy. The voice tells you what you really want. Do you know what I am talking about?'

'Sort of,' Priyanka said, her eyes darting away from the phone.

'That voice is mine,' God said.

'Really?' Esha said, her mouth wide open.

'Yes. And the voice is easy to ignore—because you are distracted or busy or just too comfortable in life. Go on, ignore it—until you get tangled in your own web of comfort. And then you reach a point like today, where life brings you to a dead end, and there is nothing ahead but a dark hole.'

'You're making sense. I didn't get it all, but you are making sense,' I conceded, more to myself.

'I know that voice. But it isn't subtle in me. Sometimes it shouts and bites me,' Vroom said.

'And what does the voice say, Vroom?' God said.

'That I should not have taken up a job just for money. Call centers pay more, but only because the exchange rate is in the favor of Americans. They toss their loose change at us. It seems like a lot in rupees. But jobs that pay less could be better. There could be jobs that define me, make me learn or help my country. I justified it by saying money is progress. But it is not true. Progress is building something lasting for the future,' Vroom said, sounding as if there was a lump in his throat. He pressed his face into his hands.

Esha put her hand on Vroom's shoulder.

'C'mon guys. This is getting way too sentimental. You can do a lot better than this. You are all capable people,' God said.

It was the first time someone was using the word 'capable' to describe me.

'We can?' I said.

'Of course. Listen, I will make a deal with you. I will save your life tonight, but in return, you give me something. You close your eyes for three minutes. Think about what you really want and what you need to change in your life to get it. Then, once you get out of here, *act* on those changes. You do this, and I will help you get out of this pit. Deal?'

'Deal,' I said. Like you won't do a deal that saves you from death. Everyone nodded.

We closed our eyes and took a few deep breaths.

Man, I tell you, closing your eyes for three minutes and not thinking about the world is the hardest thing to do. I tried to concentrate, but all I could see was commotion. Priyanka, Bakshi, my promotion and Ganesh—my mind kept jumping from one topic to another.

'So, tell me,' God said after three minutes.

We opened our eyes. Everyone's face was a lot calmer.

'Ready?' God said.

Everyone nodded their heads.

'Let's go around the Qualis one by one. Vroom, you first,' God said.

'I want to have a life with meaning, even if it means a life without Bed or daily trips to Pizza-Hut. I need to quit this call center. Sorry, but calling is not my calling,' Vroom said.

I thought his last line was quite clever, but it wasn't the right time to appreciate verbal tricks.

Priyanka spoke after Vroom. My ears became extra alert.

'I want my mother to be happy. But I cannot kill myself for it. My mother needs to realize a family is a great support to have, but ultimately, she is responsible for her own happiness. My focus should be on my own life and what I want,' Priyanka said. I wished she had said my name somewhere in her answer, but no such luck. I think ninety percent of Priyanka's brain is either occupied or controlled by her mother.

Military Uncle's turn came after Priyanka. And then he spoke the most I have heard him speak—ever.

'I want to be with my son and my grandson. I miss them every moment. Two years ago, I used to live with them. But my daughter-in-law did things I didn't like—she went for parties, got a job when I wanted her to stay at home.... I fought with them and moved out. But I was wrong. It is their life, and I have no right to judge them by my outdated values. And I need to get rid of my inflated ego and go to the US to see them and talk it out.'

Radhika's turn came next. She fought back her tears as she spoke. 'I want be myself again, just like I was before marriage, when I was with my parents. I want to divorce Anuj. I don't want to ever look at my mother-in-law's face again. To do this, I have to accept that I made a wrong decision when I married Anuj.'

Esha spoke after Radhika. 'I want my parents to love me again. I do not want to become a dumb model. I am sure I can find a better use for my looks, if they are worth anything. Any career that makes you compromise on your morals, or judges you because you are not an inch taller is not worth it.'

People now turned to look at me, as I was the only one left to speak.

'Me? Can I pass?' I said.

Everyone gave me an even harder stare. Sometimes you have no choice but to share your weird thoughts with the world.

'Okay. This will sound stupid, but I want to take a shot at my own business. I had this idea, if Vroom and I collaborate, we can set up a small web design company. That is all. But it may never work, because most of the things I do never work, but then...'

'What else, Shyam?' God said, interrupting me.

'Uh, nothing,' I said.

'Shyam, you are not done. You know that,' God said.

I guess you can't outsmart God. I just had to come to the point. I looked around and spoke again.

'And I want to be worthy of someone like Priyanka one day. I do not deserve her as of today, and I accept that...'

'Shyam, I never said...' Priyanka said.

'Please, let me finish Priyanka. It is about time people stop trampling all over me,' I said.

Priyanka looked at me and became silent. I could see she was in mild shock at my firmness.

I continued. 'But one day I'd like to be worthy of someone like her—someone intelligent, witty, sensitive and fun, someone who can seamlessly merge friendship with love. And yes, one day I want to be successful too.'

We had all finished our turns. God stayed silent.

'God? Say something, now that we've poured out our deepest secrets to you,' Esha said.

'I don't really have to say anything. I am just amazed—and pleased—at how well you have done. Knowing what you want is already a great start. Ready to follow it through?' God said.

Everyone nodded except me.

'Ready, Shyam?' God said.

I gave a small nod.

'Shyam, can I say something personal before your friends,' God said, 'because it is important for everyone as well.'

'Sure,' I said. Yeah, use me as Exhibit I for 'how not to live your life'. At least I am of some use.

'You want to be successful right?' God said.

'Yes,' I said.

'There are four things a person needs for success. I will tell you the two obvious ones first. One, a medium amount of intelligence, and two, a bit of imagination. Agreed?'

'Agreed,' everyone said.

'And all of you have those qualities,' God said.

'What are the third and the fourth?' Vroom said.

'The third is what Shyam has lost,' God said.

'What's that?' I said.

'Self-confidence. The third thing you need for success is self-confidence. But Shyam has lost it. He is hundred percent convinced he is good for nothing.'

I hung my head.

'You know how you became convinced?' God said.

'How?' I said.

'Because of Bakshi. A bad boss is like a disease of the soul. If you have one for long enough, you get convinced something is wrong with you. Even though you know Bakshi is the real loser, you start doubting yourself. And that is when your confidence goes.'

God's words shook my insides like the vibrating Qualis had a few minutes ago.

'God, I want to get my confidence back,' I said.

'Good. Don't be scared and you will get it back. And then there won't be any stopping you,' God said.

I felt the blood rush to my ears. My heart was beating hard and I wanted to be back at the call center. At the same time, anger surged in me as I thought of Bakshi. I wanted to get even with the man who had killed a part of me, who had put everyone's job on the line, who had ruined the call center.

'What's the fourth ingredient for success?' Vroom said.

'The fourth ingredient is the most painful one. And it is something all of you still need to learn. Because it is often th most important thing,' God said.

'What?' I said.

'Failure,' God said.

'What? I thought you were talking about success,' Vroom said.

'Yes, but to be really successful, you must face failure. You have to experience it, feel it, taste it, suffer it. Only then can you shine,' God said.

'Why?' Priyanka said. Obviously she was focused on my personality dissection as well. I tell you, Ganesh may have the Lexus, but she will never find as interesting a psycho case as me.

'For once you taste failure, you have no fear. You can take risks more easily. Then you don't want to snuggle in your comfort zone anymore—you are ready to fly. And success is about flying, not snuggling,' God said.

'Point,' Priyanka said.

'So, here is a secret. Never be afraid of failure. If it has come your way, it means I want to give you a real shot at being successful later,' God said.

'Cool,' Priyanka said.

'Thank you,' God said.

'If only you had given India as much as America,' Vroom said.

'Why, you don't like India?' God said.

'Of course not. Just because India is poor doesn't mean you stop loving it. It is mine. But still, America has a lot,' Vroom said.

'Well, don't be so high on America. Americans may have many things, but they are not the happiest people on earth by any stretch. Any country obsessed with war can't be happy,' God said.

'True,' Radhika said.

'And many of them have serious issues in the head. Issues only call center agents know about. And you can use them to save your call center tonight,' God said.

'The messed up heads of Americans will save our call center?' Vroom, Radhika and I spoke together.

'Yes. Think about their weak spots, and then you can win,' God said.

'Like what? They are fat, loud, thick and divorce all the time?' Esha said.

'There are more. I will give you a hint. What's behind all this war sentiment?' God said.

'Fear. It is obvious, they are the most scared and paranoid people on earth,' I said.

'We'll scare them into calling us. Yes, that will get us back our call volumes,' Vroom said, his voice excited.

'Now you are thinking. In fact, you can figure out a way to get even with Bakshi too. Not completely fair and square, but by now you deserve to bend a few rules in the game,' God said, and I thought I heard a chuckle.

Everyone smiled.

'Really, we can teach Bakshi a lesson?' I said.

'Sure, remember Bakshi is not your boss, the ultimate boss is me. And I am with you. So what are you afraid of?' God said.

'Excuse me, but you are not there with us always. Or how did we end up here?' Radhika said.

God sighed before speaking again. 'I think you need to understand how my system works. You see, I have a contract with all human beings. You do your best, and every now an then, I will come behind to give you a bonus push. But it h. to begin with you. For otherwise I can't distinguish who need. my help most.'

'Point,' Vroom said.

'So, if I listen to my inner call and promise to do my best, will you be there for me?' I said.

'Absolutely. But, I have to go now. Someone else needs to reach me,' God said.

'Wait! Help us get us out of this pit first,' Esha said.

'Oh yes, of course. I have to help you out of this pit,' God said. 'Okay, Vroom, you are balancing on a few rods now. There are two tricks to get out from such a situation.'

'What's that?'

'One, remember the reverse gear. And two, make friends with the rods—do not fight them. Use the rod as rail tracks and the rods will guide you out. Shake things around, and you will fall right through.'

Vroom stuck his neck out of the window. 'But these steel construction rods are as thin as my fingers. How do we bunch them up?'

'Tie them,' God said.

'How?' Vroom said.

'Do I need to tell you everything?' God said.

'Dupatta. Use my dupatta,' Priyanka said.

'Here, I have this half knitted scarf in my handbag too,' Radhika said.

'I think you can take it from here. Bye now. Remember, I am inside you when you need me,' God said.

'Huh?' Vroom said and looked at the phone.

'Bye God,' the girls said one after the other.

'Bye everyone,' God said and disconnected the call. I waved the phone goodbye in reflex. Silence fell on us.

'What. Was. That?' Priyanka said.

'I don't know. Can I have the dupattas please,' Vroom said. 'Military Uncle, can you open the rear door and tie up the rods under the wheel. Tear up the dupatta if you want to.'

Priyanka flinched for a second at the last line, but that was the last we saw of her dupatta and Radhika's half-scarf. Vroom and Military Uncle tied up the rods right under the wheel for the Qualis to do its ten-foot journey to reach firm ground. Several times they bent over deep and had to look right into the pit. I was glad i was not the one doing it—I would have died just from the view.

'Okay people,' Vroom sat back on the seat, wiping his hands, 'hold tight.'

Vroom started the ignition. The Qualis vibrated, as the rods below us started quivering again.

'Vrr..oom...I am...sl...ipp..ing,' Esha said, trying to grip the handle of the glove box.

In a nanosecond, Vroom put the Qualis in reverse and drove back. All of us ducked down, partially so Vroom could see, but mostly in fear.

The Qualis shook as if it was rumbling down a hill. However, we did not fall. My upper and lower jaws chattered so hard that I thought a couple of teeth would break loose.

In six seconds, it was all over. We were out of the pit and on the slushy mud road again.

'It's done. I think I am alive,' Vroom said with a grin of relief. He turned around, 'Did anyone survive?'

# #31

EVERYONE RELEASED THEIR BREATHS TOGETHER. THE GIRLS broke into hugs, and Vroom reached out and backslapped me so hard I thought I would die of a broken spinal cord.

Vroom took a U-turn and drove back slowly in first gear until we reached the highway.

'We made it,' Esha said and wiped her tears. Priyanka folded her hands and prayed a few times.

'I thought we would die,' Radhika said.

'What was that call?' Esha said.

'Something very strange—can we make a pact to not talk about it?' I said. Everyone nodded, as if I had said exactly what was on their mind. It was true. The call felt so personal, I did not want to discuss it anymore.

'Whatever it was, we are okay now. And we shall be in office soon,' Priyanka said.

'It's still only 4:40. We are just two kilometers away,' Vroom said. He soon regained his confidence and began driving at sixty an hour.

'I'm just lucky to be alive, I don't care when we reach,' Esha said.

'I do want to reach soon and find out about the layoffs. However, I'm quitting in any case,' Vroom said.

'You are?' Esha said.

'Yes, enough's enough,' Vroom said.

'What are you going to do?' Priyanka said.

'I don't know long-term—maybe get back to journalism. But as an immediate short-term goal, I'm going to try and save the call center,' Vroom said.

'Hey, you want to open a web design company? With me?' I said.

'With you?' Vroom said, looking back at me.

'I'm quitting too,' I said.

'Really?' Priyanka's eyes popped open. She looked at me as if a seven-year-old had just announced his decision to climb Mt. Everest.

'Yes, I came close to death in that pit. I could have died there, with having tried nothing in life. I am tired of soft, comfortable options. It is time to face the real world, even if it is harder and painful. I'd rather fly and crash, than just snuggle and sleep.'

Everyone nodded. I was shocked; people were really listening to me for the first time.

'Plus, I have made one more promise to myself,' I said.

'What?' Vroom and Priyanka said together.

'That I am not going to work for an idiot anymore, anywhere. Even if it means less money. I could skip a meal a day and sleep hungry, but, hell, I can't spend my life working for a moron.'

'Not bad,' Vroom said, 'looks like our team leader-in-waiting just became wiser.'

'I don't know if it is wise or not, but at least I have made a choice. We will see what happens. For now, I have a short-term goal too.'

'Like what,' Vroom said, as he drove with utmost concentration, 'don't tell me it is call documentation and all.'

'No. I have to take care of Bakshi too. Since we have nothing to lose, let's teach him a lesson,' I said.

Vroom screeched the Qualis to a halt and we all fell forward.

'Now what?' I said.

'Wait, I just had an Eureka moment. I have an idea for fixing Bakshi and the call center,' Vroom said.

'What?'

'Aha, I like it,' Vroom said and smiled to himself.

'What, damn it,' I said.

He leaned back and whispered something in my ear.

'No way, I mean how?' I said.

'Yes way, I'll tell you how when we get back. Let's meet in the WASG conference room,' he said and pressed the accelerator hard as we made the final stretch to reach the call center. We entered the Connexions main gate at 4:45 a.m. We passed Bakshi's car again.

'Want to bump it. Should we give it a nasty dent?' I said to Vroom.

'The thought crossed my mind,' Vroom said and let out a sigh, 'but I love all automobiles too much to hurt them. This Lancer is already suffering under Bakshi. Don't worry, we will deal with him inside.

Vroom took the Qualis to the parking lot. Our driver was sleeping in another vehicle, so we quietly parked the Qualis next to him. We wanted to give him a few more hours of rest before he saw his mud-coated vehicle.

'People, let's go, 4:46,' Vroom said and jumped out of the car.

At our desk I saw an A4-sized sheet stuck on my monitor with big bold letters scrawled on it.

'Check this out,' I said. It was Bakshi's writing.


WHERE IS EVERYONE? PLEA  CALL/REPORT TO MY OFFICE ASAP. WHERE ARE MY BOARD MEETING AGENDA COPIES? WHAT HAPPENED TO THE XEROX MACHINE? AGENT VICTOR'S MONITOR?


Vroom looked at the notice and laughed, 'Whatever. He'll get his answers. But first, he will answer us. Guys, conference room first,' Vroom said.

We went inside the conference room and Vroom bolted the door.

'Guys, sorry to sound like the MBA types, but I think in the next few hours we have a three-point agenda. One, to save this call center. And two, to teach Bakshi a lesson. Agreed?'

'What's the third point?' Radhika said.

'That's between me and Shyam. It's private. Okay, listen...'

And that is where Vroom revealed his plan to a) save the call center and b) take care of Bakshi. All of us jumped in our seats when we first heard it. Slowly, Vroom convinced us. Between laughter and intense concentration, everyone pooled in to refine the plan further. We concluded our meeting at 5:10 a.m. and came out of the WASG conference room.

'All set?' Vroom said.

'Of course,' all of us said in unison.

'Good. Step 1: Getting Bakshi out of his office,' Vroom said. 'Esha, you ready?'

'Yes,' Esha said and winked at us.

She picked up the phone, dialed Bakshi's number and took on the voice of an older woman.

'Sir, this is Elina calling from the main bay. Sir, there is a call for you from Boston I think,' Esha said, in a dumb-but-conscientious secretarial tone.

'No sir, I can't seem to transfer it.... Sir, I tried that, but the line does not go through.... Sir, I am a new assistant here, so I still do not know how the phones work.... Sir, sorry but can you come down sir... Yes sir,' Esha said and hung up the phone.

'Worked?' I said.

'Total sucker for anything Boston. He is coming right now. But he'll only be out for a few minutes, so let's rush.'

# #32

As EXPECTED, BAKSHI'S OFFICE WAS EMPTY WHEN WE GOT THERE.

Vroom went straight to Bakshi's computer and opened his email.

Radhika, Priyanka and I sat at Bakshi's conference table.

'Hurry,' Radhika said and kept one eye on the door.

'Just one more minute,' Vroom said as he furiously typed on Bakshi's keyboard.

I know what we were doing was wrong, but somehow doing this wrong thing was not associated with 'real, hard, painful guilt', as Esha had put it. In fact, it felt good. Once he had finished, Vroom printed several copies on Bakshi's printer.

'Five copies,' he said, 'one for each of us. Fold it and keep it safe.'

I folded my copy and put in my shirt pocket.

Bakshi arrived twenty seconds later.

'Can't believe we have such outdated telephone systems,' Bakshi was talking to himself as he came into his office. He noticed us at the conference table.

'There you guys are. Where were all of you? And what happened to the Xerox machine and agent Victor's monitor?' Bakshi said. He wrapped his arms around his middle and looked at each of us in quick succession.

'Sit down for a second, will you Bakshi?' Vroom said, patting a chair next to him.

'What?' Bakshi said, shocked at Vroom referring to him by his name. 'You should learn how to address seniors...'

'Whatever Bakshi,' Vroom said and put his feet up on Bakshi's meeting table.

'Agent Victor, what did you say and what exactly do you think you are doing?' Bakshi said, still standing.

'Ahh,' Vroom said, 'this is so much more comfortable. Why don't people always sit like this?' Vroom crossed his legs on the table.

'I can't believe you are misbehaving in times when I have to recommend rightsizing...' Bakshi said as Vroom interrupted him again.

'You are mega fucked Bakshi...' Vroom interrupted him.

'Excuse me? What did you just say Agent Victor?'

'So you are not only dumb, but deaf too. Didn't you hear him?' Esha said, trying hard to suppress a smile.

'What the hell is going on here?' Bakshi said and looked at me blankly like I was a renowned interpreter of nonsense.

Vroom pushed a printout towards Bakshi.

'What's this?' Bakshi said.

'Read it. They taught you how to read in the MBA course, right?' Vroom said.

The email read as follows:

From: Subhash Bakshi
To: Esha Singh
Sent: 05.04am
Subject: Just one night

Dear Esha,

Don't be upset. My offer is simple—just spend one night with me. You make me happy —I'll save you from the right-sizing. My pleasure for your security—I think it is a fair deal. And who knows, you might enjoy it too. Let me know your decision soon.
Your admirer,
Bakshi.

Bakshi's face turned white. His mouth opened five inches wide as he re-read the email several imes.

'What is this? What the hell is this?' Bakshi said, his hands trembling as much as his voice. His mouth was still open and vibrated like it was battery operated.

'You tell us. It is a mail from your inbox, dumb ass.' Vroom said.

'But I never wrote it,' Bakshi said, unable to hide a hint of desperation in voice, 'I never wrote it.'

'Really?' Vroom said as he lit a cigarette. 'Now how can you prove you didn't write it? Can you prove ir to people in the Boston office that you didn't write it?'

'What are you talking about? How is this connected to Boston?' Bakshi said, his face sprouting droplets of sweat through the oilfields.

'Let's see. What if we forward Boston a copy of this mail? The same people who you copied on the website manual? I am sure they love employees who do, well, *fair deals*,' I said.

'I never wrote it,' Bakshi said, unable to think of better lines.

'Or we could send a copy to the police,' Vroom said as he blew a huge puff of smoke on Bakshi's face, 'and to some of my reporter friends. You want to be in the papers tomorrow Bakshi? Here is your chance.' Vroom took out his phone, 'Oh wait, maybe I can even get you on TV.'

'TV?' Bakshi said.

'Yes, imagine the headline: 'Call center boss asks girls for sexual favors in exchange for job'. NDTV could live on that for a week. Damn, I know I could be a good journalist,' Vroom said and laughed.

'But what did I do?' Bakshi said and ran to his desk. He opened his email and checked the 'Sent Items' folder.

'Who wrote this?' Bakshi said as he saw the same mail on his screen.

'You didn't?' Priyanka said, as if in genuine confusion.

'Mr Bakshi, I held you in such high esteem. Today my faith in my role-model is shattered,' Esha said and put her hands to her face. She was good—I think she should try for an acting career.

'No, I swear I did not,' Bakshi said, as he scrambled with his mouse and keyboard.

'Then who wrote it? Santa Claus? The tooth fairy?' Vroom shouted and stood up. 'You explain this to the police, the journalists, and over the video conference to Boston execs.'

'Hah! Look I have deleted it,' Bakshi said with a smug smile as he released his computer mouse.

'C'mon Bakshi,' Vroom said with a sigh, 'it's still in your 'Deleted Items folder.'

'Oh,' Bakshi said and jerked his mouse. A few clicks later he said, 'There, it is gone. No more email.'

· Vroom smiled, 'One more tip for you Bakshi. Go to your Deleted Items, select the tools menu and choose the "recover deleted items" option. The mail will be there,' Vroom said.

Bakshi's face panicked again as tried to follow Vroom's complex instructions. He desperately clicked his mouse.

'Oh, stop it Bakshi. The mail is in my inbox as well. And Vroom has many printouts,' Esha said.

'Huh?' Bakshi said as he looked like a scared rabbit. 'You'll never get away with this. Esha you know I didn't do it. You wear tight skirts and tops but I only look at them from a distance. Even those jeans that show your waist I only saw...'

'Stop right there, you sicko,' Esha said.

'You can't get away with this,' Bakshi said.

'We have five witnesses Bakshi, they will support Esha's testimony,' I said.

'Oh, and we have some other evidence as well. In Esha's drawer there is a packet with cash, it has your fingerprints on it, in case you want to get to that level,' Vroom said.

Bakshi's fingers trembled as if he was getting ready to play drums.

'We also have a printout of your visits to pornographic websites,' Radhika said.

'You know it is not me Esha, I will finally get proved innocent,' Bakshi said, his voice sounding like a hapless beggar's. His eyes looked ready to leak.

'Maybe. But the amazing publicity will be enough to screw your career. Goodbye Boston,' I said and waved my hand to indicate farewell. Everyone else raised their hand and waved goodbye as well.

Bakshi looked at us in horror and sat down. His white face had now turned red, or rather purple—even though it was still as shiny as ever. I could see a twitching nerve on the side of his forehead. I felt an urge to make him suffer more. I stood up to pick a thick management book from his bookshelf.

I went up to Bakshi and stood next to him.

'Why are you doing this to me? I will be leaving you forever to go to Boston,' Bakshi said.

'Boston?' I said. 'You do not deserve a posting to Bhatinda. You do not even deserve a job. In fact, one could argue you do not even deserve to live. You are not just a bad boss, you are a parasite: to us, to this company, to this country. Damn you.'

I banged the management book on his hard head. Bakshi's head was hollow, as the impact made a big noise. God, it felt good. Few people in this world get to hit their boss, but those who do will tell you it is better than sex.

'What do you want? What is it you want? You want to destroy me,' Bakshi said, rubbing his head. 'I have a family with two kids. With great difficulty my career is going fine. My wife wants to leave me anyway. Don't destroy me, I am human too.'

I disagreed with Bakshi's last phrase. I didn't think he was human at all.

'Destroying you is a good, fun option,' Vroom said, 'but have more worthwhile goals for now. I want to do a deal w you. We bury this issue and in return you do some things for u'

'What kind of things?' Bakshi said.

'One. I want to have control of the call center for the next two hours. I need to get on the mass speaker.'

'The one management uses to make fire drill announcements,' I said.

'The fire drill speaker is used to talk to everyone. Why do you want it? Will you talk about this email?' Bakshi said.

'No, you moron. It is to save jobs at the call center. Now, do I have the speaker?'

'Yes. What else?'

'I want you to write out a resignation letter for Shyam and me. Layoffs or not, we are quitting Connexions.'

'You guys are quitting right now?' the girls said.

'Yes. Shyam and I will start a small website design business. Right, Shyam?' Vroom said.

'Yes,' I said. Wow! I thought.

'Good. And this time, no idiot will take credit for our websites,' Vroom said and slapped Bakshi's face. Bakshi's face turned sixty degrees from the impact. He held his cheeks but emained silent, apart from a tiny dry sob. His facial expression had a combination of ninety percent pain and ten percent shame.

'May I?' I said.

'Be my guest,' Vroom said.

Slap! I gave a slap on Bakshi's face. The face turned sixty degrees in the other direction. It was my most fun career moment. The shiny face turned hot.

'So you will do the resignation letter, okay?' Vroom said.

'Okay,' Bakshi said, rubbing his cheek. 'But Esha will delete the email right?'

'Wait. We are not done. Our business will require start-up capital. Therefore, we need a severance package of six months' salary. Understand?' Vroom said.

'I cannot do six months. It is unprecedented for agents,' Bakshi said.

'NDTV or Times of India, you pick,' Vroom said as he took out his phone.

'Six months is possible. Good managers break precedents,' Bakshi said. I guess no number of slaps could break his jargon.

'Nice. Last thing, I want you to retract the right-sizing proposal. Arrange a call with Boston. Ask them to postpone the layoffs to try a new sales-driven recovery plan for Connexions.'

'I can't do that,' Bakshi said.

Vroom lifted his mobile phone and put it in front of Bakshi's face.

'I'll make sure all of India knows you by tomorrow,' Vroom said. 'Listen, you idiot. I don't care about this job, but there are agents with kids, families and responsibilities in life. You can't just fire them. They are people, not resources. Now, which news channel is your favorite?'

'Give me half an hour. I'll set up a call with Boston,' Bakshi said.

'Good. We'll bury the email. But you get the hell out of the call center, this city, and this country as fast as you can. We need a new boss. We need a normal, decent, inspiring human being and not a slimy, blood-sucking goofball with fancy degree

Bakshi nodded as he continuously wiped the sweat from his face.

'Good. Anything else? You had some questions about my monitor?' Vroom said.

'Monitor? What monitor?' Bakshi said.

# #33

Bakshi gave Vroom the key to the speaker room. Soon, Bakshi was on his phone, calling Boston to arrange management meetings. I have never seen him work so efficiently.

Vroom went to the broadcast room and switched on the mikes. I went to the main computers bay to check for sound quality.

'Hello, everyone. May I have your attention please? This is Vroom, from the strategic group.'

Vroom's voice echoed through Connexions. Every agent looked up at the speakers as they continued to talk to their customers.

'Sorry, to bother you, but we have an emergency. This is about the layoffs. Can you please disconnect all your calls,' the speaker said.

Everyone heard the word layoffs and a thousand calls ended at the same time. New calls flashed, but no one picked them up. Vroom continued:

Idiots have managed this place, because of which we have to suffer tonight. For their mistakes, more than a third of you will lose your jobs. It does not seem fair to me. Does it seem fair to you?'

No response came back.

'C'mon guys, I want to hear you. Do I have your support to save your jobs and this call center?'

All the agents looked at each other, still in partial disbelief. Many of them said a weak 'yes'.

'Louder guys, all together. Do I have your support?' Vroom said.

'Yes!' a collective scream rocked Connexions.

I was standing at the corner hall of the main bay. Every agent glued his or her eyes to the fire-drill speaker. Vroom continued, this time in a firmer voice.

'Thank you. My friends, I am angry. Because every day, I see some of the world's strongest and smartest people in my country. I see all this potential yet it is all getting wasted. An entire generation up all night, providing crutches for the white morons to run their lives. And then big companies come and convince us with their advertising to value crap we don't need, do jobs we hate so that we can buy stuff—junk food, colored fizzy water, dumbass credit cards and overpriced shoes. They call it youth culture. Is this what they think youth is about? Two generations ago, the youth got this country free. Now that was something meaningful. But what happened after that? We have just been reduced to a high-spending demographic. The only youth power they care about is our spending power,' Vroom said, and even I was amazed at the attention every agent gave him.

Vroom continued: 'Meanwhile bad bosses and stupid Americans suck the life blood out of our country's most productive generation. But tonight we will show them. And for that I need your support. Tell me are you ready to work hard for the next two hours?'

'Yes!' a collective voice came back. The whole call center vibrated as Vroom paused to take a breath.

'Good, then listen. The call center will survive if our call traffic goes up. My plan is to scare the Americans into calling us regularly. Tell them that terrorists have hit America with a new computer virus that will take their country down. The only way they can be safe is if they keep calling us to report their status. We do it like this, pull out every customer number you have and call them. I will send you a call script on email. The mail will come to you in five minutes. Until then, get those numbers out,' Vroom said.

Noise levels rose in the main bay as hundreds of localized conversations took place simultaneously. There was a frenzy as people took printouts of all customer numbers in their database. Nobody was sure if the plan would work, but people were willing to try anything to avoid layoffs.

Vroom and I came back to our bay. He typed furiously on his computer and tapped my shoulder after a few minutes.

'Check your email,' Vroom said and pointed to my screen.

I opened my inbox. Vroom had sent the mail to everyone in the call center.

Subject: Operation Yankee Fear.

Dear All,

Operating Yankee Fear's single aim is to increase the incoming call traffic in the Connexions call center, capitalizing on Americans being the biggest cowards on the planet. This will prevent the planned mass-layoffs and help us buy more time to fix things around the place, including a marketing effort to get new clients.

Operation Yankee Fear cannot succeed without your 100% cooperation. So, please read the instructions below carefully and relentlessly focus on making calls for the next two hours. When you call each customer, the key message you have to deliver is as follows:

1. Start by saying you are sorry to disturb them on Thanksgiving Day.

2. State that 'evil forces' of the world have unleashed a computer virus that threatens to pervade every computer in America. This way the evil forces will monitor every American and eventually destroy the American economy. Tell them that, according to your information, the virus has hit their computer.

3. If asked what the 'evil forces' are, give vague explanations like 'forces that want

to harm the US' or 'organizations that threaten freedom and liberty' etc. Remember, the more vague you are, the greater the amount of fear you can create. Try to inject genuine panic into your voice.

4. To check whether the virus has hit them or not, make them do an MSWord test. Tell them to open an empty MSWord file, and type in =rand (200,99) and press enter. If a lot of text pops comes out, that means there is a virus. (Don't worry: the text WILL pop out—it is a bug in MSWord). Once that happens, your customers might start shaking in fear.

5. Tell them you can save them from this virus as a) you are from India, and all Indians are good at computers b) India has faced terrorism for years and c) they are valued clients and you believe in customer service.

6. However, if they want our help, they must keep calling the Connexions call center every six hours. Even if nothing happens, they should just call to say things are okay. (The shorter the calls, the better for us anyway).

7. Once calls rise, I will speak to Boston about the sudden rise in traffic and recommend we postpone the layoffs for two months.

> After that, we can implement a revival
> strategy.
>
> Cheers,
>
> Varun @ WASG

Vroom grinned and winked at me as I finished reading the email.

'What's with the MSWord trick?' I said.

'Try it, open a Word file,' Vroom said.

I opened an empty Word document and typed in =rand (200,99).

As soon as I pressed Enter, two hundred pages of text popped out. It was spooky, and went something like this:

*The quick brown fox jumps over the lazy dog. The quick brown fox jumps over the lazy dog. The quick brown fox jumps over the lazy dog. The quick brown fox jumps over the lazy dog. The quick brown fox jumps over the lazy dog. The quick brown fox jumps over the lazy dog. The quick brown fox jumps over the lazy dog. The quick brown fox jumps over the lazy dog. The quick brown fox jumps over the lazy dog. The quick brown fox jumps...*

'This is unbelievable. What is this?' I said.

'I told you. It's a bug in MSWord. Nothing is perfect. Now just wait and watch the fun,' Vroom said.

Vroom's email reached a thousand mailboxes and agents read it immediately.

Team leaders further assisted agents in clarifying doubts. Within minutes, agents were doing a job they knew only too well: calling people to deliver a message as fast as possible. I left my bay and passed by the main bay. I picked up random sentences from the telephone conversations.

'Hello Mr William, sorry to disturb you on Thanksgiving. I am from Western Computers with an urgent situation. America is under a virus attack,' one agent said.

'Yes sir. Your computer as per our records is affected...' said another

'Don't freak out sir. But, yes, it looks like the evil forces have targeted you,' an eighteen-year-old agent said. 'But we can save you.'

'Just keep calling us. Every four to six hours,' said one, as she ended the call.

The more aggressive agents went a step further: 'And I want you to tell all your friends and relatives. Yes, they can call us too.'

Some customers panicked, and agents had to reassure them: 'No problem. We will save this country. The evil forces will never succeed.'

A thousand agents, four minutes to a call—we could do thirty thousand calls in two hours. If they called us every six hours, we would have over a hundred thousand calls a day. Even if this lasted a week, we would hit our targets to cover the next two months. Hopefully, with a new manager and extra sales effort, Connexions could recover. And for now, no one would lose his or her job.

Vroom came looking for me in the main bay. We went back to the WASG. Vroom signaled me into the conference room.

'The response is amazing. We have just called for thirty minutes, and call traffic is up five times already,' Vroom said.

'Rocking man,' I said. 'You make me feel confident about our web design company. But let's go back to the desk, why have you called me here?'

'We have to discuss the third private agenda.'

'What's that?' I said.

'The third agenda is for you. Don't you want Priyanka back?'

# #34

'No, PRIYANKA AND I ARE OVER,' I SAID.

'Be honest dude. You spoke to God and everything.'

I looked down. Vroom waited until I said something.

'It doesn't matter if I want to or not. Look at my competition. How am I going to succeed against Mr Perfect Match Ganesh?'

'See, that is the problem. We all think Ganesh is Mr Perfect. But nobody is perfect.'

'Yeah right. A house with a pool, a car that costs more than ten years' of my salary, freaking working for the world's top company—I don't see much imperfection in that.'

'Everyone has a flaw, dude. The trick is to find a flaw in Ganesh.'

'Well how are we ever going to do that? And even if we find a flaw in him, what is the point? He is so good, Priyanka will still go for him,' I said.

'At least Priyanka will know she isn't making the perfect trade-off,' Vroom said.

I remained silent for two minutes. 'Yes, but how do we find Ganesh's flaw now?' I said and looked at my watch. It was 5:30 a.m.

'There must be a way,' Vroom said.

'The shift is over in ninety minutes, and then Priyanka goes home. What are you planning to do? Hire some instant detectives in Seattle?' I said, my voice irritated.

'Don't give up, Shyam,' Vroom said and patted my shoulder.

'I am trying to forget Priyanka. But if you search within me, there is still pain. Don't make it worse, Vroom.'

'Wow, what drama. Search within me, there is pain,' Vroom said and laughed.

'Sorry for my lame lines. Let's go back to the bay,' I said.

'Hey wait a minute. You just said *search*.'

'Yes, search within me, there is still pain. Pretty cheesy, I know. Why?' I said.

'Search. That is what we can do. Google will be our detective. Let's do a search on his name and see what comes out. There could be some surprises.'

'What? You want to do a search for Ganesh?'

'Yes, but we need his full name. Let's find out his college as well. I think he did his Masters in computers from the US,' he said and grabbed my shirt. 'C'mon, let's go.'

'Where?' I said, even as I let myself get dragged.

'To the WASG bay,' Vroom said.

Priyanka was busy on the phone, scaring Americans out of their wits. I think she can put on that voice of authority when she wants, and it is impossible not to believe her. It comes from her mother I think. Vroom spoke to her after she had ended a call.

'Hey Priyanka, quick question. My cousin also did a Masters in computers from the US. Which college did Ganesh go to?'

'Huh? Wisconsin I think,' she said.

'Really. Let me email my cousin and ask him if it is the same one. What is Ganesh's full name by the way?'

'Gupta. Ganesh Gupta,' Priyanka said as she prepared to make another call.

'Oooh. Mrs Priyanka Gupta,' Esha said in a mock high-society voice and laughed. Priyanka poked her with her elbow. Priyanka's new name sent ripples of pain down my rib cage.

'Cool. Keep calling,' Vroom said and went back to his seat.

As Vroom's monitor was broken, he took control of my computer. He searched for the following terms on google.com:

ganesh gupta drunk Wisconsin
ganesh gupta fines Wisconsin
ganesh gupta girlfriend

Several links popped out, but there was nothing we could make much sense or use of. We hit upon Ganesh's list of classmates, and found out that he was in the Dean's list in Boston.

'Damn, what a boring guy. Let me try some more,' Vroom said and did some more searches.

ganesh gupta fail
ganesh gupta party
ganesh gupta drugs

Nothing interesting came out.

'Forget it man. He was probably the head boy in school,' I said.

'You bet, one of those teacher's pet types,' Vroom said, letting out a frustrated breath. 'I give up. I am sure if I type something like this, lots will pop out, achiever that he is.'

ganesh gupta microsoft award

More links popped out. We clicked through a few, and then we hit on one with his picture. It was Ganesh's online album.

'Damn, it is him, with his buddies,' Vroom whispered and clicked on the link. 'Let's check out how ugly his friends are.'

The link opened to a webpage titled 'Microsoft Award party photos'. The party was at Ganesh's house. Ganesh had won some sidey developer award at Microsoft. A couple of his friends had come to his house to celebrate.

'Do slideshow,' I said as Vroom selected the option. We looked up once to confirm the girls were busy with their calls.

As the picture came on the screen, we saw a garden party full of Indian people. On the tables, there was enough food to feed a small town. I saw Ganesh's house and the over-hyped personal pool. It was no more than an oversized bathtub, if you ask me, even though Ganesh had made it sound like Olympic champions trained in it.

'Hey, I think we found something. Check out our man,' Vroom said. He pointed to one of the photos in which Ganesh held a beer glass.

'What is the big deal?' I said. It was hardly scandalous to hold a glass of beer. Priyanka herself could knock down them if they were free.

'Check out Ganesh's head,' Vroom said.

'What?' I said. I looked closer, and then I saw it.

'Oh no,' I said, and covered my mouth to keep my voice down.

In the picture, Ganesh had a bald spot in the middle of his head. It was the size of a Happy Meal burger and had caught the camera's flashlight.

'Unbelie...' I said.

'Shhh!' Vroom said. 'Did you see that. He has perfect hair in the Statue of Liberty picture.'

'Are all his photos in this album like this?' I said.

'Yes sir,' Vroom said and flicked through the slideshow. One boring picture after another followed—mainly people with mouths and plates stuffed with food. Every picture had one thing in common: wherever there was Ganesh, there was a shiny spot.

Vroom pushed his computer mouse away. He reclined back on his chair with a proud expression, 'As I said sir, no one is perfect. Apart from Google, of course.'

I looked at the screen and Vroom's face in amazement.

'So, now what?' I said.

'Now we invite the ladies for a viewing,' Vroom said and grinned.

'No. This is not right...' I said, but it was too late.

'Esha, Radhika, Priyanka. Want to see some more Ganesh pictures? Come here fast,' Vroom said.

The girls stopped their phone calls and looked at us. Esha and Radhika stood up.

'Where, where? Show us,' Esha said.

'What are you talking about?' Priyanka said and came on to our side.

'The power of the Internet. We found an online Come see what your new house is like,' Vroom said. I quiet about the shiny spot so that the girls could discover themselves. I saw the mixture of excitement and curiosity Priyanka's face.

'Nice pad,' Esha said, as she noticed the barbeque behind the pool, 'but where is Ganesh. Let me guess,' she said and brought her finger to the monitor. Here, this one no. But wait, he is a baldie. Is he the elder brother?'

Priyanka and Radhika looked closer.

'No, that is Ganesh,' Priyanka said as her mouth opened as wide as the bald spot. I could sense that the wind had been knocked out of her lungs.

'But I didn't notice the bald spot in the photo you showed us Priyanka...' Esha said. Radhika squeezed Esha's arm. Esha stopped talking and raised her eyebrows.

Priyanka came closer to the computer and began flipping through the images. She did not realize it, but her hair was falling on my shoulders as she bent over. It felt nice.

However, Priyanka was not feeling nice. She brought out the Statue of Liberty picture and we looked at it again. Ganesh had perfect hair.

'Maybe the guy in the online album is Ganesh's elder brother,' Radhika said.

'No. Ganesh does not have a brother. He only has one sister,' Priyanka said, her face distraught.

There was silence for a few seconds.

'Well doesn't really matter much, eh? What's a bit of smooth skin between the true love of two souls,' Vroom said. I clamped my jaws shut to prevent a laugh escaping. 'Let's go back people, enough of fun. Don't forget the calls,' Vroom said.

Priyanka retraced her steps in slow motion. She went back to her seat and took out her mobile phone. She dialed a long number, probably long distance. This call was going to be fun, and I wished I could have tapped it.

'Hello Ganesh,' Priyanka said in a direct voice. 'Listen, I cannot talk for long. I just want to check on something...yes, just one question...actually I was just surfing the Internet...' Priyanka said and got up from her seat. She moved to the corner of the room and I could not hear her thereafter.

I made a few calls and terrorized a few more Americans. Priyanka returned after ten minutes and tossed her cell phone on the desk.

Esha jiggled her eyebrows up and down, as if to ask 'What's up?'

'It *is* him in the online pictures,' Priyanka said. 'He didn't have much to say. He said his mother asked him to slightly touch up the hair in the Statue of Liberty snap as that would help in the arranged marriage market.'

'Oh no,' Esha wailed.

'He apologized several times. He said he was against tampering with the picture but had to agree when his mother insisted.'

'Can't he think for himself?' Esha said.

'Oh god, what am I going to do?' Priyanka said.

'Did the apologies seem genuine?' Radhika said.

'Yes, I think so. He said he understood how I must feel. He said he was ready to apologize in front of my family as well.'

'Well, then it is okay. What difference does it make? You don't really care about him being bald, do you?' Radhika said.

'Yeah, besides practically all men become bald in a few years anyway. It's not like you can do something about it then,' Esha said.

'That's true,' Priyanka said, in a mellow voice. I could see her relenting, and I turned to Vroom.

'Yeah, doesn't matter. Just make sure he wears a cap at the wedding. Unless you want to touch up all the wedding pictures,' Vroom said and chuckled. Esha and I looked down to suppress our grins.

'Shut up, Vroom,' Radhika said.

'Sorry, I am being mean. Honestly, it is no big deal Priyanka. No one is perfect, we all know that right? So, let's get back to the calls,' Vroom said.

## 35

For the next half hour we focused on one activity—making calls to save Connexions.

At 6:30 a.m., I went up to the main bay. Team leaders huddled around me as they gave me the news. The incoming calls had shot up already even though we had expected the big boost six hours later. Despite turkey dinners, Americans were scared out of their wits. Some had called us several times an hour.

Vroom and I went to Bakshi's office with some senior team leaders. Bakshi had arranged an urgent video conference call with the Boston office. Bakshi supported us as we presented the new call data, insights into the call traffic, and potential new sources of revenue. After a twenty-minute video discussion, Boston agreed to a two-month reprieve to the layoffs. They also agreed to evaluate the possibility of sending top team leaders on a short-term sales assignment to Boston. However, the team leaders would have to present a clear plan over the next few weeks.

'How did we do it man? I never thought it would work,' I asked Vroom as we came out of Bakshi's office.

'Promise Americans lots of future dollars, and they listen to you. Only a two-month reprieve, but that's enough for now,' Vroom said.

Reassured that Connexions was safe, I returned to my desk. Vroom went outside to clean the Qualis before the driver woke up. I had told Vroom I wanted to slip away—no goodbyes, no hugs and no promises to meet, especially in front of Priyanka. Vroom agreed and said he would be ready with his bike outside at 6:50 a.m.

The girls stopped their calls at 6:45 a.m. as our shift got over. Everyone began to log out so they could be in time for the Qualis, which would be ready at the gate at 7:00 a.m.

'I'm so excited. Radhika is moving into my place,' Esha said as she switched off her monitor. She opened her handbag and started re-arranging the contents.

'Really?' I said.

'Yes, I am,' Radhika said. 'And Military Uncle is going to recommend a lawyer friend. I need a good, tough divorce lawyer.'

'Won't you try to work it out?' Priyanka said as she collected the sweet boxes and placed them back in the bag.

'We'll see. I am in no mood to compromise. And I am not going back to his house now for sure. Today, my mother-in-law will make her own breakfast.'

'And after that, I'm taking her to Chandigarh for the weekend,' Esha said and smiled.

Everyone was busy making plans. I excused myself on the pretext of going to the water cooler for a drink so I could leave the office from there.

# #36

At 6.47 A.M. I REACHED THE WATER COOLER. I BENT TOWARDS
the tap to take a last drink at the call center.

As I finished, I stood up to find Priyanka behind me.

'Hi,' she said. 'Leaving?'

'Oh, hi. Yes, I am going back on Vroom's bike...' I said and
wiped my mouth.

'I'll miss you,' she said, interrupting me.

'Huh? Where? In the Qualis?' I said.

'No Shyam, I'll miss you in general. I'm sorry about the way
things turned out.'

'Don't be sorry,' I said, shaking my fingers dry. 'It is more
my fault. I understand that. I acted like a loser...'

'Shyam, you know how Vroom said just because India is
poor doesn't mean you stop loving it?' Priyanka said.

'What?' I blinked at the change of topic. 'Oh yes. And I
agree, it is our country after all...'

'Yes, we love India because it is ours. But, do you know the other reason why we don't stop loving it?'

'Why?'

'You don't because it isn't completely India's fault that we are behind. Yes, some of our past leaders could have done things differently, but now we have the potential and we know it. And as Vroom says, one day we will show them.'

'Point. Good point,' I said. I found it strange that she should talk nationalism this early in the morning. Not to mention during what was possibly our last time together.

I nodded and started walking away from her. 'Anyway, I think Vroom will be waiting...' I said.

'Wait, I am not done,' she said.

'What?' I said and stopped to look at her.

'I applied the same logic to something else,' she said. 'I thought, this is the same as my Shyam, who may not be successful now, but it doesn't mean he doesn't have the potential. And it sure as hell doesn't mean I stop loving him.'

I stood there dumbstruck. This was unexpected. I fumbled for words, and finally spoke shakily:

'You know what Priyanka? You say these good lines...that even though all night I tried to hate you, it's impossible. But I know I should hate you and then I should move on. Because I can't offer you what Mr Microsoft can...' I was speaking hastily out of nervousness and shock.

'Ganesh,' she interrupted me.

'What?' I said.

'Ganesh is his name. Not Mr Microsoft,' she said.

'Yes, whatever,' I kept talking, without pausing to breathe.

'I can't offer you what Ganesh can. No way I could ever buy a Lexus. Maybe a Maruti 800 one day, but that's about it...'

She smiled.

'Really? 800? With or without AC?' she said.

'Shut up, I am trying to say something deep and you find it funny,' I said.

She laughed again, though gently. I wiped a tear from my right eye. She raised her hand and wiped the other tear from my left eye.

'Anyway, it is over between us, Priyanka. And I know it. I should get over it soon. I know, I know,' I said, talking more to myself.

She waited until I had composed myself. I bent over to splash my face with water at the cooler.

'Anyway, where is your wedding? Your mom will probably blow all her cash for a big gig,' I said, straightening up.

'Some five-star hotel, I am sure. She'll be paying off loans for years, but she has to get a gold-plated stage that night. You'll come, right?'

'I don't know,' I said.

'What do you mean you don't know? It'll be so strange if you aren't there.'

'I don't want to come there and feel horrible. Anyway, what's so strange if I am not there?'

'Well, it's a little strange if the groom is not there at his own wedding,' Priyanka said.

I froze as I heard the words. I rewound her last sentence three times in my head.

'What, what did you just say?' I said.

She pinched my cheek and imitated me: 'What, what did you just say?'

I just stood there shocked.

'But don't think I am going to let you go that easy. One day I want my 800 with AC,' she said and laughed.

'What?' I said.

'You heard me. I want to marry you, Shyam,' Priyanka said.

I could not believe her words. I thought I would jump in joy, but mostly I was shocked. And even though I wanted to hug, cry and laugh at the same time, a firm voice asked like a guard inside me. *What was this all about? Hell, however miserable my life was, I didn't want pity.*

'What are you saying Priyanka? You will choose me over Ganesh? Is this a sympathy decision?'

'Stop thinking about yourself. My life's biggest decision can't be a sympathy decision. I have thought about it. Ganesh is great, but...'

'But what?' I said.

'But the whole touching up of the photo bothers me. He is an achiever on his own. So why did he have to lie?'

'You are rejecting him because he is bald? My hair isn't reliable either,' I said. It was true. Every time I took a shower, the towel had more hair than me.

'No. I am not rejecting him because he is bald. Most men go bald one day, it is horrible, I know,' she said and ruffled my hair. She continued: 'He might be fine in most ways, but the point is, he lied. And this gives me a clue about the person he is. I don't want to spend my life with a person like that. In fact, I don't want to spend my life with a person I don't know well beforehand. That is one part of my decision. There is the other big part.'

'What?' I said

'That I love you. Because you are the only person in the world I can be myself with. And because you are the only person who knows me with all my flaws and still loves me completely. I hope,' she said, with a quivering voice.

I did not say anything.

She spoke again: 'And even if the world says I am cold, there is a part of me that is sentimental, irrational and romantic. Do I really care about money? Only because people tell me I should. Hell, I prefer truck driver dhabhas over five-star hotels. Shyam, I know mom and you say I am uncaring...'

'I never said that...' I said and held her shoulders.

'I'm sorry, Shyam. I judged you so much. I am such a bitch,' Priyanka said.

She sniffed. Her puckered nose looked cuter than it ever had.

'It's okay Priyanka,' I said and wiped her tears.

'So that is it, Shyam. Deep inside, I am just a girl who wants to be with her favorite boy. Because like you, this girl is a person who needs a lot of love.'

'Love? I need a lot of love?' I said.

'Of course, you do. And everyone else does too. Funny we never say it. It is okay to scream in public if you are hungry "*I'm starving*". It is okay to make a fuss if you are tired "*I'm so sleepy*". But somehow we cannot say "I just need some more love". Why can't we say it, Shyam? It is as basic a need.'

I looked at her. Whenever she gives these deep, philosophical lines, I get horribly attracted to her. The guard inside reminded me, *'Be firm'*.

'Priyanka?'

'Yes,' she said, still sniffling.

'I love you,' I said.

'I love you too,' Priyanka said.

'Thanks. However...Priyanka, I can't marry you. Sorry to say this, but my answer to your mind-blowing proposal is no,' I said.

'What?' Priyanka said as her eyes opened wide in disbelief. The guard inside me was in full charge.

'No. I cannot marry you. I am a new person tonight. And this new person needs to make a new life and find new respect for himself. You chose Ganesh, and he is fine. You have an option for a new life. You don't really need me. So maybe it is better this way,' I said.

'I still love you Shyam, and only you. Please don't do this...' she said and came closer to me.

'Sorry,' I said and moved back three steps. 'I can't. I am not your spare wheel. I appreciate you coming back, but I think I am ready to move on.'

She just stood there and cried. My heart felt weak, but my head was strong.

'Bye Priyanka,' I gingerly patted her shoulder and left.

# #37

'WHAT THE HELL KEPT YOU?' VROOM SAID, AS HE SAT ON HIS bike at the main entrance. He showed his watch to me, it was 6:59 a.m.

'Sorry man, Priyanka met me at the water cooler,' I said and sank onto the pillion seat.

'And?' Vroom said.

'Nothing. Just goodbye and all. Oh, and she wanted to get back—marry me, she said. Can you believe it?'

Vroom turned to me.

'Really? What did you say?'

'I said no,' I said coolly.

'What?' Vroom said.

As we were talking, Radhika, Esha and Military Uncle came out of the main entrance into the wintry sunshine.

'Hi, you guys still here?' Radhika said.

'Shyam just said no to Priyanka. She wanted to marry him, but he said no.'

'What?' Radhika and Esha spoke in unison.

'Hey guys, chill out. I did what I needed to do to get some respect in my life. Quit bothering me,' I said.

The Qualis driver came and pressed the horn.

'We aren't bothering you. It's your life—let's go Esha, Radhika said and gave me a dirty look. She turned to Esha as they walked to the Qualis.

'Where's Priyanka madam? We are getting late,' the driver said.

'She's coming. She is on the phone with her mother. Ganesh's parents are coming home for breakfast. Her mother is making hot paranthas,' Radhika said, loud enough so I could hear. The mention of paranthas made me hungry. But I guess I would be the last person to be invited to this breakfast.

'Looks like their entire families are getting married to each other,' Vroom said. He lit a cigarette to take a few final puffs before we began our ride back.

The driver started the Qualis. Esha and Radhika sat in the middle row, while Military Uncle sat behind.

Priyanka came running out of the main entrance. She avoided me and went straight to the Qualis front seat. The driver turned the Qualis so its rear end faced us.

As the Qualis began to move, Military Uncle looked out from his window and said something. I could only make out in lip sync. 'You bloody idiot...' I thought it was.

Before I could react, the Qualis was gone.

Vroom stubbed out his cigarette.

'Oh no. I *am* a bloody idiot. I let her go,' I said.

'Uh-huh,' Vroom said as he wore his helmet.

'Is that a yes? You think I am a total idiot?'

'You are your best judge,' Vroom said as he dragged the bike with his feet.

'Vroom, what have I done? If she reaches home and has paranthas with Ganesh's family, it is all over. I am such a moron,' I said and started jumping up and down on my seat.

'Stop dancing around. I have to ride,' Vroom said as he placed his foot on the kick-pedal.

'Vroom, we have to catch the Qualis. Can you ride fast enough to catch it?'

Vroom removed his helmet and laughed.

'Are you insulting me? You are doubting that I can catch that wreck of a Qualis? I am hurt, man.'

'Vroom, let's go. Please,' I said and pushed his shoulders.

'No. First you apologize for doubting my driving abilities.'

'I am sorry, boss, I am sorry,' I said and folded my hands.
'Now move, Schumacher.'

Vroom kick-started his bike. In a few seconds, we had zipped out of the call center. The main road was getting busier in the morning, but Vroom still managed ninety an hour. We dodged cars, scooters, autos, school buses and newspaper hawkers as we took the road to Delhi.

Four minutes later, I noticed a white Qualis at a distant traffic signal.

'It must be that one,' I pointed out.

Just as Vroom moved ahead, a herd of goats decided to cross the road. There were fifty of them, blocking our way.

'Damn, where did they come from?' I said, nervous as hell.

'Gurgaon was a village until recently; the goats are probably asking where did *we* come from,' Vroom said as he cracked his knuckles.

'Shut up and do something,' I said.

Vroom tried to move his bike, but he only bumped into a goat's horns. He considered taking the right side of the road with traffic going the other way—but it was full of trucks that would kill us in five seconds.

'There is only one option,' Vroom said and smiled at me through the helmet.

'Wha…' I was saying when Vroom lunged his bike up on the road divider.

'Are you crazy?' I said.

'No, you are crazy to let her go,' Vroom said and started riding on the divider. The goats and the traffic looked at us in shock. Vroom dodged through the street lights, until we had crossed the herd. Once back on the road, Vroom sped up to a hundred. A minute later, our bike met the Qualis at a red light. I got off the bike and tapped the front window. Priyanka locked away. I banged the glass with my palm.

She opened the window. 'What is it? We don't want to buy anything,' Priyanka said, as if I was a roadside vendor.

'I am an idiot,' I said.

'And?' Priyanka said.

Everyone in the Qualis rolled down their windows to look at me.

'I am a moron. I am stupid and insane and nuts. Please, I want to marry you.'

'Oh really? What about the new man needing respect?' Priyanka said.

'I didn't know what I was saying. What does one do with respect? I can't keep it in my pocket,' I said.

'So you want to keep me in your pocket?' Priyanka said

'You are already in every pocket—of my life, my heart, my mind, my soul—please come back. Will you come back?' I said, as the red light turned yellow.

'Hmm. Let's see...' Priyanka said.

'Priyanka, please answer fast'

'I don't know. Let me think. Meet me at the next red light okay? Let's go Driver *ji*,' she said as the light turned green. The driver, as if enjoying my misery, took off at full speed.

'What did she say?' Vroom said as I sat on the bike.

'She'll answer at the next red light. Let's go.'


There was a mini-traffic jam at the next red light. I got off the bike and ran past a few vehicles to reach the Qualis. I tapped the window again. Priyanka wasn't there.

'Where is she?' I asked the driver. He shrugged his shoulders.

I looked inside the Qualis. Radhika and Esha shrugged their shoulders; she wasn't in there.

Someone came up from behind and hugged me.

'I told you we didn't want to buy anything. Why are you bothering us?'

I turned around to look at Priyanka.

'I don't know what I was doing at the water cooler,' I said.

'Shut up and hug me,' Priyanka said and opened her arms.

Our eyes met, and even though I wanted to speak a lot, our eyes did all the talking. I hugged her for a few seconds, and then she kissed me. Our lips locked, and every passenger stuck in the traffic jam looked at us, enjoying the early morning show. It was awkward to kiss in this setting, but I could not extract myself from her. We were kissing after six months, and there was a lot of pent-up demand. Vroom and everyone else from the Qualis surrounded us. Soon, they began to clap and whistle. The vehicles on the road joined in with their horns in sync with the applause. But I could not see them or hear them. All I could see was Priyanka, and all I could hear was my inner voice that said— kiss her, kiss her and kiss her some more..

# #38

WELL GUYS, THAT IS HOW THAT NIGHT, AND MY STORY ENDS. We did not know what, how or when things would happen in the future. And to some extent, we still don't know. But that is what life is like—uncertain, screwed up at times, but still fun. However, let me tell you where we were one month after this night. Vroom and I started this website design company with the seed capital that Bakshi gave us. We called it the Black Sheep Web Design Company. In a month, we had only managed to get one local order. It helped us break even or even show a profit—depending on whether Vroom charged the cigarettes to the company or not. No international orders yet, but we shall see.

Esha quit her modeling aspirations and continued to work at the call center. However, she works with this NGO during the day. Her job is to fundraise with corporates. I heard she is doing well. I guess when male executives hear such a hot woman ask for money for a good cause, they cannot say no. Most of them are probably staring at her navel ring when they are signing the cheque. Apart from that, Vroom asked her out on a coffee semi-date (whatever that means) for next week and I think she said yes.

Military Uncle got a visa for the US and went to make amends with his son. He has not come back, so things must be working out. Radhika is fighting her divorce case with her husband, and has moved in with Esha. She is also planning to visit her own parents for a while. Anuj has apologized, but Radhika is in no mood to relent yet.

Priyanka works at Connexions as well, but in six months she will go to college for an accelerated one-year B.Ed. We decided that marriage is at least two years away. Right now, we meet often but the first focus is career. Her mother faked three heart attacks when Priyanka said no to Ganesh, but Priyanka yawned every single time until her mom gave up on the heart attack front and closed the Ganesh file.

So looks like things are working out. As for me as a person, I still feel the same for the most part. However, there is a difference. I used to feel I was a good-for-nothing non-achiever. But that is not true. After all, I helped save lots of jobs at a call center, taught my boss a lesson, started my own company, was chosen over a big-catch NRI groom by a wonderful girl and now I even finished a whole book. This means that i) I can do whatever I really want ii) God is always with me and iii) there is no such thing as a loser after all.

# Epilogue

'Wow,' I said, 'some story that was.' She nodded, and had a sip of water from her bottle. She held the bottle tight to prevent the water from spilling over in the moving train.

'Thank you,' I said, 'it made our night go by pretty quickly.'

I checked the time; it was close to 7 a.m. Our journey was almost over. Delhi was less than an hour away. The train was tearing through the night, and deep into the horizon, I could see a streak of saffron light up the sky.

'So, you liked it?'

'Yes, it was fun. But also, it made me think. I went through a similar phase like Shyam, at work and in my personal life. I wish I had known this story then. It might have made me do things differently, or at least would have made me feel less bad.'

'There you go. It is one of those rare stories that is fun but can help you as well. And that is why I am asking you to share it. You ready to make it into a book?' she said, replacing the cap on the water bottle.

'I guess. It will take some time though,' I said.

'For sure. And I will give you all the people's details. Feel free to contact them if you want. Through which of them will you tell the story?'

'Shyam. Like I said, he and his story are a lot like mine. I relate to him a lot; I had similar problems. My own dark side.'

'Really? That's interesting,' she said. 'It is true though, we all have a dark side—something we don't like about ourselves, something that makes us angry and something we want to change about ourselves. The difference is how we choose to face it.'

I nodded. The train rocked in a soothing, gentle motion. We were silent until I spoke after a few minutes.

'Listen, sorry to say this. There is one issue I think readers may have with this story.'

'What?'

'The conversation with God.'

She smiled.

'What's the issue with that,' she said.

'Well, just that—some people may not buy it. One has to present reality in a story. Readers always say, "tell me what really happened". So in that context, how is this "God calling" going to fit in?'

'Why? You don't think that can happen?' she said shifting in her seat. Her blanket moved, uncovering a book I had not noticed before.

'Well, I don't know. It obviously does not happen a lot. I mean, things need to have a rational, scientific explanation.'

'Really? Does everything in life work that way?'

'I guess.'

'Well, let's see. You said you did not know why, but you could really relate to Shyam. What's the scientific and rational explanation for that?'

I thought for a few moments but could not think of a suitable answer. She saw me fidgeting and looked amused.

'Please try and understand,' I said. 'Calls from God don't happen a lot. How can I write about that?'

'Okay, listen. I am going to give you an alternative to the "God's phone call" bit. A rational one, okay?' she said and kept her bottle away.

'What alternative?' I said.

'Let's rewind a bit. So they drove into a pit and the Qualis is trapped, suspended by rods, right? You okay with that part?'

'Right. I can live with that,' I said.

'And then they felt the end was near. There was no hope in life—literally and figuratively. Agreed?'

'Agreed,' I said.

'Okay,' she continued, 'so let's just say that, at that moment, Military Uncle spoke up. He said "I noticed you guys are in an unusual situation here, so I thought I should intervene and give you some advice".'

'That's exactly what God said,' I said.

'Correct. And from that point on, whatever God said, you can substitute as if Military Uncle said it. He told them about success, the inner call and all those other things.'

'Really? Is that what happened?' I said.

'No. I did not say that. I just said you have the option to do that; so that everything appears more scientific, more rational. You understand my point?'

'Yes,' I said.

'So, you choose whichever version you want in the main story. It will, after all, be your story.'

I nodded.

'But can I ask you one question?'

'Sure,' I said.

'Which of the two is a better story?'

I thought for a second.

'The one with God in it,' I said.

'Just like life. Rational or not, it just gets better with God in it.'

I reflected on her words for a few minutes. She became silent. I looked at her face. She looked even better in the light of dawn.

'Well, looks like Delhi is coming soon,' she said and looked out. The fields had ended, and we could see the houses of Delhi's border villages.

'Yeah, the trip is over,' I said. 'Thanks for everything—err, let me guess, Esha right?' I stood up to shake her hand.

'Esha? Why did you think I was her?'

'Because you are so good-looking.'

'Thanks,' she laughed, 'but sorry, I am not Esha.'

'So? Priyanka?' I said.

'No.'

'Don't tell me—-Radhika?'

'No, I am not Radhika either,' she said.

'Well then ...who are you?'

She just smiled.

That is when it struck me. She was a girl, she knew the full story, but she was not Esha, Priyanka or Radhika. Which meant there was only one alternative left.

'So...that means...Oh my...' My whole body shook as I found it difficult to balance. I fell down on my knees. Her face shone, and bright sunlight entered our compartment in one stroke.

I looked up at her as she smiled. She had an open book next to her. It was the English translation of a holy text. My eyes focused on a few lines on the page that lay open:

Always think of Me, become My devotee, worship Me and offer your homage unto Me. Thus you will come to Me without fail. I promise you this because you are My very dear friend.

'What,' I said as I felt my head spin. Maybe the sleepless night was catching up. But she just smiled and smiled. She raised her hand and kept it on my head.

— 'I just don't know what to say,' I said in the blinding light.

A sense of tiredness engulfed me as the sleepless night took its toll. I closed my eyes.

When I opened them, the train had stopped, and I knelt on the floor with my head down. The train was at Delhi station. The cacophony of porters, tea sellers and passenger movement rang in my ears. I slowly looked up at her seat—but she was gone.

'Sir, will you get out on your own or do you need help,' a porter tapped my shoulder.

# FIVE POINT SOMEONE
## What *not* to do at IIT

***On the bestseller charts for over seventy-five weeks!***

Five reasons why Hari, Ryan and Alok's life is in a complete mess:

1. They have screwed up their grades bigtime.
2. Alok and Ryan can't stop bickering with each other.
3. Hari is smitten with Neha, daughter of Prof. Cherian, head of the Mechanical Engineering department.
4. As IITians, they are expected to conquer the world, something they know is probably not going to happen.
5. They can't live without each other.

Welcome to *Five Point Someone*, which begins with a disclaimer — 'This is not a book to teach you how to get into IIT or even how to live in college. In fact, it describes how screwed up things can get if you don't think straight.'

Funny, dark and non-stop, it is a story of three friends who try to survive in the revered world of IIT. Their measly five-point something GPAs come in the way of everything else that matters — their friendship, their future, their love life. Will they make it?